Liberty

Ginger Jamison

Liberty

HARLEQUIN® KIMANI PRESS™

Recycling programs for this product may not exist in your area.

LIBERTY

ISBN-13: 978-0-373-09165-2

Copyright © 2014 by Jamie Pope

Printed in U.S.A.

www.Harlequin.com

To Emmanuelle, for believing in this book, and to Christine, AKA Casey Wyatt, for kicking me in the pants when I needed it.

Chapter One

It almost awed him. Almost. And only because *awe* was not the proper way to describe what he was feeling. He knew something big was going to happen. Something huge. Something that was going to rock his world, that was going to change the course of his life. And that made him restless.

All week he had been on alert, the tiny hairs on the back of his neck standing at attention, almost as if they were on the lookout for the same unknown element. It was a part of his job to be on alert. Awareness seemed to be his constant companion for the past year.

He signed up for this.

Willingly.

And just maybe that deep, empty feeling came with the territory, along with the sand and the oppressive heat.

"What you thinkin' 'bout?" Terrell Ramon asked him as he switched his assault rifle from one shoulder to the other. Terrell was the youngest man in their squad. He had dark brown skin and big doe eyes that made him look like one of those Precious Moments figurines. He was a baby compared to most of them but he was there because he was smart, a whiz with his hands and all things technical. Terrell could dismember a computer in thirty seconds and put it back together in twenty-five.

"Looks like you thinkin' about a woman? *Ooo-wee!*" The

kid slapped his thigh. "I love thinkin' 'bout women," he drawled in his thick Mississippi accent. "My woman's waiting for me at home and she's bangin'—thick booty, pouty lips and the prettiest damn smile you've ever seen." He grew wistful. "She wants to get married. I think I might have to."

He smiled. Terrell couldn't have been more than twenty-two. "You don't sound too sure. Do you want to get married so young?" Normally they wouldn't be having this type of conversation while on duty, or at all, but they had been stuck on this detail for too long and he needed something to take his mind from the constant niggling feeling in the back of his mind. "What's she like?"

"Sandra?" Terrell grinned widely for a moment as if remembering something funny. His eyes softened, taking on a look not often seen in this place. "She's always on my ass, since we were babies. But she's good for me, you know? Don't take none of my bullshit. Funny as hell." He sobered a bit. "I guess I love her. Being here makes me realize that."

He nodded. This conversation had taken a more serious turn than he had intended, but he knew how the kid felt. It was hard being in a foreign country, thousands of miles from your homeland, your comforts, the people who made life bearable.

But they'd signed up for this. They fought this war even if they didn't understand the politics behind it.

"What about you, T-dog? You got a girl waiting for you?"

He shrugged. "I've got a girl but I don't know if she's still waiting."

"She's cheating?" Terrell raised a brow. "Fuck her. You're here busting your balls while she's banging some other dude. Forget about her. Women love a war hero. Once we get home you'll be swimming in panties."

He let out a rusty chuckle. "It's not like that, Terrell. She just wasn't happy with me when I left. I don't blame her. I wasn't the best man when I was with her."

Terrell nodded sympathetically as if he knew the complexities of an adult relationship. "What's her name?"

He shook his head remembering the beautiful woman he'd left behind. "Her name is—" Then it happened.

It.

He heard it first—a blast, an explosion—that momentarily caused him to lose his precious hearing and then he felt *it*. Heat, blistering heat, that burned and twisted and melted his skin. And then he saw *it* in slow motion, like some scene from a movie, like he was some actor playing a role. But he wasn't. This wasn't a movie. This is what he had been waiting for. He was flying through the air for what seemed like hours but must have only been seconds. When he landed, the air rushed out of him. Everything went black. And when he opened his eyes again things weren't in the vivid color he was used to, but sepia—muted colors of tan and beige, of sand.

Reality came rushing back to him all too quickly. There was yelling behind him. No. Screaming. Screams of pain. Of terror. Of disorientation. Someone was yelling orders. Someone else was yelling names. There was all of this noise around him, deafening him. He looked around, sending a silent prayer of thanks that he was able to look around, and saw images that would reduce a normal man to tears.

His unit had been hit hard. It must have been a rocket attack. Only something powerful could reduce the men he had known as brothers to shreds. He could no longer tell who was who, the dust was too thick. The men were covered with sand, with blood. Their cries of pain were indistinguishable from one another. This was almost too much to bear, and even though he had seen a lot in his time in the service, the sight of his fallen men made him want to cry.

"Tex!" somebody called.

Get up, he told himself. *It's time for you to take action. You are a marine. You were trained for this. Your life was leading up to this moment.* Attempting to stand, he put one leg in front of him but it didn't want to hold his weight. Sharp, breath-snatching pain shot up his leg and into his body. It was like somebody was grinding broken shards of sharp glass into his muscles. He couldn't walk, so he crawled on his hands and knees, scraping them, causing the skin on them to grow raw and red and bloody. There was a man down not far from him who he didn't know. No. That wasn't right. There were only sixteen of them. He had to know who the man was. But he couldn't tell.

The soldier was unrecognizable. Dirt. Blood. Open flesh. That was all he saw, along with the dark grit that decorated his face.

"I'm dying, man," the unrecognizable soldier told him. There was a slight twang to his voice. He knew him.

"Try not to," he said sincerely. "You owe me fifty bucks."

"It's my time, brother." He grinned, but the smile was mixed with blood, dirt and pain. "At least I can say I died for my country."

"Don't say corny shit like that right now. I'm going to help you."

"You can't help this—" He motioned to his torso, which was no longer covered with skin. "You look like shit, brother. Go help yourself."

"I'm fine," he said, even though his vision started to blur

and his head began to throb with a pain that was almost indescribable.

"Do me a favor..." His voice started to fade. "Tell my wife—"

"Tell her yourself," he barked.

"Tell Lexy I'm sorry, and give these to my mother."

The dying soldier began to hand over his dog tags. *No.* He shook his head. He didn't want to honor anybody's last wishes.

But he would. He had to.

He'd signed up for this.

And so he grasped the man's hand, the dog tags between them, and felt the life drain away. He felt his own life about to go with it. The spinning in his head grew out of control, his body began to seize and he slumped over in the sand as he succumbed to a world of foggy pain and darkness.

Chapter Two

"Mrs. Beecher, he's right in here."

When Lexy Beecher learned her husband was in a rocket at-tack and survived…she sighed. That probably wasn't the usual response of the wife of a marine who hadn't seen her husband in almost two years. But then again she wasn't the usual wife.

When the officer phoned to tell her the news, she couldn't bring herself to cry or laugh or even breathe a sigh of relief. She didn't like her husband and while she hadn't wished him dead she never wanted to lay eyes on him again. Her husband was a horrible man. An awful man. "A piece of no good, low-down stinky shit," as her best friend and Ryan's cousin, Di, called him. It wasn't a harsh description.

It was truth.

"He was hurt very badly."

She nodded slowly, trying to take in all the information that was being thrown at her. The doctor thought she was in shock, but she wasn't in shock. She was numb. She didn't love him. She was going to leave him. The divorce papers sat in her nightstand just waiting for him to come home. She should have served them to him years ago but she wasn't able to. She had been stuck. Everybody, including Ryan, thought they had her pegged. They thought she was weak, that she lacked the backbone, the confidence to make it in the world without him. They were wrong.

Ryan's mother was the only one who got it right. She thought Lexy stayed for love. Lexy had stayed in a marriage to a man she felt nothing for because she did love somebody. However, that person was not her husband.

Her husband had gone out of his way to make it impossible to leave him, to keep her down, to keep her bonded to him. Hell, he had almost succeeded once, but she wouldn't ever be stuck again. It took her two years to rebuild, but she regained everything—including her self-respect.

"He wasn't stable enough to move until this week," the doctor continued, but Lexy barely heard him.

After he had left for Iraq, Lexy had taken steps to reclaim her life. She began to once again save every penny she could spare. She had researched different towns and the services they had to offer. She found a cute little place where she could live for cheap, and some jobs that would pay the bills. She wouldn't need anything from him. Nothing except what she prized most.

Her freedom.

And all he had to do was sign. All she had to do was get him to sign. That task would be difficult, almost Herculean, because the one thing her husband took pride in was his power over her. He wanted to keep her shackled to him like a dog and it wasn't out of love or friendship or simple companionship. He did it because he thought he could, because once upon a time she had been stupid enough to let it happen. To him she was his property, and when he was drunk she turned into his punching bag. How could she be so blind to not realize that he never loved her? She never loved him, either; for ten years they had existed on sick codependence.

Lexy had married Ryan when she was just seventeen years

old—when she had been beautiful and naive and filled with hope. Ryan had been twenty-two, devastatingly handsome and deceptively sweet. He was everything an innocent girl thought she wanted in a husband.

"You may not recognize him," the doctor continued, pulling her out of her deep thoughts. "He has a lot of contusions, a broken leg, rib fractures, burns over twenty percent of his body and a broken nose. In addition to that he took a nasty blow to the head. He's been in and out of consciousness for over a month."

She took it all in. He had been through all of that and didn't even have the decency to die. "Has he said anything?"

"I'm sorry, Lexy."

She looked up at the handsome military doctor. "Why are you sorry, Doctor? He couldn't have said anything he hasn't said before."

"No, Mrs. Beecher—" The doctor shook his head. "He said, 'I'm sorry Lexy.' Those are the only words he has spoken since he's been here."

Lexy suppressed the urge to roll her eyes. Of course Ryan would wait until he was half blown-up to repent for his years of bad behavior. But that was Ryan. He always had a knack for apologizing. She had spent the first half of their marriage forgiving him, too. But now she was too smart to ever believe those words again. She wasn't a teenager anymore and she was all out of forgiveness.

"I know this is a lot for you, Mrs. Beecher." Dr. Andreas placed his hand on her arm. "You need time to absorb it."

She nodded once, still numb to it all.

Lexy had met Ryan the year her grandmother, the woman who raised her, died. He promised her all the things she craved. A family. A support system. He promised to take care of her. She never had that. She had come into this world an orphan. Her mother was a free spirit who died in childbirth. Her father didn't bother to stick around. She had never known them. Not the way they looked or smelled or smiled. She didn't know where her slanted dark eyes came from or the kink of her unruly hair or even the color of her skin.

She was neither white nor black but some sort of indistinguishable brown that made her ethnic identity a mystery. Rumors swirled that she was Native American, some people told her that she was interracial—part black, part white and a bit Hispanic. She was her own version of the Small World ride.

Ryan didn't see it that way. He called her half-breed or mutt or whatever derogatory name rolled off his tongue.

"He was found lying unconscious next to another soldier. His dog tags were in his hand. It was a good thing they weren't lost. We would have had a hard time identifying him. His condition was more critical than the soldier found lying next to him and yet your husband was the one to survive. This was a miracle."

Miracle.

Ha! Lexy scoffed at the idea. God didn't save Ryan. The God she knew didn't save anyone—not her parents, not her grandmother and certainly not her. Why would he start with Ryan?

She thought about her grandmother, Maybell, who wasn't really her grandmother at all, just some woman who had loved and cared for her since she was an infant. The people of her small town rejoiced in telling her that Maybell had just showed up one day with a squirmy wild-haired baby. When asked where she had gotten the child, she'd replied with a succinct, "None of your damn business."

Lexy loved that cranky old woman dearly but she was as old as an oak tree when Lexy was a child and her love of deep-fried, gravy-covered, barbecue-smothered delicacies didn't help her diabetes or high cholesterol. She died when Lexy was sixteen, leaving her devastated and a little more than brokenhearted.

"You should prepare yourself, Mrs. Beecher. He's stable now but that can change at any moment."

"Please call me Lexy," she said, attending to the man. "Ryan won't die. He's not the type of man to let go."

Ten years ago Ryan had set his sights on her and hadn't let go. She was just a child reeling from the loss of the only person who loved her when he swooped in.

She should have known then.

He was a man of twenty-two and she a girl of seventeen. He must have sensed her weakness but she couldn't fault him for that. She should have been stronger, but what girl could resist a beautiful man who held you while you cried, who gave you your first kiss, who whispered soothing words in your ear and promised to take care of you forever?

She let him take advantage of her. And even after he started drinking and raging she didn't leave at first because she thought she could change him, and then because forces outside of her control kept her firmly in place.

The only person who made those long years bearable was Ryan's mother. Lexy adored the woman who, too, had been married to a man like her son. Mary had iced her bruises and protected her from Ryan when he was at his worst. She was a sympathetic ear. A few times Mary helped her pay the one bill that was so crucial to her survival.

It was Mary who finally convinced him that drinking himself to death wasn't the right way to go, that beating his wife was something no real man would do. It was she who convinced him to go into the marines.

But now Ryan was back, in a military hospital, sixty miles from home.

Lexy felt like she was suffocating with his nearness.

"Are you ready?" The doctor put his hand on the small of her back and guided her into the room.

She saw him. Alone. Seemingly hanging in that precious state between life and death. And it was like somebody punched her in the stomach. Her body betrayed her. And for reasons she couldn't begin to understand hot tears ran down her face.

"Holy shit, Ryan. What happened to you?"

He was bandaged like a mummy. It had been a month since the blast and yet he looked like he had been carried off the battlefield yesterday.

Like a moth to a flame, she went to him, her feet unwillingly carrying her body to his bedside.

He was pale, almost a ghostly shade of white, his nose was different, straighter, his jaw seemed larger more square, but it was Ryan. His massive size was undeniable and he still had those thick chestnut locks that she used to run her fingers through when they were first married. She should have wanted to flee the room, but she was drawn to him like never before. She couldn't pull herself away. She couldn't force the tears to stop flowing.

Why are you crying, stupid? You hate him.

She had thought she was indifferent. At times she thought

she hated him. Why then did it hurt to see him this way? Maybe deep down she had a tiny bit of affection for him. There would be no idealizing him, but there had been a time when he provided her with comfort. A short time when she thought she loved him.

She peered down at him, careful not to touch him, wondering what on earth she was going to do. Her heart started to race. The air in the room all seemed to disappear. There was no way she could get him to sign the divorce papers in his condition.

Leave it to Ryan to make an already difficult task impossible.

She couldn't abandon him when he was like this. She would look like the personification of evil if she left him alone to heal. In Liberty, Texas, women stood by their men. They took care of their husbands.

Her conscience was speaking to her. The one time she wished it would fail her, it was loud and clear.

You can't leave him like this.

He would need somebody to take care of him. He would need physical therapy, supervision. Constant support. Bile rose in her throat as she tried not to remember the man who beat her unconscious during a drunken rage. But how could she forget? It would be easier if he had died. At least then he would forever be a hero and she could go on with her life burden-free. But, no. Ryan never did make things easy for her.

"He doesn't look good," she managed to choke out.

"He looked a lot worse. He's lucky. And up until now he's been alone. Talk to him. I'm sure that will help."

She looked away from the broken man in the bed. "I don't know what to say."

"Say anything." He patted her arm comfortingly. "Just say what you need to say." The young doctor checked Ryan's stats and then left her alone with him.

"What did you do, Ryan?"

Realistically she knew he hadn't caused the catastrophe, but she was in no mood to be rational now. She felt like he had gotten himself into it so she couldn't leave him. It was like before—just when she was ready to move on with her life he threw up a huge barricade.

"Why can't you let me go? You don't even love me."

He stirred then, causing a moan to escape his dry, chapped lips. Startled by the noise, she jumped back and then laughed at her stupidity.

He can't hurt you. You won't let him.

She moved close again. The military did a fine job patching him up, but they did not pamper him. He was in need of a shave, his lips needed moisture and his growing hair stuck out in tufts all over his head. She could manage those things. Pulling up a chair next to him, she sat. This would be a good time to talk to him. She could say everything she had wanted to say for years and he would have to listen to her. He had no choice. It wasn't as if he could get up and walk out.

She flipped her thick braid over her shoulder and dug in her purse, producing a pot of cherry lip balm. His hair couldn't be helped as long as his head was bandaged, but his mouth she could fix. She placed her middle finger in the pot, scooped out a generous helping and smeared it over his cracked lips. If he had been awake he would have never allowed her to do this, to put such a feminine-scented concoction on his mouth. But there wasn't a damned thing he could do about it, so she did as she pleased. She smiled as the balm made his lips slightly shiny. She never had noticed how beautiful they were. Maybe she had noticed. Maybe his lips were one of the many things she found perfect about him when she was young and stupid and thought herself in love.

They could only be described as kissable now. Full. Relaxed. Soft. She wondered how they would feel pressed against her lips. On her skin. Trailing down her body. A shiver ran through her as she studied his pout. She hadn't thought about him that way in years. Long ago he had ceased to produce butterflies in her stomach with his nearness. She was no longer seventeen or easily seduced by a man and his sweet kisses.

"Has anyone ever told you that you are very pleasant in this state? If you had been in a coma our entire marriage I would probably still love you."

He stirred again and she wondered if he could hear her. In his drunken days a comment like that would have earned her a smack in the face. But no longer would she stand for that.

She would kill him if she had to.

Lexy cradled his face in her hands. There was a long scar on his jawline visible through his beard, and a smaller one above his eyebrow. Somehow the scars made him look sexy.

How was that possible?

She hadn't been attracted to him in years. The last time she had seen him he was bloated and doughy. Now he was hard and lean. Forty pounds lighter. He almost looked like a new man. Was it possible that he could be a new man? The marines could have changed him. She hoped for his sake that they did.

"I'm not a fan of facial hair, Ry. You look like Grizzly Adams." She sniffed the air, inhaling the smell of pain, sweat and medicated ointment. "You smell like a grizzly bear, too. I'll have to clean you up." Looking at him in such a helpless state caused her anger to spike. Her emotions were so all over the place. One minute she was dedicated to completing her duty to him as a wife, the next moment she wanted to run away.

She kept thinking that if the roles were reversed he wouldn't have done this for her.

"I should let you sit here and rot in your own filth, you bastard." Her grip on his face tightened tenfold and she didn't realize how tightly she was holding him until she saw the red indents left by her fingers.

"I was so glad when you joined the marines, but when they told me you were getting deployed I worried. I don't know why. Maybe because if anybody gets to kill you it should be me. There would be justice in that. You stole my life and I won't forgive you for that."

She gazed down at his broken body, her chest painfully heaving with emotion.

"This isn't justice, Ryan. Having you blown up isn't justice for me. It's like a punishment for some awful thing I did in a past life. You'll always be an anchor around my neck drowning the life out of me." She laughed humorlessly. "You need me now. I should let you sit here and rot, but you need me and I am going to take care of you. And when you're better I want my life back. You're going to divorce me and I am never going to see you again. I am going to get my dignity back."

She stared down at the unmoving form, searching for some sign that he had heard her. But there was nothing. Ryan had always been a stubborn son of a bitch. Why would getting blown up change that? He looked awful, nearly lifeless and damaged. It was too hard to look at him like this. It was too hard to be breathing the same air as him. Panic started to seize her again.

She'd had two years without him. Two years of learning how to become the woman she should have always been. And now that was going to end. She would have to go back to being his wife. And even if it was just for a little while, it would be too long. She couldn't return to that life. She refused to live in fear of the next slap one moment longer.

"I can't do this. I can't look at you like that." Her conscience was battling with her spirit.

Stay. Remember what Maybell taught you. Remember what you learned in Sunday school.

Go. You are your own woman now. You are no longer a victim.

"Your mother will be here in the morning. She will take care of you. I can't do this."

She grabbed her purse and began to flee. But just as she reached the door, jumbled words hit her ears. She jumped, whipping around to see the source of the noise.

Holy hell.

His eyes were wide open and more hauntingly beautiful than any eyes she had ever seen. When she married him he had blue eyes. Light crystal-blue eyes, but the man she stared at did not. His eyes were gray, almost colorless, but in them was a hint of blue and a twinkle. No, more than that. They held a gleam of intelligence. They held character.

"Please… Don't leave me."

Chapter Three

His dark-haired angel was there again and lovelier than any woman he had ever known. God must have sent her to him because he was in so much pain. He hurt everywhere. His chest, his legs, his face, his stomach. He was so tired of fighting the pain, so tired of being trapped in a useless body, so tired that he was preparing to give up.

But then she came and something about her called him back, made him want to live. It was her voice...slightly husky and soft, with a light twang that rang of Texas. If he could have laughed he would have laughed at himself for being so damn poetic. But what better time to wax poetic than when hovering between life and death?

Hands touched him. Not the cold efficient hands of a doctor but the warm soothing hands of a lover. They heated his body when he had been cold for so long. He had to open his eyes and see the woman who caused him to want to fight the pain just so he could get a little closer to her.

She was beautiful but strange looking. Exotic. Her skin was the color of caramel and looked as sweet as sugar tasted. Her eyes were oddly wide and dark, almost black and slanted upward like a feline's. Her body was another matter. She just looked lush, voluptuous, fleshy but in no way fat. She looked like home felt and he wanted nothing more than to wrap his hands around her small waist and feel those curves.

He surprised himself. His groin tightened as an erection threatened to form. A man in his state should not feel such abject lust. It must be her. She must be heaven-sent because he never met an earthly woman who could lift him up when he was so obviously down.

"Wake up," his angel ordered. "Your mama is on her way." His mama? Mama? He tried to pull up an image of the woman in his head, but again his brain failed him.

"She's been worried sick about you this past year. I don't know why. You're like a roach. The world blows up and you still survive. But she loves you and the least you could do is open your damned eyes."

He pried them open, not only to please his feisty caretaker but to see her again. She was smiling, a sight that he was sure was rare.

"I love it when you listen to me. If you were this obedient before I would have liked you much better."

Why didn't she like him? He was known as charming, wasn't he? He opened his mouth to ask her but his voice failed him, too.

"Your throat must be dry," she murmured, reaching for a bucket of ice chips. "They put a tube down your throat. You weren't breathing on your own for a while."

She let the ice melt between her warm fingers before she dripped the cool water into his parched mouth. "I'm going to ask them to take the IV out today. You'll never heal if you don't eat. The sooner you heal the sooner I can leave you. Besides you're skinny enough as it is. You haven't ever looked this fit."

She took a second ice chip and ran it over his dry, cracked lips. The ice melted as soon as it met his warm upper lip. Her beautiful face was soft and relaxed as she concentrated on the task, her full lips slightly parted. He would kiss those lips soon. The image of running his tongue over them, tasting her flavor, licking the sweet inside of her mouth was enough incentive to will his nearly ruined body to heal.

"Maybe we shouldn't feed you." She touched her slender finger to her lips. "I like you this way. You're like a big giant helpless baby." She frowned. "And I thought I would never have one."

Something came over him, some kind of strength that made it possible for him to reach up, grab her hand and place it on his bearded cheek. She froze, looking almost frightened. He frowned in confusion but didn't let go. Why did she look scared of him? After a very tense moment she relaxed and lifted a slightly trembling hand to stroke his hair.

"Are you all there, Ryan? Do you understand what I'm saying to you?"

He blinked, now too tired to nod. He cursed his body for the hundredth time that day. He was never meant to be helpless.

"I always wanted a baby, Ry. Did you know that? That was the only thing I ever wanted you to give me. It was probably for the best that he never came. He wouldn't have grown up happy. How could our child be happy if we weren't?"

What? Their baby? He had been with this beautiful woman before? What happened to him? To them?

She sighed heavily. "The doctor says that I'm supposed to keep talking to you. He says you've been more alert since I've been around. Is he right, or is that something doctors say to wives of wounded servicemen?"

Was he in the military? That sounded right. Is that how

he was hurt? Was that why at night he saw flashes of fire and heard the cries of men?

Was the dark angel beside him his wife? It would explain the oddly strong pull he had to her, but he didn't remember their marriage. He didn't remember anything, only the way the intense heat scorched his skin.

"I would like to think it was me. I would like to think a small part of you actually cared."

A small part?

This woman was his wife and he was a man who loved his wife.

Wasn't he?

He had a wife? For some reason he wasn't sure of either.

"You're in pain aren't you? Where?" She pulled her hands from his face, unwrapping the bandage from around his head. "The doctor says that you got a pretty nasty head wound from the blast, but that was a month ago. I don't think you need this wrapped so tightly."

He felt lighter, better. Maybe the memories would flow now. Maybe he would remember the woman who was supposed to be his wife.

"You are still a handsome bastard," she cursed, seeming irritated by the fact. "Leave it to you to get blown up and come out looking better." She touched his cheek. "Maybe you will be better to your next wife."

His next wife? He didn't even know this one and he sure as hell wasn't going to let her go. What had he done to her? He had been raised to treat women with respect. His father showed him how by treating his mother with reverence. Hadn't he? He didn't remember his mother, couldn't conjure

up an image of his father, either. All the confusion was causing his head to ache.

His wife ran her strong fingers through his hair, stopping
at the place where staples used to hold his head together.

"I shouldn't feel sorry for you, Ryan. You put me through
hell, but it's not easy for me to see you like this." She rolled
her slanted eyes. "I blame Maybell for this. I blame God for
this and every damn Sunday I spent at church." She dropped
her hands from his head.

"Turn the other cheek the bible says." She let out a bitter
laugh. "Who knew I would get punched in it? But I'll get
my blessings later."

He reacted physically to her words. Fire shot through
his chest, causing his heart to pump wildly. What the hell
prompted her to use those words? He didn't like them. They
made him sound like a man he couldn't tolerate. She pressed
her soft chest against his and soon he forgot to ponder his
wife's bitterness as she finger-combed his hair. Desire rushed
through him and somehow he found the strength to touch
her face. She froze again as if bracing herself for something.

"Calm down," she whispered to herself. "He can't hurt
you."

Of course he wouldn't hurt her. He never hurt a woman in
his life. She was a fool to think he would. He grasped her hand,
squeezing slightly. That comment warranted an explanation.
He opened his mouth but all that came out were dry croaks.

"Hush," she breathed. Sweet warm breath hit his face and
he fixated on her full mouth. "Don't try to talk just yet. I
snuck in some beef broth. It's still warm. Do you want some?"

She stepped back from him and for a moment her strange
statement was forgotten because he was once again distracted

by her looks. She was sexy in her plain clothes, even with tired eyes and simple braid. His cock twitched involuntarily, informing him that she was one woman that he couldn't let out of his sight until he satisfied this crazy need to be with her.

"Hello, sugar?" She waved her slender fingers in front of his face. "Do you want some soup?"

He nodded, knowing that soup wasn't the thing that was going to satisfy him.

She returned quickly, placing a plastic container on the nightstand. "Can you sit up for me?"

He tried his hardest, not wanting to show any weakness.

"I'll help you, champ." She moved close to him, close enough that he could smell her clean soapy scent and put her arm under his neck to support him. A laugh escaped her lips when he put his head on the soft pillows that were her breasts.

"Perv." He didn't move for a moment—just inhaled, taking in her aroma. "If you throw up on me I'll kill you." She grabbed his chin, tipped his head back and poured the liquid into his waiting mouth. It was like he was taking his first drink after years in a desert.

"Easy, honey. Not too fast," she murmured as warm salty liquid ran down his throat. Her thumb came up to brush away the droplets of escaped soup, and rested on his lower lip. For a too brief moment she caressed it. He looked up at her, into her dark slanted eyes and she looked into his. Something passed between them, something unrecognizable, something sexual. They looked at each other for long moments until something changed and she grew uncomfortable, almost horrified. Stepping away, she shook her head.

"I think you could use some cold water." She turned her

back to him to retrieve it, but he knew she was composing herself.

He needed time, too. The heat that passed between them... He had never experienced that before with another woman. But this woman was his wife, wasn't she? The heat *should* be there.

It took a few moments but she finally turned back around. He didn't think she was going to come close to him again, but she sat beside him on the bed, wrapping an arm around his back. "You look exhausted."

No truer words were ever spoken. He could barely keep his eyes open. "It's okay, Ryan. Rest if you have to."

He took a sip of the water and then slumped against her.

He didn't want to rest. How could drinking broth sap all his energy? He used to kickbox and run five miles a day. He used to do it all.

He kickboxed? Yes. That sounded right. He ran, too? Yes. He could see himself running through a big green park.

Memories. Where were they? He could recall that, but his wife was a big question mark. He tried to set his mind to work, wanted his mind to work, but the exhaustion overtook him. His body betrayed him and once again he slipped into a foggy unconsciousness.

Lexy let her husband sleep on her chest for a little while, mostly because she didn't have the heart to move him. So she leaned back in the bed to make herself more comfortable, and stroked his hair.

I'm sick, she thought. *I am sick for actually liking my husband when he is weak and helpless. It was sick.* Maybe because she had spent most of her life at the mercy of others, at the mercy of him. But when he called to her, when he used all his strength to croak out the words, *"Don't leave me,"* something inside her told her to stop.

Maybe she stopped because now the tables had turned. She had the power. He was completely at her mercy. She could hurt him, walk out on him, beat him to a pulp and he couldn't do anything about it. Surprisingly she didn't want to do any of those things.

Why not? Why not when he had done everything in his power to try to make her a shell of a woman? But now sitting here she almost felt close to him. He seemed like he was a different man when he was hurt. He seemed almost sweet. She had made up her mind to stay because leaving him when he was like this would make her a coward. She wanted him to see her as a strong woman. She wanted him to know that he no longer had any power to keep her down. Taking care of him for the next few weeks would be her final good deed for him, and when the time came she was going to leave. Walk out and start a new life like she should have done the first time he hit her.

He opened his eyes for a moment as if he were checking to see if she was still there. She couldn't get over the fact that they had turned gray. More of a grayish blue but still much different than she remembered.

How do one's eyes change color?

She knew it was possible. She knew babies' eyes often changed color. But a grown man's? Ryan's blue eyes seemed to have more than changed. They seemed to have faded. Did pain do that to him? Did spending time in a war-torn country do that to him? Or maybe this man in the bed wasn't her husband at all…

She shook her head at the silly thought, but both things were possible. She hadn't seen Ryan in a year and a half and in that time they had barely spoken. The last time she saw him in person was when he came home for a leave shortly after he'd joined up. He was sober then, keeping the promise he made to her and his mother that he wouldn't drink a single drop. He hadn't hit her or said one word that wasn't necessary.

They had spent the week as uncomfortable strangers, barely speaking to each other. It was then she knew that the end of their marriage was really coming. It wasn't like before. There were no half-assed attempts to get her to stay. No lame little gifts to try to get on her good side. No more apologies. He never gave her any clue that he wanted their life together to continue. She had been so relieved.

After that she hadn't seen him again. He would call from time to time to tell her that he was alive. His friends heard from him more than she did. Well, that wasn't different. He had spent more time with his friends during their marriage than he had ever spent with her.

She looked down at her sleeping soldier, trying not to feel bitter. Of course this man was her husband. Who else could he be? Maybe the military switched him out and replaced him with a fairy good husband. The Ryan that she had seen last time didn't want anything to do with her and she liked it that way. But this man... He seemed to want her near. What had changed? Why had it changed?

In the end, it didn't matter. He could be a good man. He could be a brand-new man. But she was going to get on with her life. She had worked so hard to get her freedom there was no way she was going back. Hopefully he would let her go without a fight. And if he did fight, she would fight him back.

Lexy eased herself away from him, her resolve renewed. He reacted immediately, grabbing her hand. The touch made her slightly shaky. His grip was stronger than before. His large thick fingers covered her hand. He was definitely stronger, but not strong enough to keep her there. She could get away if she needed to.

"Relax, champ," she soothed, even though she was nowhere near feeling soothed herself. "I just need to shave you. Your mother will be here soon and she'll probably want to kiss you silly."

That seemed to appease him and he let go of her, closing his eyes. Last night after he had fallen asleep she snuck out to Wal-Mart and bought a few supplies that they would need. Soap. Deodorant. A shave kit. She also picked up a manlier-flavored Chapstick, but left it in the bag.

Smearing cherry-flavored lip balm on his now soft lips was more appealing. She found herself applying it again even though his lips were no longer dry and cracked. They looked kissable. So much so that she puckered up and set a soft peck upon his mouth. It had been a long time since she had kissed him like that and the urge took her by surprise. She hadn't wanted to kiss him in years. She couldn't remember the last time she had done so.

It must not have been like this, even though this kiss was simple. Just two pairs of lips brushing each other. But it caused Lexy to feel a tingle in a place she long ago thought was dead.

Ryan must have felt the power of it, too. He must have noted the difference between this kiss and the others they had shared so long ago because his eyes fluttered open and he gazed at her before he slipped back to sleep.

She stepped away from him, turned her back to him when

that wasn't enough. What the hell had she just done? Why had she kissed him? Why had she wanted to? She would never let herself forget what he had done to her. She would not let the passage of time dull her memories. She counted her scars every day. He was bad to her. She hated him. What on earth possessed her to do that?

And why did she like it? The strange reaction by her body alarmed her. She wouldn't do that again. She wouldn't kiss him. His kisses were what got her in trouble in the first place. But it had been a long time since she'd had gentle human contact. For the past ten years she'd felt empty. Maybe she would start to date again after they divorced. Maybe she would find a nice man to spend time with. Not to marry.

She would never marry again.

She filled a basin with water and draped a towel over Ryan, determined to not let the kiss bother her too much. This must be a test, she thought. God was just seeing how strong she had become. He was wondering if she really took those Sunday school lessons to heart. Yes, she reassured herself, that must be it.

She lathered him up with the spice-scented shave gel. If he were in his right mind he would have objected to this, too. As long as she had known him he had been shaving with that old-fashioned canned foam that cost less than a dollar.

Taking care to avoid his recent scars she began to shave his face. At some point he opened her eyes and studied her.

"Jesus, you're gorgeous," she muttered as she revealed a portion of his wide, chiseled jaw. "I guess I forgot how good-looking you were. I married you because you were handsome, but now I kinda wish God would have gave you more brains than beauty. Maybe we wouldn't hate each other so much."

She swirled the razor around in the water to clear it. "I guess that's why you joined the marines." She looked at him more seriously. "Why did you enlist?" Her shave finished, she wiped his face with a towel. His eyes were barely open at this point. He was lost again in that state of near slumber. "Did you do it to make your mama proud, or did you want to get away from me that bad?"

She knew she had wanted him to go.

"No," she heard a sweet Southern voice say. "He wanted to make you proud."

She found her mother-in-law standing there. Mary was an adorable, fluffy-ash-blonde-haired lady. A real lady who wore pink cardigans and pearls. A lady with a soul as gentle as her son's was brutal.

She was crying.

Just as Lexy had when she had seen him for the first time. He looked much better now and she was glad that Mary hadn't seen him at his worst.

"My baby," she whispered as she walked over to him. She looked unsure, afraid that he might break.

"It's okay, Mama. He's sleeping. He'll be okay. I'm sure."

She believed her words. Only the good die young.

The older woman hugged her fiercely.

"I asked him to turn his life around," she sobbed. "I asked him to do it for you. I know he wasn't a good husband. You have every right to leave him, but please don't leave him like this. I can't take care of him alone and he loves you, Lexy. He always has. Give him a chance."

Reality came crashing down around her all too quickly. No longer was it just her and her wounded patient in their own little world. Now there was truth and obligations and the past to relive. They would have to go home eventually. Be together as man and wife or caretaker and patient until he was well enough to be on his own. Once again her resolve took a hit. Every day she spent in his presence she would be haunted by their past.

Her insides felt like they were being ripped out. She knew she couldn't stay. She wouldn't give him another chance. She couldn't forget what he had done to her.

"Mary, don't do this to me. I'll stay until he can take care of himself, but I've got to move on."

She nodded solemnly. "I'm sorry. I'm not trying to guilt you."

The final straw had come nearly two years ago when he had smacked her. One night in a drunken stupor he had hit her for asking him not to drink. He had tried to keep her under his thumb for years but Lexy never could neatly fit. She hit him back like she had done each time he dared to raise a hand to her. She knew how bad he could be when his drinking grew out of control. But that night her fear of him was forgotten. And she paid for it with the rage he flew into. She looked like she had been the one who went to war, her face unrecognizable, too. Black-and-purple eyes, lips that were split and a bruise that covered the entire right side of her face.

Ryan hadn't looked much better. She had fought back hard that night. She kicked and punched and scratched until she had no energy left. There could be no denying what took place that night. There weren't sunglasses big enough to cover her bruises. Amazingly no one in their small town found out about their final battle. Only Mary. Ryan had taken a broken Lexy there, cradled in his arms.

"What did you do?" his mother hissed. "You could have killed her."

"I need help, Mama," he slurred and then swayed on his feet, showing her how truly drunk he was.

"You are my son, Ryan, and I will always love you, but you can't beat your wife," she yelled at him. "You need to be locked up. You are not a man. No man beats his wife senseless. Your daddy use to hit me! Remember how you use to cry? Remember how we felt?" she raged at him. "I knew you shouldn't have seen that. I knew it wasn't a good lesson for you to learn, but this is beyond what your daddy did. You are a monster."

She frantically began attending to Lexy, taking stock of her injuries. "You are no son of mine." She caught a whiff of his stench. "You stink of whiskey. Get out of my house right now. Get out! I should call the sheriff. You'll go to prison for this, Ryan. You deserve to go. Get out right now," she screamed. "And don't come back here unless you're sober. You better think hard about your life. You need to choose to be a man."

Ryan disappeared for three days afterward, nursing his extreme hangover, but he did come back. He came back and saw the damage he had done when he was drunk. It was then he admitted his drinking had gotten out of control. He only hit her when he was drunk, but he was drunk more than he ever had been. Lexy had known that Ryan had demons from his childhood, but that was no excuse to beat her. She wouldn't take it anymore.

"I'll kill him if he hits me again."

Mary's eyes widened. She knew Lexy spoke the truth. "He won't. He's changed."

She doubted it. But maybe he had. Ryan checked himself into rehab and from there he went directly into the marines.

He hadn't hit her since that day. He also had never really talked to her again, either. It didn't matter. She would not forgive or forget. And Ryan had never asked her to. He probably knew that what he did was unpardonable.

Suddenly Lexy's emotions started to choke her. She couldn't breathe. It was too much. Memories and Mary and Ryan. Tears ran out of her quickly, as if her past was trying to cry itself out of her body.

"I can't," she managed, and took off before she suffocated.

Ryan awoke to see his wife rushing away from him. Instincts kicked in immediately and he shot out of bed to go after her.

He had forgotten that his body was useless.

He remembered when pain shot through his arm, and his leg gave out as soon as it hit the cold hospital floor.

"Ryan!" some blonde woman screamed. "What the hell are you doing?"

"Need her," he managed to get out.

"Help!" the blonde woman screamed. "Help me!"

"Need her." He struggled to get up. If he couldn't he would crawl.

"Relax, honey. Relax. She needed some air." The woman gazed at him with warm blue eyes. "Mama can take care of you."

Something in her voice told him that she might not be coming back.

Suddenly a team of doctors and nurses rushed in the room. His dark angel had gone. His world went black.

His mother was the only person there when he woke up. Not the woman he had grown to depend on. She stood looking out the window, at the world outside the hospital. Seeming to sense his gaze, she turned around to look at him.

"My boy is awake," she said in her sweet accent.

"Where?" He struggled to speak, his throat still on fire as he looked around the room.

"She might not come back, Ryan. I wouldn't blame her if she never came back. You were a bad husband—a very bad husband. But God gave you a second chance and you better take it."

A second chance? He didn't remember the first. How could he have been bad to his wife? What exactly did he do?

"You've got to be sweet to her and not pretend sweet, either. You need to love her. God knows Lexy has spent most of her life under loved. That is your job, son. You need to love her, take care of her and support her, because if you don't she'll leave you. She'll leave you and you won't know which way is up. She's a good woman and your only job for the rest of your life is to be a good man. A good husband. Do you understand me?"

He nodded. It was all he could do. What had he done to deserve this lecture?

"Good. Just because you're thirty-two years old doesn't mean I can't spank you." She gave him a gentle smile and patted his arm. "The doctor said you don't have to wear the IV, especially if you're going to insist on darting out of bed. He also said that if you think you can get out of bed then that's a good sign. You've got your fight back. Just make sure you don't fight with your wife."

He frowned at her. He wasn't a fighter by nature. Most of the time he just walked away. That's what got him in trouble with... His head ached. He suddenly couldn't remember who he avoided arguments with. He shut his eyes. His world spinning. Thinking had even become too much.

His mother stayed with him for hours. His wife still hadn't returned, prompting him to think that everything his mother said was true. He tried to make the best out of a bad situation and listen to the woman who claimed to be his mama. He heard tales of his childhood of his family and the people of his small town. His listened carefully, trying to conjure up images from his life, trying to remember the things his mother spoke so fondly of, but nothing came to him.

He knew he was a person who had lived on earth for thirty-two years, who had seen and smelled and touched life, but right now he didn't even know what state he was in. All the thinking was causing his head to spin and soon he slipped into a deep foggy sleep.

When he woke again a beautiful orange light was washing over his room. His mother was gone but his wife was there in a white tank top that looked pristine against her honey-colored skin. On her shoulder was an overnight bag and in her hands, plastic bags.

"Ryan Beecher, what the hell did you do to yourself?" she scolded as she sat all the bags down except one. "I leave for a few hours and you turn the whole place upside down." She picked up his newly bandaged arm. "You're such an idiot. We're trying for less bandages not more."

He grinned at her, just glad she was back.

"He smiles," she said softly. "Are you happy to see me?"

"Yes," he rasped.

"Don't talk. Just nod." She lowered the railing and sat close to him on his bed. He felt her soft body press into his side and he instinctively wrapped his arm around her waist to keep her beside him. She tensed a little as she always did when he touched her but relaxed within moments. There was a pull between them that he couldn't describe.

"I bought you some food. Good stuff. You better have your behind out of this hospital in two weeks. This will help." She pulled out a paper bag filled with little cartons. "Dr. Andreas said I could give you soft foods like squash or mashed cauliflower." She frowned deeply. "But who likes mashed cauliflower? I got you mashed potatoes and gravy. Do you want some?"

He started to say no but as soon as the lid came off and the smell of fluffy potatoes hit his nose his stomach started to rumble with hunger.

"Take a few bites. If you're good I have something special for dessert."

She fed him. He didn't tell her he was now strong enough to feed himself. He knew that if he did she would shy away from him. Their connection would be gone. He wished he could remember her or a shard of his former life. There were certain things he knew. He was a marine, he was in his thirties and he loved beautiful women. But that was it. He was like a broken piece of glass begging to be glued back together.

"Are you up for dessert? It will make your throat feel better." She opened a foam container filled with soft red ice. "It's Italian ice. I don't think you've had it before. It's not common in Texas. New Yorkers love this stuff."

She fed him some and he immediately recognized the taste. It reminded him of childhood, a summer day, when he was a boy sitting on a park bench eating it out of a paper cup, but that was it. His memory dried up like a puddle on a hot day.

He ate most of it, watching her as she snuck a few spoonfuls. It was intimate, sharing an object that both their mouths had touched. Her lips were pillowy soft; they were perfect with no trace of lipstick. He could almost remember the way they felt, but that could have been one of his foggy dreams. He would feel them soon. He would have her.

"You're exhausted." She fingered his scar with her thumb. "You've had enough excitement for one day."

He was exhausted, eating and keeping his eyes open exhausted him. He was sick of being sick.

Tomorrow.

He would start his life over tomorrow. He would take care of his soft wife instead of the other way around.

"Lay back, Ryan. I bought you a real blanket when I was out. You won't be cold tonight."

She leaned forward, giving him a glimpse of the tops of her breasts before she placed a chenille blanket across him. The blanket was nice, but there was only one thing that was going to keep him warm tonight. He grabbed her hand, his grip strong this time.

"What is it? Do you need something?"

He sat up unassisted and put his hands on her small waist. She froze again and he silently cursed. He had to figure out why she was so adverse to his touch. He couldn't spend the rest of his life with a flinching woman. He drew her close to him and hugged her as tightly as he could manage. It took all his strength to do that. He leaned against her, losing the ability to support himself.

"You're welcome," she whispered. "Go to sleep, honey." He didn't let go of her.

She sighed.

"You want me to sleep with you, don't you?"

He looked up at her and grunted. She looked apprehensive,

but he caught her eye and held contact. He saw the moment when she relented. It was then that he laid down.

She kicked off her shoes before curling up at his side. Now he could sleep.

"No funny business, Jarhead, and if the doctor catches us I'm blaming this on you."

His lips twitched into a grin and he found the strength to kiss her forehead moments before he fell asleep.

Chapter Four

This man is not my husband.

The thought ran through Lexy's head when she first awoke in Ryan's arms. He couldn't be. He looked the same. Big. Powerful. With a presence that took up the whole room, but he didn't feel the same to her. She didn't feel the same around him as she did with her husband. She had woken up in the middle of the night to find him staring down at her with his hauntingly blue-gray eyes and for the first time in ten years she felt truly safe. She wanted to laugh because that was the reason she married her Ryan. To feel safe, to feel home. It was the thing she craved most.

As she continued to stare at him the safe feeling was replaced by something entirely different. Warmth. Desire. The urge to turn to him and strip herself naked, to feel his hands against her sensitive breasts and make slow, sensual, sleepy love, took her breath away. She never felt that with Ryan. He never made her feel anything other than disgust for him.

This man is not my husband.

The man in bed beside her was different than the one she had known. But who the hell was he? His good twin? It didn't matter. As soon as he was better she was leaving. She was probably just being crazy anyway. The military didn't make such mistakes.

However, she would store the memory of how he looked

at her that night. She needed at least one good recollection of him before she left so that the last ten years of her life weren't an utter waste.

"Your friends are coming," she told him the next morning when they were awake. "Tom and Georgie and Lance." She popped an ice chip in his mouth. "I like to call them the dim-witted triumvirate."

He frowned at her, looking confused.

"What? You don't like that name? Well, I don't care. They are dumber than horse shit on a hot day."

He grinned at her, sending a smile that was almost bone melting and out of character for him.

"I'm sad to say that you are the smartest of the bunch and that's not saying a whole lot." She placed another ice chip in his mouth. This time he grabbed her hand and kissed the backs of her fingers, which sent an unexpected tingle between her legs. It alarmed her.

That part of you is dead.

But maybe it wasn't. Maybe she just needed some gentle attention.

"Behave yourself, mister."

His eyes twinkled at her and the doubt returned. Ryan's eyes had been dead for years, or at least blurred by excessive alcohol use, but now… It had to be Ryan. War must have changed him, stripped away everything that was familiar about him.

She turned away from him ready to start the day. "I'm going to wash you today. You don't want to smell like a barn when they come, do you? But then again they smell like horse shit on a hot day, too."

He gave a stunning smile that was designed to melt lesser beings.

"Don't you smile at me, mister. They're your friends. If they're idiots what does that make you?"

He grabbed her hand again and pressed a kiss into her palm. It was sweetly seductive in its simplicity. It took a special man to try to seduce a woman from his sick bed.

"Stop that, damn it!" Her cheeks burned. She tried not to look flustered but she was. She wasn't seventeen anymore. A few kisses wouldn't reel her in. "Sit up," she ordered.

He did so and with ease and she removed his flimsy hospital gown, which was only held on by a tie at the neck. She exhaled as his powerful back was revealed to her. It was filled with lean muscle and decorated with angry red scars and burns. Her fingertips seemed to acquire a mind of their own and reached out to touch him. There were dozens of them, places where the shrapnel struck him. These weren't the wounds of childhood. This didn't happen when he fell off his bike. These were war wounds. This is what war did to him and it would haunt him for the rest of his life.

He stayed very still while she touched him. So still she almost forgot what she was doing.

"I'm sorry," she mumbled, dropping her fingers. She was glad he couldn't see her face when she went to fill a basin with water. She felt flushed. Touching him had caused moisture to form between legs and an ache that cried out to be soothed.

He lay back waiting for her, and she saw his front. The sight caused her to stop in her tracks. She had never seen him in that kind of shape before. His chest was hard and wide. His stomach was tight and flat. They, too, were decorated by burns. Less, but still angry.

"Ryan…" Her breath caught as she spotted a nasty spot on his torso that had been burned so badly the skin was no longer smooth but puckered and rough. She touched him again. Running her fingers over his road map of scars. "Do they still hurt?"

He shook his head and she knew he lied. She didn't want to feel bad for him. She had scars, too, and hers wouldn't be fading anytime soon, either.

Taking a bar of Ivory soap and a washcloth, she gently washed his arms, neck and chest. She felt his eyes on her, watching her, drinking her in. She refused to look up at him. Afraid he might be able to read her thoughts. His body was magnificent despite the scars. She liked touching it.

They never had passion in all the years they were married. Sex just seemed to be a basic need for him. It was never something they enjoyed together. It was just something she endured. She never got to be in control. She never felt fulfilled. But now she could take her time touching him. She found herself mesmerized by the feel of his skin beneath her hands. An image of him entered her mind. Him naked on a bed, his throbbing erection jutting out, begging to be stroked, to be satisfied. She was with him on that bed, above him, running her hands over his pecs, maybe following her fingers with touches from her lips. With her mouth she would smooth kisses over the places that used to be soft with fat, that used to be bloated but had now turned rock solid.

She would drive him crazy with caresses, but she would never touch him where he wanted it the most and he couldn't do anything to stop her torture. She glanced at the sheet which still covered his lower half. She dared not wash there.

Although the curiosity of seeing what his cock looked like caused her hand to move lower.

She snapped out of her daydream when she realized that she was trembling, that she throbbed for some sort of satisfaction.

What the hell was wrong with her? This was Ryan. She hated him. How could she be sexually attracted to him when she didn't like sex?

"You're all clean," she said, patting him dry with a towel when she gained some control over herself. "You smell good, too." It was then she made the mistake of looking into his eyes that were blue-and-steel-colored and graced with long spiky lashes.

"Thank you for taking care of me," he said clearly, no hint or rasp, no sound of Texas in his voice.

The ice must have helped, but she barely processed his words because he was staring at her so intently. He was staring at her like he knew the naughty thoughts that had raced through her mind.

"You're welcome," she said dumbly.

She should have looked away but she didn't. She couldn't and it was a mistake because he grabbed her by the waist and kissed her. She didn't even have time to react or maybe she didn't want to react. His kiss was soft at first, just one pair of sweet lips stroking another, but then it changed, it became something more. He cradled her face in his hands in an act so purely sweet it left her breathless as he deepened the kiss. The tip of his tongue came into her mouth and she found herself responding, melting, relenting. His kiss was tender lips and a sweet wet tongue. It made her forget it all, forget that she was kissing a man she had hated for the past ten years.

What the hell am I doing?

Her husband was kissing her and she was kissing him back. Somehow his hands wandered underneath her tank top, touching her back, her stomach, the skin of her waist. Soon one wandered up to her breast, ever so gently rubbing her nipple. It puckered. It felt unexpectedly good. She pushed her breast into his hand, prompting him to give her more of the attention she apparently craved. But it was wrong. How could she be attracted to a man who hurt her?

He's not your husband.

Then who the hell is he?

She was about to come to her senses and pull away but he pulled away from her first, leaving her bewildered.

"I want this damn catheter out right now."

"Ryan!" Her eyes grew wide. She knew exactly why he wanted it out.

"It hurts," he whimpered.

"Good!" She turned away, smoothing her hands over her flushed face. "You shouldn't be such a damn pervert."

He grinned at her. She wanted to be mad; she wanted to draw up every bad thought she had of him but she couldn't. Not when his grin lit up his face.

"There is nothing perverted about kissing you."

He pulled her close again, fluttering kisses across her throat. She allowed it. Hell, she didn't allow anything. Her body was ruling her now. She drank up his affection like a flower thirsty for water. Sweetness. It wasn't something she found often in her life and while she had it she would accept it. He rested his head on her shoulder and regarded her with his alarming eyes.

"You're my wife, aren't you?"

"I was wondering that myself," she answered.

"Tell me your name." He blinked at her, confused.

She blinked right back. "What kind of game are you playing?"

"I'm sorry." He grabbed her hand, linking his big fingers through hers. "I can't remember."

She backed away from him. "Don't joke, Ryan. Don't play with me. We've been married for ten years." He had to know who he was. She was just being crazy when she doubted that he was her husband.

"Ten years?" He looked confused. "You're so young. You look twenty-five."

"I'm twenty-seven, damn it and this is not funny." Her voice was rising as panic and fury ran rampant through her. "We've been together for three days. Why haven't you said anything?"

"I couldn't talk. But I tried to, remember? I want to remember you. I don't know your name and I don't even know how I got here."

"Look at me." She pushed her face to his. "Look at me and tell me you don't remember anything about me, about us. You don't remember the past ten years of our godforsaken marriage? How could you forget me?"

Because he's not your husband.

But he has to be.

It was as if God or somebody was playing a cruel joke on her, but for the life of her she couldn't remember what she had done to deserve it.

He studied her face, even lifted his fingers to trace the curve of her cheek.

"I don't mean to hurt you."

"It's too late for that, Ryan. It's ten years too late."

"Just tell me your name. It might help me. I want to remember you."

The past three days had been a crazy illusion. This man had to be her husband. He had to be, because only Ryan would be kind and sweet and gentle to her, not because he loved her, not because he missed her, but because he had no clue who she was and any soft woman would do. To him, she was a stranger. To him, the past ten years of drunken abuse didn't exist.

She felt as if she was about to go insane. She felt like screaming into the wind, but she didn't allow herself the luxury of falling apart.

"My name is Alexa—Lexy Beecher, and I am your wife."

His eyes widened and he searched her face.

"Tell Lexy I'm sorry," he said more to himself than to her.

"Do you remember?"

"No. I was just supposed to tell you that— I'm sorry."

"Yes, Ryan. Yes, you are."

Chapter Five

Ryan had been put through the ringer. In the span of a few hours he had been seen by a neurologist, a neuro surgeon, had a cat scan, an MRI, multiple X-rays and every other test his doctors could think of.

His mother was outwardly distraught and questioned him on every aspect of his forgotten life. She seemed to think endless questioning would spark his dead memories.

What's your favorite food?

Chicken Cordon Bleu.

Wrong.

What was your first job?

Paperboy?

Wrong.

Who was your first love?

Lexy. That one he thought he would nail, but no.

Wrong. Wrong. Wrong.

He failed every personal test. But he knew the score of the Super Bowl and could name the Supreme Court Justices and all the teams in the MLB.

He just couldn't remember his wife.

She stood quietly in the corner, looking horrified. Ten years of marriage was gone from his brain. Ten years. He didn't feel like a married man. His mother said he was a bad husband. How, he did not know. Maybe his marriage was so awful he purposely blocked it out. Somehow Lexy seemed unforgettable. He married her at seventeen, too. Was she that irresistible? Someone like him should have known better. He was twenty-two and going places. Why be saddled down with a wife? Ten years. They had no children, and half the time she seemed to hate him. Why the hell were they still married?

He had to be in love with her. They had to have great passion. When they kissed, he felt it deep inside; it shook him. She was so responsive, explosive. He was still weak and in pain but he could imagine what it would be like when he was healthy. He wanted to know all things concerning his wife. He would learn.

They were left alone for a while. His mother stepped out, too upset to be there. Lexy sat quietly, playing with her long French braid.

"Talk to me, honey," he told her. He couldn't stand her stony silence.

"I have nothing to say."

"Nothing? We've been married for ten years and I've been blown up by a damn rocket. My friends are dead and I can't remember a damn thing. I've been poked and prodded and tested over and over. You aren't the only who is having a rough day. So please spare me the self-righteous attitude and talk to me."

"I hate you." She rolled her dark, slanted eyes. "There, I talked to you. Are you happy?"

"No. Tell me why you hate me."

She glared at him, unable to hide the exhaustion from her eyes. "Go jump off a bridge."

"If I could walk I would do a backflip off of one. Maybe the fish would talk to me."

They stared at each other for a very long moment and then Lexy unexpectedly cracked a smile. Damn, she was beautiful.

"I hate you. You son of a bitch."

"Don't call my mom a bitch."

She laughed and rose from her chair in the corner. Her whole face lit up when she laughed. Why did he have the feeling that she didn't do much of that?

"If I would have known getting blown up would make you funny I would have done it myself years ago."

He reached for her hand, stroking her slender fingers till they relaxed. "Harsh. My pride is wounded along with my body. Don't you feel sorry for me?"

"Umm, let me think about it.... Nope."

"You got a smart mouth, Alexa, but I think it's damn sexy. Come here and kiss me."

"I'll pass." She rolled her eyes.

"Please." He saw her hesitate, knowing she didn't trust him but eventually she settled the inner battle she was fighting.

"Fine." She bent and pressed a light kiss to his forehead.

"Well that sucked."

"That's all you're getting. So shove it."

He tugged her closer so that her face was a mere inch from his. "Kiss me," he begged, even though he wanted to do much more than that. "I'm a wounded war hero. It's your duty." She exhaled deeply and leaned forward, kissing him lightly on the lips.

"Happy now?"

"No." He pulled her even closer and kissed her. A real kiss, one that comforted him and made this hospital stay bearable. He couldn't wait to get her home, to strip off her clothes, to touch her between her legs and make her wet for him. He would kiss her there, too. He would touch and stroke and kiss until she was coming and then he would plunge inside her and do it all again.

"*Woo-Boy!* Ry-an. You're the only man I know who can get lucky from a hospital bed," he heard a man say.

Lexy cursed silently under her breath. He reluctantly pulled away from his wife's lips and looked up to see a man in a faded T-shirt, blue jeans and cowboy boots in front of them. His mother told him that he was in Texas and born and raised here, but he felt no connection to this place.

"How the hell are you? You look like shit." The man cackled and slapped his shoulder. "Nah, you look good for getting blown to hell."

He looked to Lexy and frowned. *Who the hell was this ass?*

"This is Lance." She searched his face for any sign of recognition. But there was none, he knew. He had never seen this man before. "You work together at the shop."

Shop?

"What the hell are you introducing us for, Sexy Lexy? We've been knowing each other for nine years."

Sexy Lexy. That sounded familiar.

"Don't call her that," shot out of Ryan's mouth before he could think. She was sexy, but she was his—and not even he would call her that.

"What the hell is your problem?" Lance frowned.

"He doesn't remember anything," his wife said quietly, her cheeks red from embarrassment or anger. He couldn't tell. "Not you or me or that stupid nickname."

"No fucking way," Lance said, clearly shocked.

"When he was blown to hell, as you put it, he suffered head trauma."

"You mean—" he frowned deeply, scratching his fore-head "—that he's got, whatchamacallit... Amnesia, like in the movies."

"Yes," Lexy said drily. "Just like in the movies."

"You mean to tell me that you don't remember that time we drove down to Mexico and met them girls on spring break? One of 'em had the biggest pair of..." He trailed off when he remembered Ryan's wife was present. "Well, anyway, it was a wild weekend."

"I don't remember what happened last month much less something that happened when we were in college."

"College?" Lance burst out laughing. "If you went to college then I am the President of these here United States."

"Lord help us," Lexy mumbled under her breath.

Ryan grinned at her before returning his attention to Lance.

"I didn't go to college?" That didn't sound right. He did go. He was educated. He had a Masters of...of... Damn it. He had no idea.

"No. And we went to Mexico three years—" He stopped and looked at Lexy. "I mean eleven years ago."

"You've only known him for nine, jackass." She rolled her eyes, and Ryan felt her shrink away from him. She had grown cold to him instantly. They were fine when it was just the two of them, but when the world interfered they didn't stand a chance. Not that he blamed her. The more he learned about himself the less he liked.

"Mad Dog!" somebody chanted loudly.

Two more men appeared—one blond who was nearly Ryan's height but a few hot dogs away from being a tub of guts, and the other red-haired and slim. Ryan looked to his wife for help.

"Tom's the skinny one. Georgie's the one who's not."

He nodded, knowing he shouldn't judge a book by the cover, but these books just seemed empty.

"Look at you." Georgie slapped his shoulder. "You're as skinny as a damn stick. You better let your mama fatten you up, or better yet your wife." His eyes poured over Lexy, taking in her every feature and eventually settling on her breasts. That wasn't the way you looked at another man's wife. Jealousy flashed through him.

"How are you, Sexy Lexy? You've been hiding from me." Georgie went over and kissed her cheek. Ryan watched as Lexy stood frozen, inwardly recoiling at his touch.

"Don't call her that," he found himself telling Georgie. His fists were clenched. The urge to punch the stocky blond giant was overwhelming.

"He don't remember," Lance supplied. "Not a damn thing. Not even Mexico."

"Is that true, Mad Dog?" Tom asked him.

Ryan nodded. "The only thing I remember seeing is my wife." He emphasized the final two words, letting them know exactly where he stood.

Don't mess with Lexy.

Even from a hospital bed he was itching to knock their heads together.

"Well, ain't that some crazy shit." Tom exhaled. "I thought we was gonna go back to old times when you got back, like before you quit drinking. But hell—" he wiped his hand across his face "—if you can't remember, we'll have to start making new good-old times."

"I quit drinking?" He was a drinker?

"Yeah, we was surprised, too," Georgie said. "You could

out-drink any man in town. I'm surprised you made it home and never killed anybody."

"You let me drive home drunk?"

"We didn't let you," Lance said. "Nobody can make you do anything you don't want to. You was a mean drunk before you went in the service."

He didn't want to hear anymore, and if he could cover his ears with his hands without looking like a three-year-old he would have. His friends were assholes and he was a reckless drunk. The tales didn't coincide with the man he knew himself to be. He couldn't have been such a creep. He looked at his wife for confirmation, but she wouldn't look at him.

"Lex?"

"I'm going to find your mama." She still wouldn't look at him. "Catch up with your friends."

"Honey," he appealed to her, not wanting to be left alone with these idiots. Finally he caught her eye. Her face was washed with sadness even though she smiled at him.

"Have fun," she said before she rushed out of the room.

Chapter Six

It was too much for her and so she escaped. Seeing them, all of them, in that room together brought back memories of her marriage that she wished she could destroy. Intoxication was a constant companion to all the men she left behind in that room and she refused to live through it again. With Ryan's friends hanging around she would have no qualms about walking away from him. Injured or not. Memories or none.

"Are the boys there?" Mary found her in the outdoor meeting area the hospital had set up for families.

"Yep," she said with false cheerfulness. "Reminiscing about good-old times, except for Ryan, that is, who can't remember anything."

Mary pursed her pink-coated lips. "I can't believe he doesn't remember a thing."

"I can't, either." Lexy laughed humorlessly. "I bet you he forgot on purpose. Who wants to remember being a drunken wife beater?" She looked down at her hand, her voice taking on the heaviness her heart held. "I won't go back to that life, Mary. I won't make it."

"He'll be better this time. He promised."

"I can't risk my life on Ryan's promises. How can he learn from his mistakes if he doesn't remember them?"

"He's not the same man," Mary insisted. "I barely recognize him. Besides, Lexy, you can't leave him now. He's got no memory. He'll be lost without you. If you go, them boys will get to him and we'll be right back where we started."

Lexy sighed deeply. Mary was right about that. She was still going to leave him, but she had promised to stay until he was better. If nothing else, she had her word. She blamed Maybell for her conscience.

God gives blessings to those who deserve them. Be one who deserves them.

A few more weeks, she told herself. A few more weeks and then she would be gone for good.

"Should I tell him how things were?"

Mary looked at her, seeming not to know what to say. "You'll know when the time comes."

She made her way back to Ryan's room. Slowly. Part of her was dreading walking in, but when she did she found Georgie in the middle of a less than tasteful story that all the men, except for Ryan, seemed to be enjoying. In fact he looked miserable. She almost, *almost* felt sorry for him.

"Lex." His eyes lit up upon seeing her. "Help me to the bathroom, please?"

"I'll help you, Mad Dog," Georgie offered.

"No. I asked my wife to do it." His voice was sharp, and after he realized it he softened his tone. "But thank you for offering."

Ryan had manners?

Where the hell did he pick those up? She went to him and braced herself as he draped his arm around her shoulder. His fracture had healed in the month he had been in the hospital, but it was still weak. Walking for him was difficult. Pain shot through his leg every time he took a step, but to his credit he never uttered a complaint. The doctor said he was healing too fast, that he shouldn't be up, but Ryan Beecher was a stubborn man and had made miraculous progress since she arrived. If this continued they would be home within a week. They made it to the bathroom after a few agonizing steps.

"Come in with me," he whispered.

She didn't want to but she stepped inside and shut the door behind them. She could see the exhaustion stamped on his face, his brow contained a few beads of sweat. He pulled the lid closed and sat on top of the toilet seat.

"I don't have to go."

"Then why are we here?"

"You were right about them." He shook his head. "They are the stupidest set of assholes on the planet. I don't believe I could have been friends with them."

"Believe it," she snapped, but then smiled. "I love it when you tell me I'm right."

"Then I will tell you all the time." He grinned back at her for a moment. "Tell me I wasn't as bad as they are. They give Texans a bad name."

"Unfortunately you were their leader. You were the smart one."

"That doesn't say very much about my intelligence, does it?" he muttered, surprising her. "Oh and stay away from Georgie. I don't like how he looks at you. Plus, he's a bigot."

"You're telling me to stay away from Georgie?" she asked, dumbfounded. For years Ryan would look the other way when Georgie touched her or said something disgusting to her. He seemed like he cared. Why now?

"Sorry." He looked guilty. "I wasn't issuing an order. I would just feel better if you stayed away from him. I don't want you alone with him or any of them."

"Ryan Beecher," she said, amazed, "you've changed."

Maybe he didn't. This could be some evil trick he was playing on me. Or just maybe he's not who you think he is.

He gave her a shy, crooked grin and held out his hand to her.

"How would I know?"

She went to him and barely tensed when he rested his head against her belly. His hands came to rest upon her hips.

"You really don't remember me, Ryan?" she asked softly. "Not a thing about our life together?"

"No. But I don't think I want to remember. I have been hearing what kind of man I was and I don't like myself. That life doesn't seem to fit the man I know I am."

He lifted her top and fluttered soft kisses along her belly, dragging his dry warm lips across the place she had never been kissed before. When did he learn to kiss like that? She felt a tingle between her legs but tried to ignore it. But how could she? He had never shown so much tenderness to her. He had never paid any tender attention to any part of her body even when they were dating and she thought that he loved her. He just pawed at her then, only touching her breasts, sometimes causing her discomfort. But not now. He was...tender.

"How can you kiss me? I'm a stranger to you."

"You're my wife." He deepened the kisses to her belly—he made them slower, wetter, erotic. They felt good. She hadn't ever felt so good in his arms. "I don't know many things, but I know you. I know how I feel when you're near me."

She sighed and scratched his scalp affectionately. "What romantic bullshit." His lips never left her stomach but his eyes flew to her face. "It was good romantic bullshit, though."

"Lexy," he breathed and went back to resting his face

against her. "I can't wait to get you home so that I can make love to you."

Make love? She froze. Surprised that his words came as such a shock to her. "We didn't have a good marriage. It was awful. I was going to leave you. I *am* going to leave—"

He cut her off. "We'll have a good marriage now." He sounded so damn sure of himself she nearly believed him. "We'll make it work. I'm not the same man you married."

It was a troubling thought but she was beginning to believe that.

"It's not so simple, Ryan. You can't just wake up a new man. You hurt me."

"I'm not promising you simple, Lex." He looked into her eyes, his blue-gray ones displaying a depth of character she thought impossible. "I'm promising you that I will be the best man that I can be."

Why did he have to say that?

Her emotions got the best of her and she pulled away from him. She was leaving. No matter what he said, or how he acted, she was divorcing him. This was probably all just some sort of sick game to him. A way to keep her shackled to him. No. She wouldn't allow it. She wouldn't be suckered in again.

He rose, attempting to grab her, forgetting that his leg was weak and his body exhausted. He stumbled.

"Sit down, Ryan." She caught him before he fell. A stream of violent swear words flowed from his mouth.

"I'm sorry for cursing but I hate feeling this way. I hate not feeling like a man."

Sorry for cursing? Who was this man? Why couldn't she hate him?

"Ryan." She couldn't comprehend why she felt for him. It made no sense. This man was a monster. He beat her.

"I can't do this without you. I can't make you stay and I sure as hell can't chase you if you run, but I need you. I need you so I can become a better man."

"More romantic bullshit," she said, even though tears had clouded her eyes. "You never needed me before."

It was always the other way around. He was always telling her that she needed him, that she couldn't make it in the world without him. He told her that he saved her, but now his tune was altogether different.

"How can I trust you?"

"You can't, and I'm not asking you to. All I want is a chance."

Chapter Seven

"Welcome home, soldier," Lexy said as she unlocked the door of the small white box that was their home.

The little garden of wildflowers was the best thing about its outward appearance. The paint was chipping off the outside of the house in big chunks. The windows needed to be replaced and the yard was filled with cars.

Inside was better but a little shabby. The furniture was old, possibly hand-me-downs or pieces salvaged from a Dumpster. None of it matched, but everything was clean. It was not glamorous but he could see Lexy's touch. Little things, like the arrangement of the pictures on the walls and the curtains with the embroidered flowers, told him that she tried her best with what she had.

On the coffee table lay little pink-and-white squares of cloth that appeared to belong to an unfinished baby blanket. Looking around his surroundings helped him learn about the woman he was married to.

He looked over at her, seeing worry on her pretty face. She often looked worried or tense. He hated that. He hated that he couldn't put her at ease.

"I don't remember anything," he told her.

She shrugged and attempted to smile. "That's okay. You haven't been home in a long time and I changed some things while you were gone."

He looked around the room again, searching for something to spark his mind, but nothing came to him.

"How are you feeling?"

"Fine."

He had been cleared to come home the day before. He had worked hard after that day in the bathroom to regain his strength. He went through extensive physical therapy, torturing himself and his leg to perform properly. He did it so he could start a new life to prove to the world that he wasn't the man they thought he was, that Lexy thought he was. He would do whatever he needed to wipe that perpetual look of worry off his wife's face.

"You're tired." She touched his face in an almost motherly way. "You should lie down." He was tempted to tell her to stop acting like his mother and act like his wife, but didn't. She was right. He was tired. His body was still weak.

His mind weaker.

"Maybe for a little while," he told her.

She nodded placing his arm around her shoulder and helping him to the bedroom. He should have told her it was unnecessary. The pain no longer raced up his leg with every step. It only ached. He had a slight limp, which the doctor promised would go away.

They stopped at a small room with a large bed against the middle of the back wall. There were two small windows, one on each side of the bed with periwinkle curtains covering them like blue eye shadow.

"I changed your curtains and bedspread. If you hate it I can change it back."

Ever since they left the hospital he felt as if some of Lexy's fire had deserted her. She was quiet, more reserved, unwilling to relax around him. He loathed it.

"I don't hate it, Lex. The house looks nice."

She smiled slightly.

"I finished the quilt before the— Before they sent you home. It took me six months to finish. Your bed is so big."

He studied the piece of art he thought had come from a store. It was an intricate pattern of blue squares in different shades and textures. It reminded him of blue jeans all sewn together. It was just right for a man.

"Thank you. How did you learn?"

"My grandmother. Maybell," she clarified, "taught me how. I can quilt and crochet, too. I learned a lot of things living with an old lady." An extreme look of melancholy overtook her features. Maybell must have been special. He wouldn't forget that.

"Your underwear are in here." She opened the top drawer of the dresser. "Some of it had so many holes I could strain spaghetti in them. I threw them away. We'll need to go shopping for more. Your socks are in the middle drawer. Then the T-shirts, which you have way too many of, are at the bottom." She moved to the closet, sliding the door open. "Your work clothes are in the corner. Your jeans are folded up on the top rack. Some of your finer T-shirts are hung up in here."

He listened as if he was going to be tested later, and then something dawned on him.

"Where are your clothes?"

"In my room."

"In your room?"

"We don't share a room," she said as if it were normal for a husband and wife to sleep separately.

"Why not?"

"We just don't." She sighed. "We haven't for years." She sat on the bed and looked up at him. "We didn't have a good marriage. We don't have a good marriage. For the most part you lead a life that I wasn't a part of. You only paid attention to me when you..." She trailed off. "It doesn't matter. This is your room. Mine is across the hall. If you need me, just call me."

"Lexy..." He needed her now. There was something not right about this story, something he couldn't swallow. There had to have been something great between them. Why else would he feel this ache? "Tell me about my life here."

She tensed and he didn't know why. He hadn't even touched her.

"What do you want to know?"

"What do you want to tell me?"

"I'm in no mood to recap your whole miserable life. Just ask me a damn question."

He annoyed her? Well that was too damn bad. Most wives welcomed home their wounded husbands instead of pushing them away.

"What's wrong, Lexy?" He took her hand in his.

Her eyes lost some of their heat. "Nothing. I'm just tired. I haven't slept in two weeks."

"There's a bed in here." Ryan slid closer to his wife and pushed her down on the bed.

"I will not have sex with you." Her eyes widened and she looked frightened for a moment.

He hated that she looked at him that way, but let it pass for the moment. There must be a reason why she was afraid. But he didn't understand. Every time they kissed it was explosive.

"No, we won't make love now," he agreed. "You're too tired." He moved closer to her, gathering her in his arms.

She stiffened.

"We are just going to talk," he said as if speaking to a scared child. "Tell me about my job."

"You work as a mechanic with Lance." She didn't look at him, but at the ceiling. "Fixing cars is your passion, and restoring classic cars is your life. That fleet of shiny cars outside is your baby."

He inched closer to her and entwined his fingers with hers. "There must be ten cars out there." He felt her relax. It was a good sign.

"Plus two bikes and a pickup truck in the garage."

"It seems with all the money I spent we could have gotten a better house."

Lexy turned to face him so that they were nose to nose. Her slanted eyes widened in surprise. "You love those cars more than you ever loved me. You wouldn't give them up."

"What? They are just sitting there and I don't love anything more than I love you."

She sat up and moved away from him.

"Don't say that." She shook her head. "You don't love me. You never have."

He grabbed her arm to stop her flight. "I woke up and saw you, Lexy," he said fiercely. "*You.* Don't tell me how I feel. Don't tell me what I know."

"You wake up not remembering anything and you claim to love me. It's bullshit," she snapped. "You don't even know me."

"Did I ever know you? Did you let me? Will you let me? I want to, but you won't let me close enough to try."

"Why should I? I won't fall in love with you again. I won't go back to how things were."

He grabbed her other hand and spoke very quietly to her. "Tell me what it was like before. Tell me what I did."

She shook her head. "I'm giving you your freedom. Divorce me. You can get your job back at the shop. You can hang out with your friends. You can be with whoever you want. You don't need me holding you down."

Divorce? No way. Not without a fight. He didn't believe in it.

"You don't hold me down, baby. You lift me up."

She stared at him for a moment, tears in her eyes, and then giggled. "Oh, Ryan. When are you going to stop spewing bullshit?"

"When you love me."

"I'm afraid that's never going to happen," she said so softly that he almost didn't hear her. "You were never this smooth before."

"Tell me how I was." More than he was hungry for her, he was hungry for a glimpse of the man he used to be. Not knowing who he was was the worst feeling imaginable.

"Rest." She fingered the scar on his cheek. "You look tired."

"I want to talk to you." He racked his hands through his hair in frustration. He was frustrated with her for closing herself off to him. With himself for being unable to make his mind work. Sensing this, Lexy cupped his face in her capable hands.

"Go to sleep, honey. We can talk later."

Panic rolled around inside him. He needed to know about himself. He needed her beside him. He couldn't go to sleep now. When sleep came so did the dreams. They only stopped when she was with him.

"Stay." In one move he had her on her back beneath him and before she even had a chance to tense he kissed her. It was soft at first, an exploring taste of the mouth he was still getting to know.

She responded.

She responded to him and relaxed in his arms. She participated, reaching up to lightly hold the back of his head in place. Her lips fit with his. He had kissed a lot of women, most of them more technically proficient, but kissing Lexy felt—right.

Sweet.

Too sweet, like a young girl just introduced to the art of kissing rather than a married woman. Had he never kissed her before?

Slowly, so as not to scare her, he slid his tongue into her mouth. She moaned and met it with her own. Moaned. He felt his cock shoot to life. Getting so hard, that his zipper nearly burst. It was the softness of her body that did him in. The gentleness of her smell coupled with the loving way she touched him, the way she instinctively moved her body against his. He knew she cared about him. She showed him in the simple things she did.

He slipped his hand into her T-shirt, finding his way to her lush perfect breast. His thumb brushed across her nipple. Slowly. Back and forth until it was a hard little point of pleasured skin. She gasped. Then moaned and then pushed her hips against his, seeking release. His sex met hers and through too many layers of clothes they rubbed against each other, their skin growing damp with all the friction.

It was then the reality of the situation hit her. She pulled her lips from his, looking up at him with fear mixed with horror. What had he done to deserve that look?

"Ryan, please stop," she begged.

He did so immediately. What had he done to earn such rejection? Women didn't reject him. He had been with... A memory struck him. He was in his twenties and there was a beautiful woman at his side, smiling, flirting, throwing her perfect long auburn locks over her shoulder, flashing him a killer smile. They were by the water, a riverfront, at night. He could remember the way the breeze blew her hair and how she claimed that it was much too chilly for her to be in such a skimpy dress. He remembered opening his jacket and wrapping the slender redhead inside, holding her close while she whispered sexy things in his ear. Her name was... His memory failed him, faded away to the place where all memories were for him.

"I cheated on you, didn't I?"

She quickly rose from the bed and backed away from him.

"That's not what this is about." She faltered. "You— Yes, you cheated on me."

That was it. He knew there was a reason why she kept her distance.

"Lexy, I'm so sorry."

"It's too late for that. It doesn't even matter anymore. I'll be leaving soon anyway. Get some rest. I'll be across the hall if you need me."

He watched her flee, self-loathing washing over him. He had cheated on his wife. How many times? Once. Twice. Too many times to count? He couldn't remember. He didn't want to remember. He didn't want to be the man who hurt Lexy.

Chapter Eight

Lexy pulled up in front of Golden Hill just a little after noon the next day. Instead of getting out, instead of walking inside like she was supposed to, she sat in her car and stared mindlessly at the big brick building. She couldn't make herself move. Exhausted didn't begin to describe how she felt. Being by Ryan's side the past few weeks while he recovered had drained a little bit of life out of her. If he was the same man he was when he went away it would be easy to walk away. To not care. But this new Ryan made her feel things she had never felt before. She wasn't sure how to handle him.

She thought that maybe when she got home, got the chance to sleep in her own bed, that she could get some sleep, rest her mind and reevaluate this turn in her life. But as soon as they crossed the threshold she knew there would be no regrouping.

Ryan was really back. In her home. *Her home*. The place she had made her own. The place she spent the past two years becoming who she wanted to be. But after that alarmingly steamy interlude in his bedroom she could barely think about anything else. She felt him everywhere. Not just his presence in the house but his touch on her skin. His lips on her body. She felt his heat even though it had been hours since he had touched her. And when she went to bed last night she could barely sleep because she knew he was across the hall. She knew that only a few steps separated them.

He was going to make leaving hard. Instead of physical strength he was going to use mental warfare to try to get her to stay. And that was more brutal than any slap he could deliver.

Shaking herself out of her troubling thoughts, she focused on the task ahead. There was no use stalling any longer.

Taking a deep breath, she left her car. She needed to get on with her visit. She needed to talk to the man she thought about constantly. To explain how the past few weeks had been for her. She knew he would understand. Kyle was very sweet that way.

"Hello, Mrs. Beecher," one of the front-desk staff cheerfully greeted her as she walked in.

"Hello, Janet. How are you?"

"I'm just fine. We missed you around here." Janet looked at her curiously as if she were waiting for an explanation of her absence.

Lexy knew the staff of this building was aware that she had a husband somewhere, but she never talked about him and she didn't want to talk about him now. "I missed you all, too," she replied as she made her way toward Kyle's place.

The door was open when she got there and Kyle was sitting in his favorite spot. He always waited for her by the window. Today he wore the blue shirt she had gotten him for Christmas last year. He always wore something she bought him when he knew she was coming to visit. It made her smile each time she walked through the door. It made her feel appreciated.

"Hello, handsome."

Kyle didn't look up at the sound of her voice. She tried to ignore the tiny stab of pain in her chest when he didn't respond. Part of her wondered if he might be upset with her for not being around for so long, but a bigger part of her, the rational part of her, knew that wasn't the case.

She walked farther into the room, placing the bag with the gifts she had bought him on the table. He didn't stir at the sound of her footsteps or give any indication that he had heard her.

"Kyle? Honey?" She touched his shoulder and he finally looked up at her. Her heart dropped into her stomach when she saw him. He was thin to the point of gauntness but his eyes lit up in recognition.

"Hi, buddy." She greeted her younger brother with a kiss to his papery cheek. "I missed you."

Kyle was the brother she had never known about. She had grown up thinking she just had Maybell, and then she thought she just had Ryan. But five years ago somebody contacted her from Golden Hill Extended Care facility to tell her the money from her grandmother's trust had run out and that if she didn't make a payment soon her brother would have to find a new place to live.

A brother. A family. The news was more than a shock to her. Maybell never talked about her parents or anything pertaining to Lexy's past. The old woman had kept Kyle a secret from her his entire life. At first Lexy was furious with her grandmother. Kyle was her family and she wanted to know him, but when Lexy finally met her brother she understood why her grandmother kept him away from her.

Kyle was sick with some rare debilitating disease that literally caused him to melt away. His life expectancy was only thirty years. He needed round-the-clock care. He couldn't talk or walk or stand or feed himself. He was in constant pain. She knew Maybell, and while the world thought the woman was tough, Lexy knew that there was no way her grandmother could see such suffering on a daily basis.

For Lexy, seeing her brother's suffering was nearly impossible. But she bore it anyway because nobody should live their life alone. Everything she had done for the past few years had solely been for her brother's sake. Kyle was the reason she had stayed with Ryan for so long. For the first two years he paid for Kyle's care. Lexy would have if she could, but working as a librarian's assistant she couldn't afford to support herself much less pay her brother's huge bill.

So she asked her husband to do it, and he never let her forget it. Especially when he was drunk.

"You better do as I say, Lexy, or your brother will be out on the street," he slurred. *"If it wasn't for me he would be dead."*

She hated him a little more every time he held her brother's welfare over her head. At first she thought he was bluffing, but he wasn't. One time after she refused to have sex with him he didn't pay the bill. It was then she knew she couldn't allow him to have that kind of power over her.

Golden Hill was one of the best in the state and with such excellent care came a high cost. She looked into cheaper facilities that would solely be covered by his insurance. But seeing those places, seeing how miserable the patients were, made her realize that she could not leave him there.

So she got another job, picking up shifts at the Calloway—the restaurant her grandmother used to be the cook at. Ryan thought it was to help out with the household bills. They were in serious debt. He thought she didn't know about it. She knew his paycheck went to alcohol and cars and to a woman that wasn't her. But she didn't care about that. She only cared about her brother.

So she did the only thing she thought she could do. She told him her brother had died. She wouldn't allow him to play with somebody else's life. From then on she worked double shifts in addition to her day job, stashing away every penny she could while she paid for Kyle's care in secret. She was going to use that money to leave Ryan. But three years ago he almost knocked her into a tailspin. He had found her stash hidden in a coffee can in the back of a kitchen cabinet. She thought he was going to get angry about it, but he didn't. It never occurred to him that she might leave him. He just looked at her, told her it was stupid to keep so much cash in the house and then went to deposit it in their bank account.

She never saw that money again.

She couldn't protest him taking it because that would cause him to ask questions. She was so close to leaving him. It was hard to pretend the loss of three thousand dollars didn't nearly kill her.

Looking back, it was a blessing in disguise. She had no plan then. No place to go. Nobody to lean on. Now she was smarter. She had opened up a bank account that he couldn't access. She visited a counselor at a women's center who helped her make a plan. All the pieces had recently just fallen into place. And then Ryan got hurt.

And she hadn't worked for a month—at either of her jobs. Their property taxes were due and Lexy had spent a lot of money caring for Ryan while he was in the hospital. And she still had to pay Kyle's bill. It would take her a little while to recover. But she tried not to let it get her down. Maybe by the time she was ready to leave, Ryan would be well enough to survive on his own. Then they could both move on with their lives.

"I'm sorry I was gone for so long." She took Kyle's hand in hers. It was softer than the last time she held it. The muscle tone noticeably different. "Ryan got hurt and I had to go take care of him."

"Oh, Mrs. Beecher, it's nice to see you again." Dr. Hebert walked into Kyle's room. "How's your husband? I was sorry to hear that he was injured. I hope it wasn't too gravely."

"Ryan will make a full recovery," she said with no doubt in her voice. There was no other option. He had to get better so that she could leave.

"That's good. Please thank him for his service to our country."

"I will." She looked back to her brother. "How's Kyle been? He doesn't look as good as before."

"No." The doctor shook his head sadly. "His illness is progressing. His body is reacting the same way any patient with his type of dystrophy would react. He's had a few small seizures this week, but as you know at this point all we can do is make him as comfortable as possible."

She nodded. She knew Kyle would only get worse but still it was hard for her to hear it. "I stopped and got him some ice cream before I came here. Do you mind if I give him some?"

"What kind?"

"Double-fudge chocolate swirl."

"Good choice." He nodded. "Normally I would encourage my patients to eat fat-free, no-sugar-added frozen yogurt, but in this case I say whipped cream and hot fudge are in order."

Lexy smiled at the doctor. "A man after my own heart. I've bought that, too." She turned to pull a towel out from her brother's nightstand and placed it over his shirt. "You want some ice cream, honey?"

His eyes lit again and she wondered what was going on in his brain. Did he understand what was happening to him or was he blissfully unaware of the course of his future?

Dr. Herbert had the bag in his hand when she turned back around. "Thank you. I feel really terrible that I wasn't here for so long." She pulled out a spoon and began to feed her brother. A memory of her feeding Ryan in the hospital entered her head, but she didn't feel the same way feeding him as she did Kyle. And that bothered her more than she could express.

"Don't feel bad. Half the people stick their family in this place and never walk through the door again. You weren't here because you couldn't help it. I know how far you have to travel, Lexy. There is no way you could have been in both places. And you were where you needed to be. With your husband. Everything that can be done for your brother is being done. There is no need for you to feel guilty."

"Is there anything else I should be doing to help him?"

Dr. Herbert shook his head. "You're a good sister. And I know paying for his care must be a financial strain."

"I'm happy to do it," she said quietly. It was more than a strain but it was the most important thing to her.

"Keep visiting. His time left on this planet is limited. Just be here for him."

When Ryan woke up the next morning his wife was gone. She left him a note telling him to eat the oatmeal she left warming on the stove and that there was fresh coffee in the pot, but she gave him no clue as to where she went. He hoped she would stick around today, not because the urge to be near her was nearly overpowering but because he still had so many questions about their life together.

Nothing in their home seemed familiar or felt right, but this had to be his place, their home, because the man in the pictures with Lexy looked like him. Not exactly. The man's eyes were different, his face a little fuller, but they were so similar in appearance they had to be the same man.

Of course they were the same man. How could they not be?

But what kind of man was he? A cheater? A drinker? He hated to hear those things about himself, but those must be the reasons she was so averse to him. And they were valid. But it seemed to go against everything he stood for. He wasn't the type of guy who would cheat on his wife. He wasn't a drunk. Or maybe he was. He simply couldn't remember.

Lexy *did* remember and she thought he was her husband. And Mary thought him to be her son. And his friends… To them, he was the same man who went off to war. He needed to remember, to find out who he really was. And if he wasn't the man he should be then he was going to have to change all of that.

This town was the place he grew up. Something had to trigger his memory. After he ate and showered he put on clothes that didn't feel right against his skin and he stepped outside their little house to go to town. The yard, the garage, the driveway were filled with cars, all in various states of disrepair. He shook his head. It seemed like such a waste. The money that had gone into the cars could have gone to giving them a better life.

He disregarded the pickup truck, ignored the Trans Am and chose the classic black Mercedes to drive to town in. It was beautifully restored. A collector would go crazy for a car in this condition. He mentally calculated how much he could get for it if they sold it. How much they could get for the expensive tools that took up half the garage. He would have to do proper research on it later. Lexy said he loved his cars but as of right now he felt no attachment to them. He might one day soon when his memories returned.

He started the car and went into town, only knowing the way because he paid close attention when Lexy was driving him home. Even then she seemed to test him, asking him if wanted to drive. It was almost as if she thought he was faking, like he was using his memory lapse to deceive her in some way. It was clear she didn't trust him and he wasn't sure whether to be sympathetic or annoyed by it. There was no way he could fake it. It was the worst feeling in the world not knowing who he was. Not remembering his wife. Or what he did to cause her to want to leave him.

Nothing looked familiar as he drove down Main Street. Liberty was a cute little town, quaint with redbrick buildings lining the street. This is not what he had imagined when he pictured a small Texas town. He had been to Austin…. A memory hit him hard. He was at a concert with some friends. He vaguely remembered a singer belting out a bluesy melody. He thought harder. His head began to ache but he couldn't remember any more than that. So he stopped trying to think and kept driving.

He saw kids playing in the park as he turned the corner. He saw the grocery store and a little drive-in restaurant whose rich-smelling food made his stomach growl, but none of it seemed familiar. After four hours of not a single familiar sight, he went home just as lost as he was that morning.

He found Lexy on the couch, her hand over her eyes. She must have just gotten in because she still had her purse draped over her shoulder.

"Hi, Lexy." He couldn't describe the little lift in his chest upon seeing her. She was familiar. In a world where he knew nothing she was his constant. "Lex, honey?"

She didn't respond. Didn't stir. He walked a little closer to see that she had fallen asleep. Poor baby. She had been running herself ragged trying to take care of him this past month. She must be exhausted. He needed to find a way to thank her. Without her he would have died.

He turned around and walked out.

When he walked back in she was awake but still on the couch rubbing the chords of her neck.

"You're home." She looked mildly surprised to see him. "I thought you were going to stay out with your friends longer."

"I didn't see my friends today. I drove around town for a little while and then I picked up dinner."

"Oh." Her eyes widened. "I was going to cook. What did you end up eating?"

"Nothing yet." He lifted the bag to show her. "It's all in here. Relax I'll get us some plates."

"Wait." She blinked at him. "You bought me dinner, too?"

"Of course I did." He bent to kiss her forehead. "Where do we keep the good plates?"

"We don't have any good plates." She frowned at him. "But the regular old plates are in the cabinet to the left of the sink."

"I'll be right back. You relax."

But she didn't. She got up and followed him to the kitchen. Watching him suspiciously as he put the food on plates.

"You got chicken, biscuits and gravy?" She placed her hand on his shoulder, forcing him to turn around. "Ryan, do you remember?"

"No. Why?"

"Are you telling me that you didn't remember that chicken, biscuits and gravy from The Sycamore is my all-time favorite thing to eat?"

He shook his head. "I didn't. It was a lucky guess."

She narrowed her eyes. "What are you up to?"

Her tone made him bristle but he tried not to let it show. It was obvious that he had done a lot of things wrong in their marriage. "I have to be up to something every time I get you dinner?"

"Yes! You never brought home dinner before. It's not going to work, Ryan. There's no point being sweet now. It's ten years too late."

"Damn it, Lexy. It's just dinner. There's no ulterior motive. You took care of me for the last month. The least I can do is pick up dinner."

She turned away from him, rubbing her hands over her face in frustration. "Dinner? That's all this is?"

"Yes. That's all this is."

"I'm going to leave you, Ry. There's nothing you can do to change my mind. When the time comes you are going to let me go without a fight. You owe me that."

He nodded. He wasn't sure why a sinking feeling entered his gut. He didn't remember her or their time together. A divorce could be a blessing, but right now it didn't feel that way. He felt like he was in danger of losing something good.

"Sit down, Lex." He pulled a chair away from the table. "Let's have dinner together. I promise not to declare my undying love for you until at least dessert."

She gave him an unwilling smile. "When did you get a sense of humor?"

"My wife is telling me she is going to leave me. I think I need something to laugh about."

Her smiled faded away. "It's for the best."

He nodded again and motioned for her to sit down.

She finally did and he served her a heaping portion of her favorite meal. He watched her in silence for a few moments. So this was her favorite meal. He could tell just by the way she ate it. With her first bite she closed her eyes and moaned, tilting her head back as if savoring the moment. If she looked like that when she ate, what did she look like when she was made love to? Would she close her eyes when he slid his tongue across her lips, or his mouth between her breasts? Would she moan when his slid his hands along her naked body? How would she behave when he pushed inside her? He had a feeling that Lexy was more than what she presented to the world. He was dying to see that side of her.

"What?"

She caught him staring. "Nothing." He shook his head. "You're a beautiful girl, Alexa."

Her cheeks went rosy. "I'm not a girl. I haven't been one for a very long time."

She had clearly been through a lot but there was still an innocence about her. And he could still remember her kisses. More like a sweet girl's than a full-grown woman's. "What did you do today?"

She looked startled for a moment. "Nothing. Why?"

"You were gone all day. I was just curious."

"Oh, I—I..." She looked away from him. "I ran some errands."

She was lying to him. Badly. But he wasn't sure why. What

was she hiding? He didn't say a word; he just took a bite of his food. "Damn, this is good."

"Sometimes I just need some time to myself. Okay? Is that so wrong?"

"There's nothing wrong with that, Lexy. I understand." She had spent the last month at his side. Any person would need time alone. "You don't have to tell me how you spend your time."

"Stop it, Ryan!" She threw her fork down.

"Stop what?"

"Being understanding. This is not you. I don't like it."

"Tell me how I'm supposed to act." He reached across the table and took her hand. She stiffened, but as soon as he ran his fingers down her palm she relaxed slightly. "You don't want me to be civil to you. You hate it when I bring you dinner. You throw silverware when I try to be understanding. Tell me what you want from me."

"I—I…"

In one swift move he yanked her from her chair and into his lap. Her eyes went wide, but he ignored the startled look on her face and pulled her against him. She was so soft and she smelled good and she was the only damn thing in his life he knew was right.

"What?" He slipped his hand beneath her shirt, touching the small of her back. It was tight. Her whole body was tight. He didn't like it. He shifted her, pulling one leg over his lap so that she straddled him. Her wide-eyed expression turned to shock. He knew she felt his erection stirring, but he didn't care. He wanted her to know what she did to him without even trying. "Tell me how you want me to act."

He stroked his hands up her back making sure his fingers

came in contact with every inch of skin he could reach. She shut her eyes. Had she always been so sensitive to his touch? Had she always behaved like this each time they were together, like every touch was a new experience? Or was his touch a new experience. If it was, he was a bigger asshole than he thought he was.

"Treat me like you did before you left," she moaned. "Like you didn't care about me at all."

"That's never going to happen." He dragged his lips down her throat, leaving hot wet kisses behind. "I can love you. I can hate you, but I could never be indifferent to you."

She pulled away from him, but he wouldn't let her get far. "What are you doing to me?"

"This." He cupped her face in his hands and pulled her mouth to his. He tasted surprise on her lips and a little bit of the sweet iced tea she had been drinking. She was delicious. He pushed his tongue past her lips and this time she opened her mouth a little to allow him entrance. For one long glorious minute she allowed him to kiss her. She didn't kiss him back, but she was soft and pliant and she draped her arms around his neck, keeping him in place.

She broke the kiss, her eyes still closed. "Enough."

"Okay," he said, but it wasn't enough. Each touch, each kiss made him hungry for more. "Just answer one question."

"What is it?"

"How could you be so sweet to me, take such good care of me when you want to leave me?"

She blinked at him, then her expression turned troubled. "I don't know. I grew up with Maybell who was old when I was just a little girl. Sometimes it seemed like I took care of her more than she took care of me. Then there's Kyle."

"Kyle?"

"My brother. He died a couple years ago," she said quickly. "And we live in Liberty, Texas. Little girls are brought up learning how to take care of their husbands. It's been ingrained in us since birth. There were times when I wanted to put arsenic in your food but there was never a time I didn't think about making you dinner."

"Maybe you should stop, then." He hated saying that but he knew he couldn't take the hot and cold without snapping. It seemed cruel to reel him in with her actions and push him away with her words. "I think I can manage to do things on my own."

"But you can't. You never could and just because you're out of the hospital doesn't mean you're all better. I know you're in constant pain. I can see it in your face."

"It's not more than I can manage."

"You can't even make coffee," she continued as if she hadn't even heard him. "You've never made more than a sandwich in your life."

He knew he wasn't as useless at she made him out to be. It just wasn't him. "Why do you care anyway? You're leaving me. It might be time I learn to do things for myself."

"Ryan."

Right now he couldn't be around her without saying or doing something he might regret, so he cleared his plate and went into the garage that he supposedly loved so much. Not knowing where he stood with Lexy was too much. She either had to walk out of his life completely or be his wife in every sense of the word. For him there could be no in between and he knew after their first kiss he couldn't just stand by and watch her go. He needed to figure out how to redeem himself in her eyes. He needed to find a way to keep her in his life for good.

Chapter Nine

Patsy Cline must have known how Lexy felt when she sang "Crazy."

Patsy's moody voice poured from the little radio she kept in the windowsill of their small kitchen, placing Lexy in a trance.

Yes, Patsy had to know what she was feeling. The woman was psychic.

She had lived with Ryan for more than a week now and it wasn't getting any easier. He was just so...everywhere. After two years living without him she couldn't seem to get used to having him around. Even when he wasn't home she felt his presence in their tiny house. She might have been able to tolerate it more if the man she lived with was anything like her former husband. But she saw no traces of the man she had once known.

After he brought her dinner that night he seemed to go out of his way to prove to her that he wasn't the man she thought him to be. That he wasn't as useless as he was before. When he went out he told her where he was going and when he was going to be back. And then he came back! He didn't smell like alcohol or cigarettes or women. He was kind to her. He washed the dishes after she cooked and picked his underwear up off the bathroom floor. He acted like she always prayed he would. And it caused her to be wound tighter than a clock. Ten years of history told her that this wasn't possible. She knew drunken Ryan. She knew mean Ryan. She didn't know new Ryan. And the not knowing was driving her to distraction.

He sat across from her every night and told her about his day. He asked questions about hers. He spoke of a world that was entirely new to him. They had conversations. They had been married for ten years and she could count on one hand the amount of conversations they had before he went off to the marines.

She thought she might have hurt his feelings that night over dinner. He didn't like to be reminded of the man he used to be. He didn't want to believe it. This past week must have been a show for her benefit. For her to think that she had been wrong about him. Or he was just trying to get into her good graces. Trying to gain her trust. But that wouldn't work, either. She wouldn't let him lure her into a false sense of security because as soon as he did he would change back and she would be once again trying to cover up her black eyes.

But there were no signs of the old Ryan yet. Not a single slip back into his usual behavior. Maybe because his memories were buried somewhere in his bruised mind. Or maybe this was how Ryan was when he was sober. She never knew him as sober. She kept waiting for him to come home drunk and that made her so tense she wanted to jump from her skin.

His nearness also caused her skin to prickle… No, to tingle. It was the way he looked at her. Like he was hungry for her. Which was shocking because he hadn't visited her bed for nearly three years. What shocked her more was that she dreamed about him doing so, even though it was the last possible thing she wanted. But she couldn't deny that she woke up embarrassingly wet in the middle of the night, her body aching for something it had never experienced.

During the day when he was near her the urge to reach out and stroke his muscled body was difficult to deny. Every time she looked at him she thought about how she felt sitting across his lap, about how his hands knew exactly how she liked to be touched. She was so angry with herself for that. For wanting more. She couldn't let her body betray her. She could handle Ryan when he was sick. She could leave him if he grew violent but what she couldn't handle was Ryan when he was sweet.

"Lexy," Ryan called. "I'm home."

He was right on time, too.

"I'm in the kitchen."

He found her there turning down the burner that held a pot of dirty rice. He brushed a kiss across her forehead. He was the one who asked her to keep her distance but every time she was near him he was doing something to get closer to her.

"How was your day?" she asked as he moved past her to wash his hands at the kitchen sink.

He sighed heavily. "Can I tell you something?"

"Sure."

"I went to work today and realized I have no idea what the hell I'm doing."

She laughed at his defeated statement. "Well, of course you don't. You don't remember how."

"You would think that something would come back to me, though. Even if I couldn't explain what I was doing, like some sort of muscle memory." He shook his head. "They showed me how to rebuild a carburetor and I did it eventually, but I didn't like doing it. I didn't like getting that black gunk under my nails and I hated lying on my back under rusty cars all day."

He looked over to her and she could see the torture of not knowing who he was was eating away at him.

"I just thought I would enjoy it more. Cars are supposed to be my passion."

She didn't want to acknowledge his pain. She didn't want to feel sorry for him. Because she was leaving him. A few more weeks and Ryan would be on his own.

"You're such a girl," she laughed trying to keep the mood light. "Real Texas men don't care about a little grit under their nails. You say that to the wrong person and they'll run you out of town."

He smiled back at her, causing his eyes to twinkle.

"You have a pretty smile, Lexy." The way he said it, softly, made her cheeks grow warm. She turned her attention back to the pot to avoid his gaze.

"What are you going to do about work? You could quit, but when your memory comes back you'll realize how much you love it."

"I'm not going to quit. We need the money. How did you make it when I was gone?"

"You sent enough money to keep me afloat. We're in debt, though. Ever since you decided to invest our money with Georgie we've been in big trouble. But I work at the library and waitress at the Calloway on the weekends. I haven't worked for a while, so things will be tight for a couple of weeks."

"How tight?"

"I'm a little worried, but I can pick up a couple of doubles. And if my tank top is tight enough I'll bring home good tips. We'll be okay. Don't worry."

He frowned. "I don't want you working double shifts. I should be the one to fix this. But if you want to wear that tank top around the house, I'll tip you good."

She bit her lip trying to suppress a smile. New Ryan was a bit of a flirt.

"How are you going to fix this? You planning on knocking over a bank? Are you going to pay the bills with your good looks alone?"

He winked at her. "I am good-looking, aren't I?"

"You're too good-looking. That's why I'm married to you. If you were ugly I might have had a chance."

That wasn't true. All she wanted was somebody to love her. She hadn't cared what that person looked like. Ryan came along and promised to love her and take care of her and fill up the emptiness that she felt. His good looks just added to his allure.

"You were seventeen when we got married?"

Seventeen and stupid.

"Yes. We dated for two months and you charmed the pants right off of me." She threw a look at him. "Literally."

"Your parents must have hated me."

"No parents. I didn't have anyone. My grandmother died just before we met and then you came along and I fell hard for you."

He lost that twinkle in his eye and leaned on the counter next to her.

"You did love me once."

"Of course I did. I had this sick puppy-love devotion."

"It must have been more that puppy love. I couldn't even wait till you were eighteen. Unless you wouldn't sleep with me until we were married."

"Nope." She smiled sadly. "Second date."

It had not been a good first experience, either. They had been kissing and before she realized what was happening she was in pain and he was pumping in and out of her so hard she bled. She was so stupid then. She hadn't even cared that he hurt her.

He shook his head. "You don't seem like the easy type."

"You were my first."

"Am I your only?"

She looked up at him. There was no grin on his face, no twinkle in his eye. He was serious. "Of course. Do you see the men in this town?"

"I won't cheat on you again, Lexy. I promise you that."

"Don't make promises, Ryan. It doesn't matter to me one way or the other."

He had cheated on her frequently, mostly with one woman. Gloria Rodgers. She was a big-haired, big-breasted wildcat and Ryan loved her. She was almost positive that Ryan was going to leave her for Gloria. She waited in vain for that day to come.

"It should matter," he said sharply.

"Why? I'm leaving, Ryan. In a few weeks I'll be gone. The love in our marriage died nine years ago. Why should I care now? I remember what it was like all those years with you coming home smelling like booze and sex. I remember every—" She stopped herself from saying *slap*. "It all. Nothing changed just because you can't remember what a bastard you were."

He pounded the counter, causing the pot and Lexy to jump. "Damn it, Lexy. I'm not him anymore. I knew I was wrong before. Actually, I don't know anything because you won't tell me. But I know who I am now. You married me. You stayed married to me. How can you blame me for wanting to be with my wife? I feel like I've been living with a fucking roommate."

She saw his eyes flash with hot anger. This is what she was waiting for. This is what she was used to. She could handle an angry Ryan.

"Don't act like you didn't know this was ending. We talked about it. I can't forget how you treated me. I can't pretend that the first eight years of our marriage didn't exist. You don't even want me anymore. So let's just make everything simple and go—"

He grabbed her wrist and pinned her against the counter. "No. You don't get to tell me what I want or how I feel. All I'm asking for is a shot. You won't even let me near you. I see you every day and I want you so bad it hurts. I could understand if there was nothing between us. I could understand if you felt nothing. But this is something, Lex, and you can't deny it."

"Let me go, Ryan." She twisted her wrist to break free but he was too strong for her. Not again. She would not be abused again. She would kill him first. "Let me go."

He refused and instead bent forward to kiss her neck, not as sweet as before but steamy hot kisses that felt surprisingly good in spite of her anger.

"Please stop." She willed herself to stay calm. She would no longer be a victim.

This time he listened and backed away from her. She could clearly see the disgusted look in his eyes.

"You can't keep doing this to me."

"I'm not doing anything," she yelled at him, close to tears. When he was gone she never cried, but that all changed the moment his broken body entered the United States.

"Yes, you are. You make me want you. When I was in the hospital you fed me and washed me. You held my hand when I was in pain. When we kiss, you push your body into mine. You can't tell me that you don't feel anything. And now you cook for me and wash my clothes and smile at me and look at me with those eyes even when I asked you to stop. There may not have been anything before but there is something now."

"I'm your wife. I was supposed to do all those things."

"You're also supposed to love me." He grasped her shoulders. "Treat me like I'm a man. I should be able to touch you. I should be able to sleep beside you. I shouldn't have to act like a horny teenager stealing kisses and jerking off in the shower."

"You're not listening to me. I can't be with you again."

"Why not?" he roared. "You won't even explain it to me." The grip on her shoulder grew tighter. His eyes were icy but she knew that there was extreme heat hidden behind them. She knew what was going to happen next. She knew the sting of his hand. She wouldn't let it happen again.

Behind her there was a block of knives. She grabbed one and pointed it at him. He dropped his hands and backed up immediately.

"Calm down, Lexy."

Tears dripped from her eyes and she hated herself for crying. "I won't let you hit me again."

"Hit you?" he asked, shock clear in his voice. "I never hit you."

"Bullshit," she screamed, feeling hysterical.

"I don't—"

"Remember," she finished for him. *She* did. She threw the knife on the counter and took off her shirt so that she could reveal her scarred body to him.

"Maybe these will serve as reminders. This—" she pointed to her left side, where a square-shaped scar graced her body "—is where your belt buckle stuck to my skin. And this round one—" she pointed high on her right breast "—is where your thumb dug into me while you were forcing your drunk self on me. And here—" she showed him her lower belly "—is where I landed when you threw me into the kitchen table, all because I asked you not to get drunk anymore.

And this one—" she moved her French braid to show him the base of her head "—is my favorite. It was from the last time you hit me. I hit you back and you tried to kill me. I don't even remember how it happened but every time I feel it, it reminds me that I'd rather be dead or in jail than go back to life like that. I'll kill you, Ryan. If you ever put your hands on me again I'll murder you."

He was staring at her in horror, and if she didn't know any better she would think his eyes were filled with tears.

"I did that to you?" He took a step away from her, looking down at his hands. "I hurt you? Lexy...I didn't know. I'm..." He was shaking like he couldn't believe he was capable of such things. "I'm so sorry, baby." Those tears that she thought she saw in his eyes were now dashed across his cheeks. But she couldn't be sure because he turned and walked from the house.

Chapter Ten

He hit his wife. No. He didn't believe it.

No!

He would never hit a woman. He would never *beat* a woman, but the scars were there—all over her beautiful body. They were her battle scars. Only a coward would hit a woman. Only a monster would hit a woman so soft and sweet and half his size. He was supposed to take care of her. He hit her? No, he didn't believe it. Somebody hurt her, but it couldn't have been him.

It did explain a lot, though. He now knew why she shied away from his touch.

He found himself at his mother's house. He didn't know anybody else in town, least of all himself. He knew something wasn't right about his life. It was like he woke up as somebody else. He didn't even feel comfortable in his own clothes.

"Ryan? What's the matter? Why are your eyes red?" Mary rose from her place on the couch and rushed toward him. "Please tell me you didn't hurt Lexy."

He paused, almost not believing what he was hearing. "You knew I hit my wife?"

"Well..." She pursed her lips. "Yes. What exactly did she tell you?"

"That I nearly killed her. That she would kill me before I hit her again."

Mary sat on the couch and slowly looked up at him. "Did you hit her?"

"No," he yelled. "I didn't hit her. I couldn't hit her. What kind of man does that make me?"

"Not a good one," she said softly.

"You need to tell me the story because I can't go on like this." He couldn't have his wife live in fear. He would let her go before that happened.

"You were always a little crazy about Lexy. You saw her and you had to have her. I thought you loved her in a different way than your daddy loved me. You ran away and got married so quickly…" She rubbed her eyes and then looked at the floor. "Your daddy used to hit me."

"What?"

"He'd hit me if dinner was late or if I didn't iron his shirts right. Usually just a slap. I think that seeing your daddy hit me made you think it was okay for you to hit your wife. I was hoping that you loved your wife more than that. I was hoping that you wouldn't hurt her."

"She has scars all over her body. What did I do to her?"

"At first you were just like your daddy. You slapped her around a little when you were drunk. I thought that was an improvement because your father didn't need to be drunk to hit me. But…" She pulled out a wicker box that rested beneath the coffee table. "Sometimes you hit her real hard and she would bruise, or her lip would bleed. And then there was the time when she was pregnant that you pushed her and she hit her stomach on the table." Tears began to stream down her face. "She lost…" She choked on her words but she didn't have to finish. They had no kids. He killed his own child. He was the lowest form of human existence. He didn't think he was capable of that.

"You felt real bad after that. You quit drinking for a month. I'm sure if you knew she was pregnant you would have been more gentle with her."

"Are you insane?" he whispered. "How could you make excuses for me? I don't deserve excuses. Tell me the rest, Mom."

"You used to call me Mama," she said softly, but handed him three photos.

"You did this to her. I don't know how it started, but you did this."

"Shit." His face felt wet and hot, his stomach queasy. Before him were pictures of a woman he didn't recognize. Her delicate features were indistinguishable. Purple-and-black bruises were splattered across her skin like paint when it should only be the rich color of honey. Those slanted eyes that he loved so much were shut, not because Lexy closed them but because they were too swollen to be opened. Her cheeks, which should have showed the graceful curve of her bone structure, were puffed out to three times their size. He had literally been blown up—his nose broken, his face burned—but he still looked better than she had. She was deliberately beaten. Some man tried to kill her.

"You stopped drinking after that. You got sober and joined the marines."

"Don't." He put his hand up to stop her. "You let this happen to her. You knew your son was a monster and you turned a blind eye. She could have died that night, but what makes me sicker is that she was getting the crap kicked out of her for eight years and you let it happen. You should have helped her get away. You should have picked up the damn phone and called the cops. You are guilty in this, too. You enabled an abuser."

"What did you want me to do?" she cried. "Have you locked up? Is that what you wanted?"

"Yes," he barked. "It's what I deserved. You should have strung me up by my toenails. You should have kicked the shit out of me." He shook his head, knowing in his heart that he wasn't that type of man. "I didn't do that to her. There must be some kind of mistake. I'm not your son."

Somehow Lexy knew he would be here. Sure enough his car was parked in front. Not the old pickup he had been driving for ten years but the old black Mercedes he restored not long before he left. Her head told her to go check a bar, but her heart knew that this Ryan wasn't a drinker. Either the blow to his head had changed his personality or the man she had pulled a knife on wasn't her husband.

"Lexy." Mary rushed out the front door, looking troubled. "He's in the backyard," she said softly. "He's not the same. He's not the boy I sent off to war."

"I know."

A few minutes later she spotted him sitting on the picnic table, his back to her, his eyes focused on the clear Texas sky. He turned, sensing her presence.

"Lex?"

He looked surprised to see her. He should have been surprised. She was surprised she came here. She was surprised that his tears affected her. She was surprised that he had any tears for her at all.

"What's wrong, champ?" She came up to him and leaned

against the picnic table. "You found out you weren't husband of the year, so you go off pouting?"

"This is not funny, Lexy. You don't get to make a joke about this." He held out the pictures Mary had taken of her. She didn't look. She didn't need a reminder. She relived it every day.

"Don't blame your mama," she said softly. "She doesn't know any better. She did what she thought was best."

"She's guilty of not protecting you and you know it."

"I don't think she knew how."

"Bullshit!"

She saw a stubborn set to his face that she had never witnessed before.

"Ryan…"

"Don't call me that. I don't know who Ryan Beecher is but he's not me. I didn't do this to you. I couldn't. You didn't marry me and you know it."

"Then who are you?" It was a question she had been trying to answer for days. "Why do you look just like my husband?"

He shook his head, at a loss. "I don't know. I wished to God that I didn't." He turned his blue-gray eyes on her. "I wish you would have told me about how I treated you sooner."

"Why?" She shook her head. "It wouldn't have changed anything."

"I would have known why you tense up every time I touch you. I would have known why you seem afraid."

"Well, now you know," she said simply.

"You should have left, Lexy. Why didn't you leave him? You deserved better than that. You deserved more."

"Ryan, you—"

"Not me." He shook his head firmly. "He." Ryan locked

eyes with her. "I won't hurt you and I won't ever force you, but I will not stop wanting you. You should leave me tomorrow. I won't stop you."

"I can't leave you," she shocked herself by saying. This is what she always wanted. "Not now. You can't even get around town by yourself."

"I'll learn. You have to go. I know I won't hurt you, but you don't know that. I'd rather be alone than have you live in fear of me."

Her heart was beating faster than it ever had before. She was supposed to hate him but for some reason she couldn't bring herself to.

"Who are you?" she whispered. "You look just like him. When I see you, I see him."

"I don't know who I am, but if you are going to stay then you need to separate who I am from who he was. You know I'm not him." His voice broke and he looked up to the sky, trying to check his emotions.

She must be crazy. She believed him, not that he wasn't her husband, but the fact that he truly didn't think he was her husband. She had never seen him this affected by anything, not even his father's passing. Maybe war did this to him, maybe an alcohol-free mind helped.

She found herself wiping away the tear that ran down his cheek. His pain made her uncomfortable.

"You have to believe me, Lex."

"Hush, honey." She couldn't believe him. Not fully. She wouldn't allow herself to trust him.

"I'm not him. This is not my life."

She couldn't say she knew what he was going through, but could image what it must feel like to wake up and find out you weren't a good person. Her body rebelled once more as she wrapped her arms around him in some sick need to comfort him.

"I cannot forget. I cannot stop myself from flinching. I'm always going to wonder if you're going to turn into a monster."

"Then go."

This is what she had been waiting for. She should run. She should pack all her suitcases and never look back, but something was preventing her from doing so.

He's right. He's not Ryan.

But that couldn't be it. She had made a promise to herself. She would not run away. She would not be a coward. She would leave on her own terms with her head held high. She would show him how strong she had become. She would show him what turning the other cheek meant.

"I am going to leave, but now's not the right time."

He gently cupped her face in his hands, causing her to tense. His eyes flashed with something—sadness? anger?— she couldn't tell. But she couldn't help her reaction. Ryan had rarely touched her gently.

"I'm not going to stay away from you," he warned, his eyes locked on hers. "You need to understand that. I want you, Alexa. If you stay I'm going to do everything in my power to keep you here."

She blinked at him. Her brain was telling her to run, but her body was saying something far different.

You never felt this way about your husband.

"Ryan…"

"I'm going to kiss you." He slid his hands down her back, pulling her closer.

Her heart lodged in her throat. "Please don't." She couldn't bear his touch—she would lose her mind.

He raised his hands in surrender. "Then you kiss me. You control it. I'll do what you want."

She froze at his words. *Control?* That was the one thing she never had. She leaned toward him even though her brain was screeching at her to stop. She didn't stop. She couldn't.

Grasping both of his hands she held them tightly with her own so he couldn't touch her. So he couldn't take it any further than she wanted. All she wanted was a kiss, which was madness.

You should be packing your bags.

She ignored the rational side of her brain, her lips brushing his. Too softly at first. She wasn't used to kissing. She wasn't sure how to do it properly and when she opened her eyes to look at him she found him staring with the most intense burning gaze she had ever seen.

"Try it again. Kiss me harder." He shook his head. "Kiss me however you want."

She tried again, her lips meeting his fully this time. But it was a dry kiss, the extreme heat that she was used to from him was missing. She pressed harder, liking the way his lips felt against hers but unable to gain the satisfaction that kept evading her.

She backed again a fraction of an inch and spoke into his mouth. "What am I doing wrong?"

"Nothing," he breathed, sitting very still, never once attempting to touch her. "You're innocent."

"Tell me how to do it."

"No. You're in control. You need to do what feels good for you."

She nodded, not fully understanding what he meant but she leaned forward and ran her tongue along the edge of his upper lip.

He groaned.

Ah, wetter. Softer. She swept her tongue along the seam of his mouth, ordering him to open it. He did, but he still didn't kiss her back. She grew frustrated with his lack of attention and kissed him harder, deeper. Her tongue swept inside to taste the softness of his mouth.

She broke away, panting. Slightly aroused. Slightly confused.

"Tell me what you want from me, Lexy," he whispered roughly. "Tell me what to do."

"Kiss me back," she ordered softly. She felt his cock twitch beneath their hands, which rested in his lap. She had an effect on him. Pride spurred her on. "Kiss me slowly. Use your tongue."

He nodded but didn't move, waiting for her to close the tiny gap between them. This time when she placed her lips upon his, he responded. Slow deep licks inside her mouth, nibbles to her lips. Kissing was like this? It was supposed to be wet and sloppy and alcohol-scented. But this was heavenly and yummy and caused her to want to crawl into his lap again and rub all the places that tingled against him.

He broke the kiss. She stared at him, bewildered for a moment.

"That's enough for today. We'll try again tomorrow."

Run. Get away from him. He's dangerous.

But she couldn't listen to the thoughts in her head. Her body had awoken, and right now tomorrow was too far away.

Chapter Eleven

"Lexy, why don't you get out of here?" Jemma Fisher, the librarian, said to her. "It's quiet in here today and you worked so hard this morning we won't have anything to do all week."

"Oh, I couldn't leave." Lexy looked up from the stack of books she had been cataloging. "I missed so much work already and I'm scheduled for another two and a half hours." She had been working so hard to keep her mind off the troubling turn her life had taken. Keeping busy helped push all that stuff away.

"You were taking care of your husband, not cruising around the world. You deserve a little time for yourself. It's okay to do that sometimes. And if you are worried about us not paying you, don't. You work harder than any other assistant I've ever had. I don't know what I would do if you ever left."

Jemma's words hit Lexy square in the chest. Lexy had worked in the library since she was fifteen years old. First as a volunteer, then checking books in and out at the circulation desk. But now she did everything that Jemma did as the head librarian. They had worked together for twelve years and Jemma had no idea that Lexy was planning to leave town. Even though Jemma had seen her nearly every day she had no clue about the problems she had with Ryan. Lexy hid them too well. She had become a pro about lying to Jemma, and the world and herself. And she had been lucky, too. Jemma was away taking care of her ailing father when things between her and Ryan were at their worst, when he beat her so badly she couldn't go to work for two weeks.

Jemma would have helped her, Lexy knew that, but she didn't want Jemma to know that she had stayed with a man who had abused her for so long. She was ashamed of it, embarrassed by it. Jemma always had such faith in her. Lexy didn't want her to know she had been so stupid.

Even now she was keeping a secret from the woman. Jemma had no clue that she had been searching for a way to leave Liberty. Most of the time Lexy ignored the little pull in her chest when she thought about leaving town. She had grown up here. Her best friend Di and her family were here. And Ryan's mother, Mary, was the closest thing to family Lexy had.

This place was her hometown and it was as beautiful and quaint as a little town could get. Despite everything that happened to her here she couldn't hate her town. She only hated her husband.

Or at least she used to. She wasn't sure how she felt about Ryan now. Confused was the only emotion she could clearly define. He cried. She had never seen him do that before. He was gentle. That was something new for him, too. He was understanding and kind at times and he acted like he wanted her. And there was something about him, an attraction, that made her want to be near him. That's why she kept her distance.

She had promised herself she wouldn't kiss him again. She couldn't even blame him for kissing her. He left the choice up to her. He gave her some of the control she had been missing her whole life and it confused the hell out of her. Plus, she had lied to him about Kyle. The guilt didn't come the first time. She was so happy about being able to take Kyle's care from him, but now she felt dishonest. Her weekly visit was going to take place tomorrow and she was going to have to lie to him again.

The old Ryan never asked how her day was or where she had spent it, but the new Ryan did. He asked her every day. He listened like he cared. When he came home from work he always wanted to talk to her.

Either he was the world's best actor or something more than a memory lapse had happened to him. This change could only be spurred on by an act of God. If this had happened six years ago she would have been grateful for it. She used to pray that he would change, that he would be the husband she always wanted him to be. But now it was too late.

"I love my job here, Jemma," Lexy said, looking at her boss. "And you, too. I never tell you that, but I do."

"You're a sweet girl, honey." Jemma gave her a quick squeeze. "My dream for you is to go back to school and get a degree so you can take over my job here."

"School," she said as if she had never heard the word before. "You think I could handle that?"

"Of course. You used to make excellent grades in high school. All while holding down two jobs and taking care of your grandmother. You can do anything you put your mind to."

"Oh...thank you." College wasn't something she had ever thought of. She had only wanted to be a good wife and mother. She never thought there was anything else for her. But those plans didn't work out.

College? It was a dream she was going to put into her back pocket.

"Get out of here, Lexy. I know you are working that second job at night. Go home and relax before you have to leave again."

"Thank you, Jemma. I'll do that."

But she didn't go right home, instead she went to the supermarket to pick up some things for the house. She wouldn't have time tomorrow. Kyle's nursing home was an hour and a half away, and after she left him she would be going straight to her job at the Calloway. She had to dip into her savings to pay his bill for the month. Which meant she was going to have to work like a maniac until she made up for the loss. It was going to be a while, maybe six weeks, until she was comfortable enough to make her move. She was going to live closer to her little brother. She was going to see him more and not have to hide her visits from the world.

"Lex?"

She froze upon hearing her name. Ryan. She turned around to face him. He was wearing his old clothes, the jeans sagged around his hips, the button-down shirt he wore was made for a much bigger man, but he was still handsome—in a much different way than when she had been a girl. Her husband used to have a baby face. The weight loss must have done that to him, turned him all into hard lines and angles. There was something about him that pulled her closer to him.

"What are you doing here?"

"We're out of milk, bread and eggs. I thought I would pick some up. What are you doing here? I thought you were at work."

"I was. Jemma let me go early." She blinked at him. "You don't go get the groceries. I didn't think you knew where the store was."

He grinned at her and took a tentative step closer. "Is it okay if I touch you?"

She nodded. Ever since he learned the kind of man he was before the marines, he had gone out of his way to respect her wishes. He only touched her with permission. And that wasn't a lot because Lexy had done her best to avoid him. She always said yes when he asked and usually hated herself for it afterward.

He touched her cheek with the backs of his knuckles. "I'm smarter than I look," he said softly. She shut her eyes while he stroked her cheek. "I hate that you look so damn tired." He dropped his basket and wrapped his arm around her waist pulling her into his hard chest. "I should be the one working the second job."

"No," she said. Guilt pounded in her chest. "You are still healing. I don't mind working," she lied. She did mind working almost sixteen hours a day. But she had to do it so that she could get away from him.

Only right now, walking away wasn't going to be as easy as she thought it would be.

"Will you at least let me take over some of the household stuff? I can pick up groceries. I can do the laundry. I can even scrub toilets."

"Did you learn that in the marines?"

She wasn't sure when it happened but she had her arms wrapped around him and her head on his chest. His words were erotic to her. *Pick up the groceries… Do the laundry.* They were words she never knew she needed to hear.

"I think I must have learned a lot in the marines." He kissed her forehead. "You go home now and rest. I'll get what we need."

"Okay," she said, but she didn't move. In his arms, in that moment, she felt sleepy and warm and safe. She didn't want to move.

"How do BLTs sound for dinner? I can fry bacon with the best of them."

"Sounds nice."

"You smell nice." He brushed a kiss across her cheek and for some reason she turned her face up to him to give him more access. She didn't want this. This closeness. This intimacy. But her body did and she couldn't deny it that.

He sprinkled kisses all over her face. This was another first for her, for them. He didn't treat her this kindly even when they first were dating. She felt butterflies in her stomach and warmth tingle between her legs. She wanted him to lay his big heavy body on top of hers and make her feel good all over.

"Ryan? Lexy?" Tom, one of Ryan's best friends, approached them. "Well, ain't this a sight to see. Since when do you kiss on your wife in public?"

Lexy pulled away from her husband. She had lost her mind again. She was leaving him. She should be breaking away not getting closer to him.

"Look at her," Ryan said, his expression almost sad. "I couldn't help myself."

"I'm going to go now," she told him, barely able to meet his eyes. "I'll see you at home."

He nodded, and then, as if he couldn't help himself, he grabbed her waist and set a quick kiss on her mouth. "Goodbye, Alexa."

Only three men in his unit survived the rocket attack. And he was one of them. One man walked away with no physical injuries at all, and the other was still in the hospital, half his body covered in burns. Both of them were unreachable.

The military had given him a list of the men in his unit and their ranks, but not much more. No pictures. No addresses. It frustrated him to no end because he knew there had been a mistake, but when he tried to explain that to the military they treated him like a nut job.

He knew he wasn't Ryan Beecher. All he needed was something to trigger his memory. All they sent him was Ryan's personnel file. He studied the photo of the man that was supposed to be him. Ryan looked like him. Exactly like him. But he wasn't him. He wasn't a man who would hit his wife.

One of those men who died that day in the desert must have been him. The real him. His real family was off mourning someone who wasn't dead. They would never know unless he solved this mystery. He studied the names on the list, read each one about a dozen times. None of them stood out, but each one of them had a specialty—a doctor, a mechanic, an engineer, a systems analyst. They were a special unit on their way to some destination when the attack came. The marines would not divulge anything else. It made him wonder what exactly happened that day.

It also frustrated him that, no matter how hard he searched his mind, he could make no connections.

It was blank.

Lexy was proving to be his only salvation. Maybe there was a reason he was dropped into Liberty, Texas. Maybe it was to make life better for her. To show her how a man was supposed to treat a woman. To set her up more comfortably. He couldn't express the amount of shame he felt at seeing how they lived. She was wearing threadbare clothes, while he—

her husband—was spending money they didn't have on cars. Yes, he would find out who he was and return to his life, but before he did, he would fix things for Lexy, and in the process make her feel good.

He had no qualms about sleeping with another man's wife. Ryan Beecher didn't deserve Lexy. Besides he was probably dead anyway. For the time being Lexy was his wife and he was determined to treat her that way.

He sat at his desk in his new office. He confessed to his co-workers that he was no good at fixing cars so Pep, the ruddy-faced, white-haired owner of the shop, sent him to work in the office. The place was a mess, records were scattered all over, the books were a disaster. It was as if they only cared about the car side of the business. Ryan took it upon himself to check the books.

Pep's shop, while successful, was bleeding money. Workers clocked in and never clocked out, a supplier was charging double for parts and Pep had gotten in the habit of loaning money to anyone with a sob story. In three days Ryan put an end to all of it and in the process saved Pep a lot of money.

Pep was so pleased, he made Ryan manager and book-keeper for the shop and gave him a substantial increase in pay. Apparently Ryan had a head for numbers. He liked knowing that about himself.

"Hey, Mad Dog!"

He looked up to see Georgie, his supposed best friend, in the doorway, his shirt stretching over his large gut, the buttons ready to pop off. Georgie was Pep's nephew and often visited Ryan at the shop.

"I heard you moved on up in the company." He sat his

girthy body in the chair across from Ryan's desk. "I guess we should start calling you Big Dog instead of Mad Dog."

Ryan attempted a smile but his face wasn't up to it. He wanted to like Georgie but he found that every time he was near him he wanted to punch him in the face.

"We're going to the Eagle's Nest tonight. You wanna come? We'll have a few beers, eat some ribs, talk about old memories." He grinned. "Make some new ones."

"No, thanks. I'm going home to see my wife. Plus, I quit drinking."

"You quit drinking whiskey. Beer don't count. Come on, Ryan. We ain't seen you in over a year. Why can't you come out with us? We want it to be like old times, before you joined up."

Ryan didn't want to go back to old times. Not that he thought he was the person this whole damn town thought he was, but on the off chance he was, he didn't want to risk regression.

"Did you know I hit Lexy?"

Georgie frowned at him and scratched his head. "Well, yeah. You popped her real good once in front of me, but she's got such a smart mouth I understood. Some women don't know their place."

Was everybody in this town an idiot?

His friends knew. His mother knew. The whole damn town probably knew and yet nobody lifted a finger to help her, nobody stood up for her, nobody was her champion. She never had a shot, did she? It was no wonder she didn't leave the man who nearly beat her to death.

"There is never a reason to hit a woman. You should have

kicked my ass when you saw that. My wife shouldn't be afraid of me."

"You don't sound like the man I used to know," Georgie said, shaking his head in disbelief. "It's nobody's business how you handle your wife."

Was that a mantra in these parts? Or was it that nobody cared?

"Why aren't you married, Georgie?"

"Because you stole Lexy from me." He smiled, but Ryan could see the hard look in his eyes. Georgie really did have something for Lexy. He didn't like that.

"You never had Lexy." He was certain about that.

"No, but I saw her first," he said sharply. "It don't matter. I wouldn't want to be saddled with Lexy anyway. Not with that smart mouth of hers. Besides, I like raising hell with you. Come out with us tonight. We'll get that memory working."

Before Ryan could respond a knock was heard at the door. A curvy blonde in a tight T-shirt and even tighter jeans stood there. She smiled at him and not the smile that one friend gives to another, but a smile that was entirely more intimate. This woman was another forgotten memory.

"Hey, Ryan." Her thick Texas accent oozed with sweet syllables. "I almost didn't believe the rumors." She nodded at Georgie in acknowledgment. "You look real good. If I didn't know any better I would say you're a different person."

Maybe this woman was smarter than she seemed.

"He almost is," Georgie chimed in. "He don't remember nothing. He don't like fixing cars and he won't come out with us."

"I'm sorry," Ryan said. "I'm afraid I don't know who you are."

"It's me, sugar. Gloria." She looked hurt. "Everybody calls me Glory. We've been knowing each other for years." She paused and ran her baby blue eyes all over his body. "We're real good friends. You don't remember me?"

"Are you friends with my wife?"

A beat of irritation crossed her pretty face. "No, Lexy and I don't run in the same crowd."

"I'll leave you two to talk," Georgie said slowly, lifting his larger body from the relieved chair. "You got a lot of catching up to do." He took his leave.

"You really don't remember me?"

"I don't remember anybody. Not even my wife."

A look crossed Glory's face that he couldn't read. "You were always crazy about Lexy," she said in a quiet voice. "How is the old ball and chain?"

"Beautiful."

Her big baby blues searched his face, looking for something he knew she wouldn't find.

"You should take Georgie's advice and come out tonight. I'll be there. Maybe I can jog your memory."

Ryan stood in the doorway of Lexy's bedroom, watching her for a moment. He had come home early from work, needing to talk to her. Meeting Glory unsettled him. A dozen more questions popped into his mind about who this woman was to him. She seemed to know him better than most. He couldn't ask the men he worked with in the shop. He couldn't count on his so-called friends for truthful answers, so he came home to her.

She must have fallen asleep just after her shower. The brush she used on her damp hair lay discarded on the bed beside her.

She had worked till 2:00 a.m. last night at the Calloway, and then spent all day today working in the library. He hated that she worked so hard to keep them afloat. He could understand it if she loved him—or Ryan Beecher—but he couldn't understand her busting her ass for somebody who clearly didn't care about her.

He was going to make it better for her, he promised himself. He had taken steps toward her security. Lexy would never be without choices again.

He studied her in her sleep—her breath slowly going in and out, her chest rising beneath that ratty bathrobe. Her honey skin looked so soft, so touchable. How could any man mistreat her?

He barely knew Lexy and yet he wanted to be with her. He lusted after her. He craved her touch, her kiss, her scent on his skin. But she didn't want him. No, that wasn't true. She wanted him. He felt it in his bones. It was in her touch, the way she kissed him. The memory of the little moans she made when their lips touched made his cock grow hard at the most inconvenient times. He wanted to take care of all her needs but she didn't trust him. Not that he blamed her. The man everybody told him he was, was scum. He needed for her to see that he wasn't the same man she married. Which was hard to do because when he looked in the mirror he saw Ryan Beecher, too.

She awoke with a start, and gasped, fear filling her eyes.

"Shit," he cursed. He never meant to frighten her. "I'm sorry. I came to talk to you but you were sleeping."

"I'm sorry." She sat up, holding her bathrobe tightly around her. "I'm not used to large men hovering over me while I sleep."

"I didn't mean to scare you."

She nodded, wrapping her arms around her, trying to protect herself from a threat that wasn't present.

"I'm sorry," he apologized again. Thoughts of what her husband must have done to her churned his stomach. He didn't want to think about it—there was no point. He couldn't kill a man who was already dead.

"It's okay," she said, but the tension didn't leave her shoulders. "Did you need something?"

"Yes." He walked toward her. "I'm going to get in that bed with you."

She looked up at him with those slanted eyes, the wheels turning in her head, thinking, wondering if she should keep him away. He wouldn't be sent away yet.

"Move over."

"No sex."

"Okay." He climbed in next to her, wanting to collect her in his arms. But she wasn't ready for that yet. "You've been avoiding me, Alexa."

Ever since he met her in the supermarket that day she had been avoiding him, using work, exhaustion, anything as an excuse to stay away from him. She couldn't look him in the eye.

"I have been," she finally admitted. "A little."

"I don't want you avoiding me. I miss you."

"You miss me?" She turned over and put those pretty, exotic eyes on him. "You're full of it."

"Usually, but not today."

He was sent here to this small Texas town for a reason. God was playing some cruel joke on them, and if He wasn't,

He'd better have a damn good reason for cursing Ryan with a woman who drove him insane.

"You're home early. Are you feeling okay?" She reached out and gingerly touched the scar on his face. He captured her hand and gently kissed the backs of her fingers.

"I'm fine." He was in pain but in a place she was not ready to soothe. He wanted to kiss her again. He dreamed about it. His mind often wandered to those few times she had let him get close enough to her. His nights were painful, with his manhood straining against his boxers, begging for relief. It was made even more painful since he knew she was right across the hallway, that he could bring her so much pleasure if only she would give him a chance.

She frowned, her gaze intently studying him. "Are you sure you're feeling all right? You've got a funny look on your face. Are you sure it's not your head?"

"Relax." He gave her fingers a gentle squeeze. "I just came to talk to you." He wanted to do more than talk—he wanted to run his hands all over her curvy body and feel her naked skin on his.

But he couldn't. Not yet.

"We're broke."

She blinked at him, her slanted eyes still sleepy. "You had to wake me up to tell me something I already knew?"

He ignored her dry tone and went on. "I need to know why we are broke. We both have full-time jobs. This place can't require that much upkeep."

"Georgie." She rolled her eyes. "He's a dreamer. First it was alpacas and then it was mail-order junk. He always had something that he swore was going to make you rich fast."

"Please tell me I didn't believe him." Nobody, not even the old Ryan could have fallen for that.

"I don't think so, but Georgie was your best friend. I think you felt like you owed him."

"Did he save my life?" he asked, unable to keep the disbelief out of his voice.

"No." Her pretty mouth quirked up in the corners in a slight smile.

"Why did I owe him?"

She turned away from him, unable to meet his gaze.

"What, Lex?" He touched her face, turning it toward him so he could see her beautiful dark eyes.

"It doesn't matter. It was years ago."

He stroked her cheek with his thumb, willing her to trust him. "Tell me."

"Georgie has—had a thing for me. I met him before you. He used to hang out at my job and try to get me to go out with him, but I didn't like him. And then you came along and you didn't hit on me. You just talked to me and I thought you were so handsome then. So when you asked me out, I said yes. I don't think he has forgiven either one of us for that. He thinks you stole me from him."

"I didn't steal you. Georgie never had a chance. Did he?"

"That's not what Georgie thinks. We married so quickly, and I think he thought it would fall apart. And when it didn't, he became more…" She stopped speaking and looked up at the ceiling again.

"Say it," he urged her.

"He never made it a secret about wanting me."

Ryan tensed. That day in the hospital came rushing back to him. Georgie ogled his wife's body. He put his fat, spitty lips on her smooth skin. That look of lust in his eyes was unmistakable.

"What do you mean?"

"Before you left he would..." She trailed off. "He would touch me and sometimes you would act like you didn't see."

Ryan swore.

"You always stopped it before it went too far."

"I'll kill him." Nobody got to touch his wife. Not even Ryan. He would slowly tear Georgie limb from limb.

"Don't get all worked up. He hasn't touched me since you joined the marines. I think you might have warned him."

"Warned him! If he touches you again, he's dead. No warnings. You're *my* wife."

She was quiet for a moment. "I'm your wife, but sometimes you don't sound like my husband."

He cupped her face in his hands. She looked wary for a moment, but just for a moment. "I'm not him, Lexy. You know it, don't you?"

She shut her eyes. "I'm not sure what I know anymore."

He wasn't going to win this fight. He didn't have to win. He just wanted her.

"Lexy. I want to kiss you. Do you want me to?"

"Yes," she choked.

"It's not wrong to want to kiss me. It's not wrong to want to be with me."

"But you say you aren't my husband. And if you aren't, then you have no right to me. I am somebody else's wife."

He sighed heavily. She had a point. "Right now I am your husband. What do you want to do?"

"I want to go shopping."

"What?" He shook his head in disbelief.

"You need new clothes. Can we go?"

"We can go shopping later. Let me kiss you now."

"I need to brush my teeth."

"You brushed them this morning."

"But I ate raw onions for lunch."

He gently stroked her face with the backs of his fingers. "Raw onions. Raw sewage. I don't give a shit."

"That's gross."

He saw the moment she gave up her fight.

"I'm going to kiss your neck."

"Okay," she consented and lay very still, shutting her eyes as if she were bracing herself.

He placed his nose in the crease of her neck, rubbing it along her smooth skin so she could get used to his touch. She smelled good, not like the perfumed necks he was used to but clean, like soap and shampoo and skin. It was Lexy.

"I really hate my clothes, Lex," he told her as he kissed her under her right ear. "Why does one need twelve Budweiser T-shirts?"

"Because, sweetness, you get one free when you buy fifty twelve packs."

"Mmmm." He ran his nose along her throat, and like a good girl she tilted her head up so that he would have free access to her silky skin. "You smell so good," he muttered as his kisses grew a little longer, hotter, wetter. "I hate beer."

She moaned, "You're a whisky man."

"No." He nipped her with his teeth. "But I could get drunk off of you."

"Beautiful words, honey, but I'm still not going to have sex with you."

"Deny, deny, deny. I won't stop trying." He delivered a

particularly scorching kiss to the spot on her neck that all women seemed to have.

"Where did you learn how to do that?" She unconsciously leaned into his kiss.

"The marines."

"Oh, I forgot," she moaned again. "You boys must get lonely in Iraq."

"You're such a smart-ass. I don't know why I want you so much."

"We all want what we can't have." She grinned up at him and his heart stopped beating. It had been days since he had seen her smile, and now that it had reappeared it warm his insides. "I hate that I find myself liking you."

She sat up. Her expression tortured. Her confusion was palpable.

"Why *are* you still here, Lexy?"

She shook her head, silent for a long moment, as if weighing her words. "Because for now I have to be."

That wasn't the truth. She could blame it on him if she wanted to but he could take care of himself. Her presence here baffled him. She didn't seem like the kind of woman who would stick around to be mistreated. She could have left him years ago. There had to be something he was missing.

Or maybe a little part of her knew that he wasn't her husband but some other man who had come to take his place. Maybe she wanted what he could give her even if she was too afraid to admit it to herself. His hand slipped down to stroke her thigh.

She jumped, but instead of pulling away he stayed there gently touching her. She was naked beneath her dowdy bathrobe. All he had to do was pull the tie open. One tug and he could see all the creamy smooth skin he imagined at night.

"Hands above the waist, mister," she said with a catch in her voice.

"Okay," he agreed easily. He slid his hand up her thigh to her hip. His fingers made wide lazy circles. She relaxed under his caress. After long minutes of touching he moved his hand to her trim waist. He stroked the skin there with his thumb over and over until she was sighing with pleasure.

"Is that better?" When she nodded he moved his touch higher and higher until it reached the underside of her breast. He stroked her naked skin, pulled her nipple between two of his fingers, gently plucking it until it was hard and ready to be suckled.

"Ryan…" She stiffened slightly. "Please don't touch me like that. I can't think when you do."

He didn't want her to think. He wanted her to feel.

"Tell me what you want from me." He was learning that in order to touch her he would have to relinquish control. In a past life he would have never agreed to it, but she was different. He would wait for her.

"Give me your hand," she ordered in a quiet voice as she lay back down. She locked her fingers with his, resting her face on their joined hands.

"Where's your wedding ring?"

She looked at him as if he had three heads. "You never gave me one."

Of course her husband never gave her one. He marked her body in a different way, a way that didn't show love but brutal dominance. She deserved more than this. More than this little house, more than near poverty and a husband who hurt her. Every day he spent with her made him that much more sure he wasn't her husband.

"How do people know you're married if you don't wear a ring?"

"Everybody knows I'm married. It's you who should wear a ring. Maybe it will keep you faithful."

There was anger in her voice mixed with sorrow. She had dealt with too much from Ryan Beecher. He didn't know how she could hold her head up. But she did, and he admired her for it.

"Who is Glory Rodgers?"

"Your mistress." She rolled her eyes. "Excuse me. Poor people don't have mistresses. She's your sl— Your girlfriend."

"That proves it. I know I'm not your husband. Why would I mess around with her when being near you makes me hard enough to drill holes in steel?"

She locked eyes with him then looked away. "There was a time that I thought you were going to leave me for her."

"You should have left him." He bent down to kiss her mouth, feeling sad for her wasted life.

She kissed him back for a moment, then looked away. "I should have, but I didn't realize that was an option for a long time. Besides, I would have missed this beautiful body if I had." She gave him a shy look and gently touched his chest.

"Why did you stay? I'm serious. I want to know." He studied her face and saw her walls begin to go up.

"I don't want to talk about this now."

"What do you want to do?"

She opened her mouth and then closed it and then opened it again, looking helpless.

"Tell me," he urged.

"I'm not ready for it all yet."

"Okay, then tell me what you are ready for."

"I want to—to—" she pulled her lower lip between her teeth "—touch you. But I don't want you to touch me."

"Okay." Before she could react he pulled the tie from her bathrobe, causing it to fall open. He tried to hold back a groan but barely managed it.

"Ryan!"

He greedily took in her body. He had never seen her without clothes before, and while he dreamed about seeing her naked since the day he woke up in the hospital the real vision was worth the wait. Her breasts were full and round with pretty chocolate-colored nipples that he longed to suck into his mouth. Her waist was small. Her hips flared out, looking like the perfect things to hold on to while burying himself deep inside her.

"What are you doing?"

He pulled off his shirt and settled on his back. "You're going to have to tie me to the bed."

"Excuse me?" Her eyes went wide.

"If you don't want me to touch you then you're going to have to tie me to the bed. I want you too much to keep my hands to myself."

"Oh… Um… Maybe we shouldn't do this." Her face turned scarlet. "It was a dumb idea anyway."

"No." He tossed the tie to her. "Do it. It's time for another lesson. You're in charge."

She looked adorably unsure for a moment. "Are you sure about this?"

"No, but if this is the only way I can have you, then this

is the way I'll take you." He folded his hands together and rested them against the headboard. "I just have one request."

She looked wary but nodded.

"Please take off your robe. I need to see all of your body."

She looked away from him as she slipped it off her shoulders and sat back, allowing him to take in his fill. It was clear she was embarrassed by her nudity, but she made no move to cover herself.

"You're so pretty, honey." He reached out to touch the smooth expanse of skin that covered her chest but he remembered her request. "Tie me to the headboard, Lexy. I'm afraid I won't be able to stop myself."

She climbed on top of him, her naked body straddling him, giving him an excellent view of her sex. She wasn't totally bare there, not shaved bald like most women he had encountered and it caused his cock to throb painfully.

She was aroused. The smell of her moistening sex filled the room and it took everything in his power not to touch her. She made quick work of tying him to the bed and once she was done she sat on top of him, seeming as if she was at a loss.

"Tell me what you're thinking."

"I thought about you like this," she admitted, her cheeks turning even redder than before.

"Yeah?" Her admission caused his chest to swell. "Tell me about it."

She trailed her fingers across his scarred stomach. "It was when you were in the hospital and I was washing you." She placed her lips where her fingers had been and delivered sweet wet pecks to his skin. "I don't know what it was about knowing that you couldn't hurt me that…"

"Turned you on?"

She looked up at him, her plump lower lip pulled between her teeth. "I think I'm sick. It's not normal to think that way."

"No." He pulled against his restraints needing to comfort her, but he could go nowhere. "You are not sick. What we do is never wrong and who dictates what's normal?"

She nodded and kissed him just above his belly button. Her kisses felt so innocent on his body he wanted to instruct her, tell her how to give them both pleasure, but he refrained. She was in charge.

She slid her body along his, bringing those beautiful breasts into contact with his chest. His nipples tightened with her touch. He hissed, involuntarily writhing beneath her so that her sex lined up with his.

She looked up at him wide-eyed, as if she hadn't known that those two parts should come together but then she pushed back against him, her wetness rubbing against his jeans.

Take me out, he wanted to beg. He wanted to slip inside her wet warmth so badly, but he knew it wasn't time. He knew that for now it was his job to put up with this torture for her pleasure.

"It hurts there," she whispered, setting a kiss on his jaw. "Why does it hurt there?"

"You're aroused. That's why you're wet. Your body is preparing itself for sex. For me."

She looked up at him, puzzled for moment. "But I don't like sex. It hurts."

"Aw, baby. It's not supposed to hurt. It's supposed to make you feel good. When you're ready I can show you."

She mulled his words over for a moment before kissing him. She then lightly set her hands on his shoulders, still unsure of her every move. It was as if she hadn't been married for the past ten years, as if she were new to loving. He would show her how good it could be. He met her gentle mouth with his own, matching her every stroke with a deeper one. He pulled her tongue into his mouth and sucked on it, mimicking the movements of sex, trying to explain to her without words how good it could be.

"We have to stop," she whimpered. "It hurts too much."

"No," he said more forcefully than he intended. "I can show you how to make it feel better. Lexy, have you ever touched yourself?"

"What?" She looked horrified. "No, of course not."

He smiled gently at her. "There's nothing wrong with that, honey. Sit up. Let me show you how to make yourself feel good."

She obeyed his directive, sliding herself upward until her legs were spread open across his stomach. He could see the wetness on her lips, could smell her sweet-scented arousal filling the room.

"The thing that throbs is called a clitoris or a clit. If you stroke it, it will make you feel good."

She slowly moved her fingers to her clit and stroked once. She jumped at the contact.

"Again, sweetheart. I promise you it will feel good."

She stroked again, her fingers moving in slow little circles. He wanted to put his mouth there to suck on her, to taste her arousal but right now he could only imagine it, only watch and dream of how good it would be when it happened. She finally relaxed, her eyes drifting shut, her mouth slightly open, the tip of her pink tongue darting out to lick her lips.

She moaned softly, taking to self-pleasure like it was natural. It was the most erotic thing he had ever seen. He wouldn't leave here until he had her, until she trusted him, until she knew that sex could be good and fun and addictive.

She opened her eyes and stared down at him. "I want to kiss you."

"Kiss me. Place your body against mine and move against your hand."

Her chest met his once again, their nipples touching. He groaned. She moved them against him, her eyes closing as she learned that she could receive pleasure from more than once part of her body.

"Lexy, kiss me. Move against me."

She pulled his lower lip between her teeth, nipping it until he cried out. Then she licked it. Smoothing her pouty lips across the place she had bruised.

Her hand settled between her legs and he could feel her grinding against it. He could hear the wetness of her sex, feel the pressure from her hand as it bumped his too hard cock. He pushed his tongue into her mouth, wanting this experience to be over but at the same time never end. It was too much. Too erotic. Made that way because he could not touch her.

"What's happening to me?" she cried out.

"You're coming."

As soon as the words left his mouth she shook as her first orgasm hit her hard. She cried out, her eyes filled with tears, but she kept moving against her fingers, riding wave after wave of aftershock until she was spent. She collapsed against his chest panting.

He could take no more.

"Untie me now," he ordered.

She bolted upright, afraid to disobey. She pulled the tie loose and sat beside him, her body tense. She was bracing herself again but he didn't touch her. He lay back on the bed, pulled his hard aching cock from his pants and fisted it.

"See what you do to me?" He watched her as she watched him in amazement as he pulled on his cock. "You make me hard. I go to bed like this every night. I wake up like this every morning. I spend every shower jerking off because I know I can't have you yet."

He stroked himself furiously. He had never been so aroused before. He had never been watched. He looked at her, imagining her tight wet folds surrounding him, squeezing him, milking his seed. He would kiss her breasts, and lick her mouth and finger her clit until she cried out his name. Fantasy became too much. He hissed as he balls drew up tight, preparing to explode.

"I want you, Alexa. Nothing will change that."

He came hard, his hips leaving the bed as he spilled himself all over his hand. She watched in silent horror. Then she took her bathrobe and gently cleaned his hand. Her touch surprised him. He wasn't sure how to react, but then she crawled into his arms and began to weep.

Maybe it had all been too much.

"Oh, Lexy. I'm so sorry, honey."

"No!" She looked up horrified. "It's just   It's just… Thank you."

Lexy wasn't sure why she was crying. She wasn't sad. Overwhelmed? Yes. Confused? More than she had ever been. Who was this man? Ryan never respected her wishes. He had never gone out of his way to see to her pleasure first. Her heart kept telling her that the man who was holding her while she cried was not the man she had married, but her brain was telling her something entirely different. Nobody could change that much.

He had to be Ryan Beecher, not because she wanted him to be, but because if he wasn't, this kind man belonged to somebody else.

She needed to leave him. Forget her promise. God would understand. She couldn't risk her sanity by staying here. She needed to make plans tonight.

The doorbell rang and she bolted from bed, throwing a tank top over her naked body and shorts over her hips.

He sat up, staring after her. "Where are you going?"

Away from you! "The door bell is ringing."

"So? Lexy, please don't do this. Please don't shut yourself away from me."

"I'm not. Somebody has to answer the door."

Ryan followed her, buttoning his jeans as he went.

"You're going to answer the door like that?" he called after her.

"Yes."

She practically ran toward the door. Ryan was so intense and when she was alone with him she didn't trust herself...or her body, to be more exact. It had been so long since she had been touched in a nice way that when Ryan did, she nearly lost her mind. Not nearly. She had. He hadn't touched her at all and she still went insane. She had just experienced something with him that she hadn't thought possible. It was sensual and scary and wonderful. And she wanted to do it again.

She reached the door prepared to open it, when he yelled, "You're not wearing a bra and your shirt is see-through."

She froze, turned around and looked down. Sure enough

she could see her breasts straining against the cloth, her nipples erect little points still aroused from Ryan's attention.

"Why didn't you say something?"

"I did."

He was looking at her, a knowing little smile curling his lips. She felt her insides melt. She had to leave him. The sooner the better.

She covered herself with her arms and glared at him.

"Oh, don't look at me like that."

He gave her a soft peck and opened the door. She jumped behind him.

"Beecher?" A large, barrel-chested man stood at the door in full military uniform.

"Sir." He saluted the man, only wearing blue jeans.

Lexy might have laughed if the man before them didn't look like a bull ready to charge.

"At ease," he barked. "You aren't in the military anymore. You don't have to do that." He frowned deeply at Ryan and then spotted Lexy who was peeking at him from behind Ryan's shoulder.

"Hello, Mrs. Beecher. I'm sorry to bother you this evening." His face and voice softened. Apparently somebody taught him to be nice to women.

"No problem," she squeaked, thoroughly embarrassed.

Ryan covered her hands with his. It was then she realized that she had wrapped her arms around his middle in a move to shield herself from their guest. That was odd for her. She never turned to her husband for protection. And today she did it without thinking.

"Introduce me to your wife."

"Uh, I would, but I have no idea who you are."

The man's eyes narrowed. "They said you didn't remember. I wasn't sure if I believed it."

"He really doesn't, sir," Lexy interjected. "Not me. Not his mother. Nothing."

The man shook his head. "I was at the hospital the day you arrived. You really don't remember."

"I'm sorry, sir. I don't."

"I'm your commanding officer, Beecher. You don't remember me making you do suicide drills for two hours because you mouthed off?"

"I'm sorry, sir."

She could feel both men's frustration. She had a fair amount of her own. She could not rest easy until she knew Ryan remembered their life together. She could leave then with no guilt. Her life with him would have closure, not this electrifying newness that kept her awake at night thinking about him.

"I'm Major Daniel Lee."

"I recognize your name." Ryan's head snapped up. "Sir, I don't think we have met."

"How would you know? You don't remember a damn thing?"

"I see their faces sometimes," he responded quietly. "Not clearly, but I see the men in my unit and I hear them yelling and I remember the heat of the fire." He looked into the major's eyes. "It's like trying to catch a fish in a pond, everything is murky and when you reach your hands out to catch it, it slips under the surface. I want to remember. I've been trying because I'm stuck without my mind. I'm not the man I used to be."

"Beecher?" The major looked dumbfounded. "I remember you being a giant idiot."

"Me, too," Lexy said, moving slightly away from the stranger she was infatuated with…and terrified of.

"Sir, you knew me before? Can you say that I am the same Ryan Beecher that you knew?"

Lexy saw the spark light behind his eyes. This was the thing he was looking for to hold on to.

"We spent every day together for months. We needed a mechanic and you were the best we had."

This Ryan couldn't fix cars. He liked numbers. He wasn't the best mechanic the marines had to offer. How could a blow to the head change a man so completely?

"Could I be a different man?"

"Ryan." She wanted him to stop speaking, to stop questioning. If he wasn't Ryan Beecher who was he? And where was the real Ryan? Was he living someone else's life or did his life end that day in the desert? Or was he locked inside the man standing in front of her?

He had to be the man she married ten years ago. His commanding officer had seen him daily over the past year while she had been a thousand miles away. He couldn't tell the difference. He had to be Ryan. But why did he act so differently?

"I think there was some sort of mistake. I don't think I'm Ryan Beecher." His voice took on a pleading tone. "I've come here and nothing is familiar. I wake up and they tell me I've been married for ten years to a woman I don't recognize. They tell me I'm a drunk, that I'm a cheater, that I used to hit my wife. That I'm half a man and I know it's not right. You seem familiar to me, but this place—this is not right. I know it's not right. I don't feel right."

"Son." The major wiped his huge hand across his troubled brow. "I'm sorry. I don't have the answers you're looking for. You do look like him, just like him and if your wife and friends think you are him then you are. The U.S. Military does not make mistakes this big."

"But they could! I want to see their records. I want to know who the other men were who died. I need to know for sure."

Her heart was breaking for him. He didn't want to believe he had hurt her. She didn't want to believe it either, but it happened. The last ten years had not been imagined.

"Sweetheart." Lexy touched his arm. "He doesn't know anything."

Ryan spun around looking slightly bewildered. His blue-gray eyes filled with an emotion she had never witnessed in her husband.

"I don't want to be him, Lex. I just can't be him."

"I'm so sorry, honey." She wrapped her arms around him and held him tightly. "I'm so sorry." She squeezed her eyes shut, feeling her insides go to jelly. What was she doing? After what they had been through, comforting him seemed ridiculous.

But she had to do it. "I'm afraid you might be stuck with me."

"Don't make a joke. This isn't about being stuck with you."

"What is it about then?"

"Mrs. Beecher," the major said, "I know your husband doesn't mean it the way it sounded. I can tell that he cares about you and appreciates all the time and effort you put into nursing him back to health." He looked at Ryan, his expression hard. "You may not know who you are, but while you are here you are her husband and you will take care of her like you are supposed to."

Ryan looked shell-shocked for a moment, but glanced at Lexy and nodded.

The Major stayed a little longer and assaulted Ryan with questions.

Tell me what you remember.

Where were you?

What is the last thing you saw before the explosion?

Who was there?

Ryan couldn't answer them. He only saw faces in his dreams. He couldn't tell Major Lee who they were. It left him mentally exhausted and Lexy found herself wanting to scream at the major to stop.

And then he did. He left them alone in a silence so thick it could have been cut with a knife. She watched the man she was now married to sit in a chair with his head cradled in his hands. He was miserable. She knew the feeling because she spent so much of her life being miserable, feeling empty. It was the worst feeling in the world. It was like drowning in darkness. It was like suffocating. It was unbearable when one had to go through it alone.

He didn't have to go through it alone.

"Ryan." She knelt before him, resting her hands on his knees. "Will you hold me?" He looked at her for a long hard moment and then swept her up into his lap. "Things won't always be this bad," she whispered into the warm skin of his neck. "You'll get your memory back and then you'll know who you are."

"I'm afraid of that, too. I don't want to be him, but I don't want to think about not being him."

Lexy didn't know what to say to that. She almost felt the same way. She didn't want to be married to an abuser but...

she was growing to like the man he was. She couldn't say she wouldn't miss him when she left.

"What do we do now?" she asked, placing a soft kiss on his temple.

"The only thing we can do."

"What's that?"

"Play the hand we were dealt." He looked up at her and suddenly that lost look disappeared from his eyes and a hard resolve took its place.

Chapter Twelve

"What the hell is he doing here?"

Lexy had asked herself the same question a half dozen times that night. She turned to look at her best friend, Di, and then to her husband, who was sitting at the back of the restaurant reading a book and nursing a Diet Coke.

"He says he worried about me coming home so late."

"He's never cared before."

It was true. Ryan hadn't cared that she worked late nights or that on occasion she had to deal with drunken customers. He just cared that she brought in money. But not this Ryan. He wanted her to quit. Told her he didn't think it was right for her to be working while he sat at home alone.

So he was here. He showed up an hour into her shift. She thought for sure that he would stay home and rest after the trying meeting with Major Lee. But he was there, his eyes following her everywhere she went, and when she looked at him her face flushed in memory of how they'd spent the afternoon. He seemed to know what she was thinking every time they locked eyes. He was making it hard for her to concentrate but she couldn't say that she didn't want him there.

Her old husband didn't handle stress well and would turn to alcohol and wild nights to soothe his worries. Not this man. He turned to her. It was unsettling and satisfying at the same time.

"I don't trust him, Lexy. I think this is a new way of controlling you."

"You think?"

Di and Ryan were first cousins, but the two never got along. And when Di finally found out how Ryan treated Lexy she became her biggest advocate. She was the only other person in her life who knew Kyle was still alive. She promised to be there the day Lexy finally left Ryan.

"I know so. You're supposed to be leaving him. What's taking you so long?"

She had asked herself the same question. The simple answer was that she needed more money to make her escape, but if she had to she could get away. There were other reasons, ones she didn't want to think about.

Physically, Ryan was much better than he had been. He still walked with a slight limp when he was tired. And sometimes his headaches would get so bad he couldn't lift his head up; but he could take care of himself. That's all she promised at first. To take care of him until he could take care of himself. But he didn't remember his life here...

And he wasn't at all the same man she knew when he left. It all made her wonder.

"I'm going to leave. I had to stop working for a while to take care of him. So I depleted my meager savings. Once I get them back up I'm out of there."

"You should have left him to rot in that hospital." Di looked at Ryan in disgust. "You should have told me the first time he hit you. I would have shot him right in the temple."

"And that's why I love you, Di."

Di looked at her, her big blue eyes filled with sorrow. "Why didn't you tell me sooner that he was mistreating you? I would have helped you."

"I was ashamed," Lexy said softly. "I didn't want anybody to know."

Di nodded. "You could stay with us, you know. I can make the kids share a room and you can stay with us as long as you need."

"I'm not going to be a burden to your family. You guys have a hard enough time without me underfoot."

Di and her husband had three small children. Lexy couldn't see herself intruding on their time together. She didn't want to. If she was going to start a new life she was going to have to leave Liberty behind. It would pain her to do so, but it was what would have to be done.

"The offer is good for whenever you need it." She looked back to Ryan. "I can't believe he's reading for fun. He was dumb as a box of bricks all through school."

She followed Di's eyes to see her husband with his face buried in a thick book about economics. "He does a lot of surprising things."

Her mind again wandered to the afternoon when he let her tie him to the bed. She knew he wanted to touch her. He told her she wasn't sick, but she thought she might be a little abnormal. She liked watching him strain against his holds. She liked that she got to kiss and touch and be in charge, be on top, to take pleasure from him when he could do nothing in return. But... As much as she liked the power she had over him she missed the way his hands felt as they brushed her body. She didn't like sex before. She wasn't ready for it now, but thoughts of it with him kept flooding her mind.

"How's he treating you?"

"Fine." She shook her head. "He's actually been very good to me, Di."

"Are you sleeping with him?"

She looked at her friend, surprised by the question. "I'm not sure that it's any of your business."

"I'm not judging you, honey." They both looked at Ryan. "He sure does look different than before. Ryan's always been on the hefty side. Even when we were little kids he had to work at it not to get fat. Now look at him."

"He thinks there's been some sort of mistake," she finally admitted aloud. "He doesn't think he's my husband. Sometimes I'm inclined to believe it."

"Lexy, that's insane."

"I know. I know. But he hates fixing cars. That was his life. And he loves numbers and little puzzles. He came to the library the other day and took out a book of IQ tests! That's not the man I married."

"I'll say."

"Plus, he's sweet to me. He doesn't touch me unless I say it's okay. He doesn't cuss—"

"He's had a blow to the head. Maybe that knocked some sense into him." Di placed her hand on Lexy's shoulder. "Listen, honey. You're an adult and I'm not about to tell you what to do, but please keep your guard up."

"I'm not sure I know how to let it down."

"Well if you do and he acts up I've got six acres behind my house and a lot of places to hide a body."

Ryan watched Lexy as she floated from table to table that night. She worked hard at her second job. So hard that the lines of exhaustion never left her face. Tonight he couldn't stomach sitting at home alone, wondering what she was doing and if she was okay.

So he came to the Calloway and sat down at a table in the back. He didn't want to bother her. He just wanted to make sure she got to her car safely at the end of her shift. Liberty was supposed to be a safe town but he still didn't like the idea of his wife leaving at a bar alone sometimes well after midnight. There was no point in him staying home and trying to get some sleep. He never could rest until he knew that she was safe in her bedroom.

She smiled at a male customer as she brought him another drink. He tried not to let his jealousy flare as the man glanced at her breasts. She wore a white tank top that stood out against her caramel skin and hugged her body tightly, and a pair of butt-hugging jeans. *Of course* the guy stared at her. She was sexy tonight. But not in the same way as the other waitresses who plied on the makeup and big hair. He could see why his friends called her Sexy Lexy. No matter what she did her allure never left her. And Ryan found himself in the same boat as all the other men in town—wanting something he couldn't have.

Yet.

She disappeared into the back and he forced his eyes to leave her and return to the book in front of him. He had read the same page about fifty times. There was no concentrating while she was in the room. Plus, he was sure that he read this book already. The concepts seemed too familiar.

His boss, Pep, had asked him to take a look at Pep's personal finances since he had done a good job with the shop's. At first he refused, claiming he didn't know enough about the stock market to help. But Pep insisted and bought him a whole slew of books to get him started. He enjoyed reading them and that made him a little more sure that he wasn't Ryan Beecher, but some man in his place to take care of Lexy.

He shut his book, tired of pretending to read, and looked around the Calloway. It was a family restaurant that turned into a local hot spot at night. There was a dance floor and a little stage where they held open-mike nights once a week. Couples tipsy and sober alike moved around the dance floor. Some country song was playing. He never thought he would be a fan of country music, but the more he heard it the more he saw the beauty in it.

"Hey there, soldier." Lexy slid a tall glass of cranberry juice and a plate of fried chicken in front of him. "I thought you might want a little snack."

He wasn't hungry, but he picked a piece up and bit into it. "This is amazing."

"My grandmother's recipe. I told you she was the best damn cook the Calloway ever had."

"You did." He nodded at the glass of iced tea in her hand. "You planning on joining me?"

"I'm on my break." She took the seat next to him. "I was going to sneak out and make out with my boyfriend in the alley, but you seem nice. Maybe I'll sit with you instead."

"I'm honored. Can I hold your hand?"

"Yes." She blushed. She had been shy with him all evening. He knew that steamy interlude in her bedroom played in her mind as much as it did in his. "I feel sixteen all over again."

So did he. Like he was in the grips of first love all over again.

"Well maybe I don't." She gave him a quick, wicked smile. "Boys usually were more interested in grabbing my breasts than holding my hand. But you get what I mean."

"I can do both if you want."

"Maybe later." She smiled again. "Why are you here, Ryan?"

"I don't like you working late."

"I know."

"I want you to stop, but I'm not going to ask you to. If you want to have some extra money just for yourself that's fine, but now that I'm making more at the shop I don't think you need to work so hard."

She stared at him for a moment, something flashing in her eyes. It looked like guilt. "Will you dance with me?"

"What?"

"I want to dance. Will you dance with me?"

She was avoiding his question; but she rarely asked him to do anything, so he got up, took her hand and led her to the dance floor.

"I didn't think you were going to say yes," she told him as she wrapped her arms around his neck. "You wouldn't even dance at our reception."

"Tell me about our wedding." He slid his hand down her back as they swayed to the slow song playing.

"There's not much to tell. We ran off and got married at a little chapel in Lubbock. We weren't even going to have a reception but your mama was so angry at you for not giving me a real wedding you asked her to throw us a party in her backyard. It was nice. All your friends and family came, but you wouldn't dance with me. I danced with your uncle Fred three times, but I have never danced with you."

"I'm not him, you know. If I were your husband I would never miss the opportunity to dance with you."

Her expression turned pained. "Stop saying things like that. I'm going to leave. I have to."

"It sounds like you're trying to convince yourself more than you are trying to convince me. It's okay if you want to stay, Lexy. We can make things work. You know we can."

"Let's not talk about this," she sighed. "Let's just keep dancing."

"Fine." He pulled her closer. "But we have to have this conversation eventually."

She nodded and shut her eyes and continued to dance.

"Mind if I cut in?" They both looked up to see Georgie standing there. The alcohol on his breath was overwhelming.

"I do," Lexy replied for him. "I get kinda testy when people try to dance with my husband."

"Always such a smart mouth, Lexy." Georgie stared at her lips for a long moment and Ryan could almost read his thoughts. "I thought that would have been fixed by now."

"It doesn't need to be fixed," Ryan said. His hand curled into a fist. "I like it the way it is." He squeezed Lexy against him. "And I'm too damn selfish to share my wife with anybody. Hell—" He dropped his voice in warning. "I don't even like anybody looking at her, much less touching her. I'm not sure what I would do if anybody did. I might kill them."

He remembered what Lexy said about Georgie and how her husband used to turn the other way while Georgie harassed her. Not this time. He was making it crystal clear how he felt about Lexy.

Georgie locked eyes with him. "A lot has changed since you joined up, Ryan."

"A lot has."

The music stopped and Lexy pulled away. "I have to get

back to work." She gave him a worried look. "My shift is almost over. You can go home. I'll be there soon."

"No. I'll be here when you're finished. We'll go home together."

She nodded and went back to work.

That left him alone with Georgie. "What are you doing here, Mad Dog? You know the Calloway is for the tame crowd. You should have come out with us tonight."

"I'm here to make sure my wife gets home, not to have fun."

"Why?" Georgie frowned at him. "You never used to care before. You know Lexy was working the whole time you were away and nothing happened to her then. Why is she so important now?"

"She's my wife."

"And I'm your best friend. I've known you longer than her. We've been raising hell since we were kids. I'd never thought you would let a woman change you."

"Change me? I was a drunk before and I hit my wife. If you don't think that calls for a change I don't know what does."

"But you didn't have to throw away us for her. She's always thought she was better than everybody else. But she's not. She's two steps away from trash, just like—"

Ryan reached out and grabbed Georgie's shirt. "Watch your fucking mouth," he said in a low voice. "Just because I won't hit a woman doesn't mean I won't knock the shit out of you."

The confrontation had caught the attention of a few other dancers. He didn't want to embarrass Lexy, especially here, so he let go of Georgie's shirt and smiled. "Stay away from my wife," he said through his teeth. "Or I'll break your neck."

Something changed in Georgie's face. His dim-witted expression changed to one of cool rage. "You can't keep up this act for long, Ryan. You're just like us. You're going to fuck up and she's going to leave you. You only have us. We're your only friends."

Someone was moaning—low, deep moans that jarred Lexy out of her sleep and caused her eyes to spring open. They weren't coming from her. It wasn't some erotic dream gone awry. The moans were coming from across the hall. From Ryan's bedroom.

Immediately the worst possible thought flew into her head. Ryan was cheating on her in their home. She wouldn't stand for that. They may not have been a conventional married couple, but sleeping with another woman under her nose was going a step too far.

She would leave him as soon as the first rays of light crossed the sky.

She listened more. The moans grew louder but not passionate. There were no creaking bed springs or the heavy breathing. There were no sounds of a woman in bliss. They were moans of pain. Suddenly she heard the bed shift under Ryan's heavy weight and then the crash of his lamp hitting the floor. Before she could process the sound she was on her feet and at his bedroom door.

"Ryan," she called to him, but he was already there.

"It's okay. I just knocked over the lamp."

Something wasn't right—his voice was strained, as if he had been yelling for hours.

"You were having a nightmare." It was too dark to see him clearly but she felt him. His pained silence spoke volumes.

"I saw their faces again and the explosion. I saw the kid I

was talking to get blown away. I remember we were talking about his girlfriend."

"Do you remember? Do you know who you are?"

"No…" tore from his throat. "I just remember my unit. The way they looked— They're all dead, Lexy. I survived." He smacked his chest. "Why didn't I die?"

The doctor had warned her about this. He said he would have flashbacks, that he would have visions so vivid that he would think he was there again. This was posttraumatic stress and without help he would suffer for years.

She turned away from him, leaving him alone in his doorway.

"Come to me," she said softly. She lay back in her bed waiting for him. Her feelings were an indistinguishable jumble. She didn't want him to hurt. She didn't want him to be alone with his thoughts tonight.

"Are you sure?"

Her heart skipped a beat at his question. He was suffering and still respecting her wishes. This was not the man she married.

"Come."

That time he obeyed and slipped under the covers beside her. His skin was damp and cold. He was eerily quiet. This wasn't the good-natured, passionate man she had come to know. The man beside her was damaged.

"Do you want to tell me?"

The doctor had said that if he talked about the event that it would be better for him.

"I can't. I'm sorry."

She wrapped her body around him, burying her face in his neck. She kissed him there, needing to comfort him and herself. He relaxed slightly and she felt herself giving her kisses freely, softly, slowly finding his throat and his ear and the scar on his face. It was when her lips touched his that she realized that she had climbed on top of him. Her nightgown bunched at her waist. Her body was rubbing against his. He was hard but not demanding. All he did was lightly caress her thighs, nothing more. He was incredibly sweet in that moment.

She cupped his face in her hands and kissed him deeply, touching her tongue to his. He reciprocated, letting their mouths mate in a sea of sweet moisture.

She didn't want him to change. It was selfish and wrong, but she needed him like this. Now he was hers. She could touch him and bear his contact. She could find pleasure without fear.

Her hands were wet. Tears were falling fast and hard from her husband's eyes.

"Oh my God," she whispered. "Am I hurting you? Is it your ribs?" She tried to crawl off him.

"No." He held her tightly to his body. "I need you with me tonight. I can't go back to being alone."

"You don't have to." She kissed his wet face, gently rubbing her hands over his hard body. "Tell me how to make you feel better." She felt almost frantic. This was new. This was not the husband she knew and the feelings that ran through her body were completely foreign to her. She wanted to comfort him.

"I'm fine." He wasn't. He was tense and hurting.

"Let me touch you." She rubbed her lower body against his, feeling his erection between her legs.

"Lexy, I want to be inside you."

She wasn't ready for that yet. In order for that to happen she had to trust him and she didn't yet.

"Let me touch you. Teach me how." She moved to his side,

resting her hand on his lower stomach. "I don't know how." She slipped her hand onto his hard large penis. She touched him gently there, amazed by how smooth something that felt like steel against her could be.

"Lexy." He sucked in a ragged breath.

"I was never allowed to touch before." She kissed under his ear. "It's crazy. I've been married ten years and never was allowed to feel my husband in my hand." She ran her hand down his shaft and cupped his heavy testicles in her hand. "I want to make you feel good. Teach me."

He looked at her, torture in his eyes. He wanted to make love to her. It was simple and for the first time in a long time she felt like she wanted to make love, too.

"Rub it," he said after a long moment.

"Like this?" She ran her fingers over his head, playing with the drop of moisture that seeped from it.

"Yes," he moaned. He grabbed her hand and stroked himself with it. She felt a shot of heat between her legs. "Like this, baby."

She shook his hand off and stroked him the way he showed her, finding her own rhythm, adjusting her strokes to his moans. And then it was over. His whole body jerked off the bed and he called out her name in the form of a growl. She felt strange, triumphant in a way.

"Do you feel better," she asked, giving him a long lingering kiss.

"Lexy." He stroked her face with his thumbs. "I—"

"Did you know that when a camel is thirsty it can drink up to twenty-five gallons of water in three minutes?"

She wasn't sure what he was going to say but she had a feeling he was going to tell her that he loved her. She couldn't hear that. Not from his mouth. Ryan had regularly claimed he loved her before they got married, and then he said it only after he hit her. In the past few years he hadn't bothered to say it at all. Lexy, like anybody, wanted to be loved but she didn't want it to be a lie. And she didn't want to hear it from a man who couldn't remember who he was.

"Is that true?"

"I don't know. A little girl who comes for story time at the library told me that."

"Does she tell you a lot of things?"

"Yes. She comes in every day with a new fact to tell me. She makes me laugh."

"I want a little girl one day," he said softly.

"You want a girl?" She looked down into her husband's face to see if he was serious.

"I want a lot of kids, Lexy. I want a little girl I could spoil and boy I can roughhouse with and teach to be a man."

"I can't have kids, Ryan," she said as tears suddenly filled her eyes. "After I lost the baby, I—"

He cut her off. "I want a bigger house, too, and a yard that's not filled with cars. And maybe we can find one of those wooden swing sets. The ones with the yellow slides."

She was too stunned to speak for a moment. After she had miscarried, Ryan felt guilty and tried everything in his power to get her pregnant even though the thought of being intimate with him made her ill. He forced himself on her every night, but she was never able to conceive again. She had bled a lot when she miscarried, so much so that she had been in the hospital for two days.

Her body was broken and Ryan never forgave her for it. He turned cold to her and looked at her as if she were no longer a woman. She felt like a failure, too. She hadn't done anything right in her life. She had even messed up the one thing a woman was put on this earth to do.

But this new man didn't seem to care. He glossed over it as if any obstacle was surmountable.

"We could take them to Disney World."

"I've never been before," she said, playing along. "The kids would like it."

She was planning a future that would never happen. She was leaving soon. Or he would remember, or turn back to his old self—and she couldn't bear that. There was no saving this broken marriage. Her new memories with this new sweet man wouldn't be enough to make her forget.

The next morning Lexy woke up much later than usual. Ryan was gone, but his scent still lingered on her pillow as well as the knowledge of what took place between them last night. What the hell was she doing to herself? She couldn't blame him. He wasn't the one who invited him to spend the night in her bed. She was off today, and instead of getting out of bed and preparing herself to go visit her brother she grabbed the pillow that he slept on and hugged it to her chest. She almost wished that she hadn't woken up alone that morning. She felt empty.

"What is wrong with me?" she asked herself.

The last thing she was supposed to be doing was liking her husband. This was the man who nearly beat her to death in a drunken rage. How on earth could she want him near? She rolled over, frustrated, and glanced at the clock. She needed to get out of bed and make the long trip to see her brother. But today she wasn't looking forward to the drive because she knew she would spend it thinking about how badly her life had gone off track once again.

When she arrived at Golden Hill, Kyle wasn't in his usual spot by the window. He wasn't even out of bed today. She knew something was wrong the moment she walked in and Dr. Andreas met her by the door. Dread rolled over her. He only waited for her when he had bad news.

"He had a very long seizure this morning when the nurses were trying to get him ready. I need to warn you, Mrs. Beecher, that he looks unwell. But usually within a few hours the paralysis goes away."

"Paralysis?" Her heart stopped beating. "Are you sure he didn't have a stroke?"

"I am. The part of the brain that the seizure took place in affects the left side of his body. Mostly his face. We have increased his medication to try to prevent another one from happening, but as you know his body becomes exhausted after these episodes. He may not realize you are here today."

"I still want to see him."

"Of course you do. I just wanted to warn you first."

She swallowed hard as she walked into the room. Kyle was blankly staring up at the ceiling. She had to grip the back of a chair because her knees had gone weak.

A hand touched her shoulder. Dr. Andreas hadn't left her side and she was glad for it. She didn't want to be alone right now. Kyle was almost unrecognizable. The left side of his face drooped. His eyes had that drugged, glazed look. He didn't know she was there. She wasn't sure he knew the world existed in that moment.

She wanted to weep for him, but she held her tears back. Crying wouldn't help. He was twenty-four. His life expectancy was thirty. For some reason she expected to have all of those remaining years with him. She wasn't prepared to think about him going early. She wished her husband was here. She had taken such pains to keep Kyle a secret from him, but she wanted him here. She wanted him to hold her. She didn't want to carry this burden alone.

"Talk to him, Lexy. That might help."

Another doctor had told her the same thing, only that time he was talking about her husband. That time it worked. Ryan came back to life. She took her brother's soft hand in hers, kissed his cheek and talked to him about anything she could think of. None of it helped. He didn't look at her once.

Ryan went into work early that next morning even though he didn't want to leave Lexy's side. She had done something special for him. She had given a little part of herself to him. He wanted more of that. More time with them together as husband and wife. But he knew that if given the chance to overthink things she would. He couldn't bear to go backward with her now. They were so close to making things between them right.

He was going to spend every day with her showing her how good things could be.

He had finished most of his work by the time the last mechanic rolled in at ten. "You were supposed to be here two hours ago," he told the young mechanic who looked like he was still recovering from a bender. "Go home. You're not working today. If you think I'm going to allow you to work on people's cars while you stink of alcohol, you're dead wrong."

"Why not? You used to."

He wanted to argue the point but he couldn't, even though

he knew deep in his gut that he wasn't the man Liberty thought he was, he didn't know for sure. "Well, I'm not a drunk anymore. The marines knocked that right out of me. Get out of here and expect a write-up tomorrow morning. You may be able to find another job, but this shop is Pep's life and you should respect him enough not to mess up his good name."

"Whatever," the kid said and walked out, slamming the door behind him.

Lance stood there staring at him, his mouth slightly open. "Holy shit, Mad Dog. Don't you think you were a little rough on him?"

"No. It's time for him to learn how to be a man. I wish somebody would have done that to me when I was his age. I probably would have turned out better for it."

Lance shook his head. "Georgie's right. You sure are different."

He nodded. "I'm not the same man."

He left the shop and headed to the library. He was anxious to see his wife. Pep had left all the responsibility of running the shop to him, which meant he was now in charge of all the mechanics. He had to crack down hard on a lot of them. It didn't earn him many friends—and while he knew he was doing the right thing for the business, the lack of friends sometimes got to him. He didn't remember much about his time before he woke up in the hospital, but he vaguely remembered feeling bonded to the men in his unit, of feeling like he belonged to something bigger than himself. He tried not to let it bother him. Everything happened for a reason.

"Ryan!" Jemma greeted him with a smile. "Are you here to take out another book? We just got the new Walter Mosley title. I think you would like it."

"No, thank you, ma'am. I'm here to see Lexy. I was hoping I could take her out for lunch."

Jemma frowned at him. "You're here for Lexy? She's not working today."

"She isn't? But she told me..."

"Maybe she meant she was working at the Calloway. Sometimes she picks up a lunch shift when they need her to."

"Oh." She hadn't mentioned that to him. But maybe she had. Maybe he was just getting his wires crossed.

"She doesn't usually work today," she said absently. "I wish she did but the county will only pay for a part-time assistant."

"Thank you." He walked out of the building and drove straight to the Calloway. Lexy had told him she was working every Friday, since he had come home. Every Friday he had asked her about her day and every Friday she told him something about the library. Jemma must be wrong. Lexy wouldn't lie to him. Or would she? He remembered back to the night he'd brought home dinner. She had lied to him then, but he wasn't sure about what.

Lexy's car wasn't in the parking lot when he pulled in. He got out of the vehicle anyway, just to check. When he went inside they told him what he already knew. Lexy wasn't there. She hadn't worked a lunch shift since before he came home.

He was angry. He was more than angry. He felt betrayed. Why was she lying to him? The only reason he could think of was that she was cheating on him. He knew he hadn't been a good husband before. He knew that she probably needed somebody to turn to, but he never expected this. She should have left him. She should have never made him think they had a chance.

He went home to wait for her. He was going to end this today. Their sham of a marriage had gone on long enough.

She came home two and a half hours later. He stood up ready to confront her, but when he saw her he was unable to say a word. She looked miserable, and when she clapped eyes on him tears started to stream down her face.

"How did you know I needed you today?" She launched herself at him, wrapping her arms and legs around him. He held on to her tightly, bewildered by her actions. She didn't smell like sex or men's cologne. The scent coming from her hair reminded him of his days in the hospital. Whatever she had been doing today didn't involve making love to another man.

"Lexy… What happened?"

"I'm glad you're not sick anymore," she sobbed. "I don't think I could have taken it. I couldn't have watched you die. I don't want to think about you dying."

"Honey—" he sat them down on the couch and cupped her face in his hands "—I'm not going to die."

"Promise me."

She kissed him. It surprised him and took his breath away at the same time. Her kisses were different than before. They were hungry. They were needy. He felt her every emotion through them. "Promise me." She ripped her lips away from his. "I need to hear you say it."

"I'm not going anywhere. I promise." He wasn't sure what brought this on but he knew it wasn't his time to go yet.

She nodded, the tears falling faster than he could catch them. "Take me to your bedroom."

He blinked at her. Had she really said the words he always dreamed would come from her lips? "Are you sure?"

"Yes."

It was all he needed to hear. He picked her up and carried her to his bedroom and as soon as she landed on his bed she started to peel off her clothes. He wanted to do it. He wanted to undress her little by little and kiss every inch of her beautiful body. But it seemed Lexy wasn't in the mood for slow lovemaking.

"Please, Ryan. I need you now."

He got distracted by her chest. Her nipples were hard little points that begged for attention. He palmed her breasts in his hands, testing the weight of them. Kissing the fleshy tops. She knelt on the bed before him, offering herself to him, letting out little hisses of pleasure when his thumbs brushed her nipples.

"Do you like the way that feels?"

She nodded, pulling her lower lips between her teeth. He stroked them for a few moments until she started to writhe beneath his attention.

"Stop," she whispered.

He obeyed her command and watched her as she rose from the bed and slid her jeans down her hips.

"Take off your clothes. I want to feel you on top of me."

He moved immediately to do her bidding, but apparently he didn't move fast enough. She took matters into her own hands, tugging his jeans down as he tried to remove his shirt. "Slow down, baby. We've got all day."

"We don't." She wrapped her arms around him, squishing her breasts against him. He was hard before but feeling her naked chest against his made him rise to epic proportions. Even though his body was screaming at him to bury himself inside her and pump them both into oblivion, he had to stay in control. This was the first time for them. For him in his new life. He wanted it to be special.

He gently pushed her down on the bed, allowing himself just a moment of space from her. When she touched him he couldn't think. And thinking about making love to her was all he had done since he'd laid eyes on her. He finished pulling off his clothes as he took her body in. So pretty. So curvy. All his. She was worth the wait. Worth the pain.

He lay down beside her and smoothed his hand over her belly then across her hips. But that wasn't enough for her. She pulled him on top of her, wrapping her legs around him. His cock brushed against her opening. She was so wet. He had barely touched her and she was ready for him. It made him ache.

"Please," she begged. "Make me feel better. Make me feel something else." She pulled him into a kiss, but her frantic plea caused him to break away.

"What happened to you, Lexy?"

"I need you." She kissed down his throat. "Please."

She began to move her body against him. His cock rubbed the outside of her wet lips. It felt too good. He had to slow down or this was going to be over before it started. He pulled himself away from her and spread her legs apart, her sweet aroused smell filling the room. He opened her with his fingers and stroked her clit once, twice, until her back arched and she rose off the bed. He had never been with anybody so sensitive to his touch. It made him feel primal, like he wanted to own her. But he knew it was the other way around. He knew he was a slave to her.

"More," she moaned. "Kiss me."

He set his lips on her and sucked her tongue into his mouth.

Her kisses were drugging and he forgot all about his control and lost himself in her mouth. She wrapped her arms around him, throwing one leg over his hip. They lay on their sides, facing each other. She was open to him again—his cock was nudging his way into her entrance, but he caught himself just in time and placed his fingers there instead. She pushed against them and he started to move his hand in and out of her slickness. He wanted to go slow but she wouldn't allow it. She wanted release as quick and as hard as she could get it. He was going to give her what she wanted and then he was going to spend the rest of the afternoon making slow love to her.

When she wrapped her fingers around him and started stroking, he was powerless to stop her. This is not the way he wanted it, but it had gone too far now. He couldn't think straight anymore. He could only feel. He buried his tongue in her mouth, kissing her so hard he bruised his lips. But she didn't seem like she wanted sweet and gentle.

She moved furiously against his hand as she fisted his cock. The sounds she was making, the way she smelled, and felt… It was too much for him. His balls drew up tightly and he begged his release to hold off but then she broke, her body lifting off the bed, a little scream tearing from her throat.

He exploded just after that in one of the most intense orgasms that he had ever experienced.

They lay together sweating and panting for what seemed like hours. Neither one of them had the energy to move, and Ryan felt himself drifting off into a deep sleep. Lexy kissed his throat and slid her hand down his chest.

"Can I stay here for a little while," she asked shyly.

"As long as you want." He lifted her off the bed and deposited them beneath the covers. She buried her nose in his neck just before she drifted off to sleep.

He lay awake for a little while longer. She was keeping secrets from him. Something happened to Lexy today and, although the need to know nearly killed him, he promised himself he wouldn't say a word. She had turned to him when she was in need and that's all he ever wanted.

The towns of Liberty and Terran played softball against each other every year for bragging rights in early June. Nobody could remember how or why the games started but every year the towns would bring out their fittest men to play the seven innings. Neither team was very good. Their fittest players had beer bellies and ran as fast as some children walked but everybody from both towns came out to celebrate. It was an excuse to drink beer and socialize. Afterward the people would split off and have cookouts and drink more beer.

Lexy sat in the stands alone because Di was with her little girl, who had fallen down and cut her leg. It was the end of sixth inning and Liberty had two outs and the bases loaded. The game could go either way. Ryan was up to bat again and Lexy smiled unwillingly. The more time she spent with this new man the more time she wanted to spend with him. He had done something amazing for her yesterday. He let her be wild and out of control. He let her take from him everything she needed and he didn't ask a single question. Even though she felt terribly guilty for keeping Kyle a secret from him she was grateful to him for that.

The old Ryan would have never done that for her. He never would have made her feel safe.

He looked for her in the stands, like he always did when

he was up at bat, and grinned at her. She waved at him and he winked, causing a surge of foolish schoolgirl pleasure to flow through her. He looked good in his uniform, which was gray to match his eyes, with pants tight enough to show off his powerful thighs and firm behind. Beneath his shirt lay his muscled arms and chest, which made her remember how good she felt when he held her close yesterday.

"He looks good, don't he?"

"Huh?" Lexy was too busy gazing at her husband to realize who was sitting near her. Gloria Rodgers had come to sit on her left.

The woman who Ryan cheated on her with.

"*My* husband does look very good. Thank you."

She heard the crack of a ball against the bat. She watched as the ball flew gracefully over the fence, scoring four runs for the team. She stood up and screamed like a crazy person.

His eyes found her in the stands and mouthed, "That was for you."

She blushed. He was trying so hard to win her over. She was feeling herself unwillingly slipping, falling...

It was terrifying.

"He doesn't remember a thing, does he?" Glory asked, obviously not knowing that Lexy didn't want to hear her voice.

Lexy remained silent and watched Lance strike out, ending the inning.

"He's not the same man, is he? Aren't you worried about him?"

Her temper sparked. Glory was crossing the line. "Why are you talking to me? You screwed my husband for years and I didn't say a word. I didn't slash your tires or set fire to your house or scratch your eyes out. You had my husband. Wasn't that enough?"

Glory nodded as tears streamed down her face.

"He doesn't want me anymore," she said as if her heart was shattering.

"Nobody likes a whore."

"Damn it, Lexy. You don't have to be such a bitch."

"I'm a bitch?" Something inside her snapped. "You were fucking my husband," she said in a fierce whisper, "for years, and laughing at me while you were doing it. I hated him for hurting me and part of me will always hate him. But you— you are a woman. We grew up together. You saw me every day and looked me in my face, knowing what you were doing was killing me. And you didn't even care. How could you live with yourself?"

"I love him," she said quietly. "I used to love him. But he never loved me like he loved you. I tried to get him to leave you, but he wouldn't even think about it. He used to talk to me about you. He would be in bed with me and talk about how good you were. How do you think that made me feel? I knew him before you. I dated him before you, but he never even cared about me. He used me for my body but he wanted your heart. He wanted you to fight for him."

"He wasn't worth fighting for. I was praying he would leave me for you. Maybe he could have knocked the shit out of you sometimes."

"He hit you?" Glory's big blue eyes filled with shock.

"Don't act like you didn't know. You had to know. He left me bleeding to warm your bed."

Glory was as close to Ryan as Georgie was. She had to know.

"I didn't know. I swear! He never hit me. But then again, I never had a smart mouth like you did."

"Not an excuse. There was never an excuse to hit me." She cradled her head in her hands as it started to throb.

"He's really stopped drinking? The man I knew would never give up his whiskey."

"Well, that shows you that you don't know my husband at all."

"Lex," Ryan called, concern in his eyes. "Are you all right, baby?" He stood at the fence, giving Glory a glare that would melt ice.

"I'm fine." She wasn't really, but she wouldn't give anyone the satisfaction of knowing she felt awful.

"Are you sure?" He looked ready to climb over the fence and take her away.

"Yes. We're just chatting. Go play. I'll see you after the game." He nodded and tossed one more hard look at Glory before he left.

"He won't even look at me anymore. Don't you ever think he's not the same man?"

The game ended shortly after that. Liberty had claimed the victory largely due to Ryan's homerun. There was raucous celebrating on the field for a few minutes before the crowds began to disperse.

Lexy spotted Ryan alone near the picnic tables. This was hard for him, being in a place he had lived all his life and yet not really fitting in. He wasn't shy or a loner. People liked him. He had even made friends, but she knew he didn't feel comfortable.

One of his teammates called out to him. He looked up

and grinned as a can of beer was tossed his way. He looked at it for a moment and then tossed it to Richie Thomas, the nineteen-year-old busboy at the Calloway. She knew Ryan didn't know she was watching. He could have had the beer, but he was keeping his promise. He quit drinking. He was taking care of her. He was being the husband she always needed.

He's not the same man.

Glory's words came back to her. She was right. He wasn't—but she didn't want to think about it. Life might never be this good again.

She grabbed a beer from the cooler and walked toward him. Whiskey was his demon—he could have one beer.

"You know," she said as she approached him, "it's illegal to give alcohol to minors."

"You saw that?" He grinned.

"I did. I brought you one to replace it." He took it from her and looked at it before he tossed it to another teenager.

"That wasn't a test. You can have a beer, Ryan. You earned it. You brought victory to our town. Celebrate." She leaned against him. "You looked good out there."

He laughed. "Thank you. Everybody played the best they could."

"No, honey, I meant you look good in your uniform. I think you should wear it around the house."

He glanced at her, surprised. She surprised herself. She was flirting, and with her husband of all people.

"Only if you put on that white tank top you wear to bed."

She smiled knowingly. He liked it because it was so worn it was see-through and she never wore a bra with it. "I'll think about it." She let her head rest on his shoulder, and for a moment shut her eyes as the rays of the setting sun warmed her face.

"What did Glory say to you?" he asked very softly.

"That you're not the same man she fell in love with."

"I'm not, Lexy. I think there was a mistake, a mix up. I'm not him. I'm not the man you married." He sounded so positive she wanted to believe him.

"Then who are you?" She wrapped her arms around him and rested her head on his beating heart. "It doesn't matter who you are, just stay away from Glory."

"I want you to trust me."

"I don't know if I can."

He held her close to him for a few moments and she felt safe enough to let her guard down. It felt good to be held by him. Behind them they heard children running, playing little kid games and the pop of cans being opened. They heard Di's voice speaking with her husband and men laughing at dirty jokes. They smelled hamburgers and grass and beer and dirt. And then there was Ryan's scent—aftershave and skin and the slight smell of sweat.

"What are you thinking about?"

"How good you smell," she said without thinking. She felt his arms tighten around her and something warm pass between them. He moved away slightly to cup her face in his hands. Hands that were soft and clean without gunk or calluses to bruise her skin.

"Can I?" he whispered.

God, yes, she wanted to say. She wouldn't admit to him how much she liked his kisses, how she hoped that he would give her one each time he saw her, how they made her feel.

He pressed his lips to hers, his eyes still opened. They were

that beautiful shade of blue gray that she had never seen before. She saw how he felt in his eyes and hoped hers didn't
give as much away. He let his lips flutter against hers for a
moment before he kissed her fully and she immediately went
slack against him. His lips were warm and still sweet from the
Gatorade he had been drinking throughout the game.

She kissed him back, pressing her chest into his, her body
beginning to react. Her nipples tightened and an ache began
to form between her legs. He sucked on her tongue, her lower
lip, and she sucked on his in return. A moan escaped one of
them. She wasn't sure who, but Ryan broke the kiss and began
to flutter tiny little sweet pecks around her mouth while he
still held her face in his hands. Warmth spread through her
and even though the kiss was over she would feel its after-
effects for hours.

"Damn," they heard.

"Damn, is right."

"You've never kissed me like that," Di complained to her
husband.

"If I did you would try to knock my head off," Stanley
shot back.

"That's because it's never happened before. I would think
you were up to something."

Lexy's face immediately burned with embarrassment. She
got lost in that kiss and forgot that they were visible to the
whole town.

"We might have done that on national TV. The whole
damn town is looking at us." She buried her head in his chest,
trying to hide from the dozens of people staring at them.

"It's all right, baby." He cupped the back of her head. "You
just stay like this. They'll get bored in a minute."

Chapter Thirteen

Lexy was shy with him that next week. He knew she was embarrassed that the whole town watched them kiss. They had both taken their fair share of teasing about it, but she was a private person. Reserved. He suspected that she never kissed her husband in public before. He suspected she never let herself get lost in the moment with him.

But she was slipping.

Every day she kept revealing a little more of those secret parts of herself to him. Little by little she was uncovering her true self. And it scared her. She wasn't as tough as she wanted him to think. She was sweet and soft and a little bit wild.

And that's why she kept her distance from him. They shared no kisses or touches. They barely talked that week. The only time he got to spend with her was on her breaks at the Calloway. He still went there every night she had to work. Even though she assured him it wasn't necessary, he still walked her to her car and made sure she got home safely. It was one of the longest weeks of his life. And then came Thursday.

"I want to take you to lunch tomorrow. You think you can sneak away from the library for an hour or so?"

She looked up at him, her eyes widening for a moment. "Oh, not tomorrow. We've got to inventory the children's section. But Monday should be fine. Why don't you come get me on Monday?" She quickly looked away from him and down at her plate as if her peas were suddenly fascinating.

She was lying to him again. Right to his face. His gut said she wasn't cheating on him but he really didn't know. Why was she keeping how she spent her Fridays a secret from him? He wanted to let this go. He wanted to trust her, but he knew there was no moving on until he knew.

"Monday? Okay. It's a date."

The next morning he waited at the end of the road until she pulled up. He knew following her was a crazy idea. It made him seem insane. But he was insane. Lexy made all rational thought leave his head. He had to know what she was doing.

The drive was a long one, almost an hour and a half before she stopped and then it was at a supermarket. This couldn't be her destination. And for a moment he felt like he was unforgivably invading her privacy. Maybe she just liked to go for long drives once a week. Maybe she just needed time to clear her head.

He was just about to go home when she came out with a small bag. But no matter how hard he strained his eyes he couldn't see the contents of it.

He couldn't just let it go, so instead of going back home he continued to follow her. She pulled up to a large brick building with manicured lawns and people milling about them. Some of those people were in wheelchairs. He looked up at the building's sign, confused.

Golden Hill.

Was this a nursing home?

She got out of her car. He knew he should just go away, let her keep this one secret from him, but he didn't. His brain couldn't stop his feet from moving.

"Lexy."

She turned to face him. Fear clouded her face. "Ryan? Wh-what are you doing here?"

"I'm sorry." He shook his head. "I know this was crazy. I know it's a breach of your trust, but I just have to know how you spend your Fridays."

"You knew I was lying to you?"

"Yes. I need to know if you are cheating on me."

"Cheating on you?" She rolled her eyes skyward. "Oh, Lord. I won't even let *you* have sex with me. What makes you think I'm having it with another man?"

"Then why are you here?"

"I should have realized you were going to find out," she said more to herself than to him. "You're not the same man." She took his hand. "Come on. There's somebody I want you to meet."

She led him into a room where a small young man lay in a hospital bed, staring up at the ceiling. His skin was pale. His eyes were unfocused. He barely looked alive. Lexy dropped her bag on his nightstand and sat on the edge of his bed.

"Kyle, honey. I'm here." She took his hand. "I wish you would look at me. I brought somebody to see you."

Tears filled her eyes again and Ryan had the distinct feeling that he was suffocating. He took a step closer to his wife, placing his hand on her back.

"Who is he?"

"My brother," she whispered.

Her brother. He remembered her telling him that he died.

She looked up at him. "I lied to you about everything." The first set of tears slid from her eyes. "I didn't always know about Kyle. My grandmother kept him a secret from me.

Kyle's been sick from birth and he spent his whole life in one facility after the other. Maybell put him in here the year she died. She left all of her money to this place for his care, but the money ran out and if I didn't find some way to pay for his care they were going to kick him out. So I—I asked you to pay for it. But every time you got mad at me, you threatened to stop. And then one time you didn't pay at all. I couldn't let you play with his life like that so I told you he died. That's why I started working at the Calloway. I needed to find a way to pay for his care. You never seemed to care where I spent my Fridays or why I was working so hard. But then you got hurt and you changed…and I lied to you again. I couldn't risk you turning back into him. I couldn't risk Kyle. I lied to you twice and now Kyle really is dying. I don't want to lie anymore. God is punishing me for it."

"No, baby." He pulled her off the bed and into a tight hug. "No. No. No. He was an asshole. You did what you had to do to protect a person you love. God would never punish you for that. You're a better person than I could ever be."

"Why does everything have to be so hard?"

"It doesn't, Lex. I'm going to make things better for you. I promise."

Kyle turned his head as if he finally noticed he wasn't alone in the room.

"Lexy, look."

"Hey!" She dashed away the tears on her cheeks before she went back to her brother. "Were we making too much noise for you? I'm sorry. But I brought Ryan to meet you, love. And if that's not good enough I got you some ice cream, too."

Like she had been doing it forever, she reached into his nightstand, draped a towel over him and began to feed Kyle ice cream. Ryan grew uncomfortable watching her feed her brother. He felt like he was witnessing something intimate. But it all made sense now. She had cared for him so well in the hospital because she had been caring for her brother for years.

He found a new respect for Lexy Beecher that day, and he promised himself that she would never have to work an extra hour again.

Lexy was downstairs in the children's section of the library when Ryan came to get her for lunch. She was surprised to see him today. They had made this date on Thursday, but in the light of everything that had happened she didn't think he was still coming to pick her up. She hadn't seen much of him all weekend. He told her that he had something to take care of. But she thought he was avoiding her on purpose. She thought he was upset with her. She couldn't blame him. She had lied to him for weeks. Years actually, if she counted the time before he was hurt.

When she saw him at Golden Hill her heart froze. She thought her old husband was going to return, that he was going to rage and scream… But he didn't. And his reaction made her feel about a thousand times worse.

"Hello, Ryan." She rose from her spot on the floor and dusted off her pants. He looked different today. He wasn't wearing his work clothes but he didn't have anything on that she recognized. Everything fit. The black T-shirt molded to his hard chest. He wore dark blue jeans that didn't sag on his hips and new black boots. Not the cowboy kind but the motorcycle kind. He looked damn good.

"Hey. You ready to go?"

She nodded. "I thought you weren't going to take me to lunch today."

He frowned. "Why not?"

"Because I'm a liar and you're mad at me."

He looked at her for a long moment. "Do you care if I'm mad at you?"

She bit her lower lip, torn between ignoring the question and telling him the truth. "A few months ago I would have said no, but right now I'm feeling a little different about it."

"I'm not mad at you." He gave her a small smile. "Come on."

She thought he was going to take her to a restaurant, but they pulled into their driveway. Eating lunch at home was fine with her. She needed to be back to work in less than an hour. This was probably quicker.

He stopped the car and stared at her expectantly.

"Did you go grocery shopping this morning? We barely had any food in the house."

"I guess you'll have to get out and see."

"Okay…" She got out, unable to shake the feeling that he was up to something. "Those BLTs you made the other week were good. I wonder if we have any bacon left."

She had her key in the door just as he placed his hand on her shoulder. "Lexy?"

"Yeah?" She faced him.

"Didn't you notice anything?"

She smiled at him. "Did you get new clothes? You look very handsome. I'm sorry I didn't say anything before."

"It's not my clothes, Alexa. Look around the yard."

She looked around seeing nothing out of the ordinary. The

grass was neatly cut. Ryan had been dutifully trying to maintain the upkeep of the house. "I don't see anything."

"Exactly."

She looked around again. There was nothing there. The yard was empty. Her heart lodged itself in her throat and she found herself gripping his shirt. "The cars are gone! You got rid of the cars?"

He grinned at her. "I got rid of the cars. And all the tools in the garage. I had no idea how much that old Ford was worth."

The cars had meant everything to Ryan. The old Ryan. He would have never gotten rid of them. He spent more time in the garage than he ever had with her. "Why did you do it?"

"I don't want you to work nights anymore. You don't have to worry about Kyle now. His care is paid up for the next two years."

His words sent her reeling. "Why did you do that?"

"I just told you why, baby. I want you at home. I should be the one to sacrifice—and getting rid of those cars *wasn't* a sacrifice. It was the right thing to do."

"But you love them."

"I don't love them." He cupped her face. "I don't love *them*."

She shut her eyes. Why was he doing this to her? Yes, she worked to pay Kyle's bill, but she also worked so she could get away from Ryan. He made it so she didn't have to work anymore. She had enough in her account right now to walk away. But he also made it so she didn't want to leave.

Where was her resolve? Her strength? The anger she carried around for so many damn years? She had expected many things when he first woke up in that hospital, but she never expected him to turn into the man he was.

He pressed a kiss to her forehead. "Are you okay?"

"I'm processing."

"Well, stop for a minute because I have one more thing for you."

"You're taking me to Disney World?"

"No, but I can if you want." He pulled a little gray box out of his pocket. "I got this from Shelby's Jewelers in town. If you don't like it, we can look for another one." He slipped a simple diamond solitaire on her finger. "I'll wear one, too. I don't want people to think you're not married."

"Every person in town knows we're married."

He nodded and kissed her forehead again. "But I want you to feel married."

She sighed heavily. There was so much she wanted to say to him, but she couldn't find the words.

"Come inside. I got lunch before I picked you up. It's going to get cold."

Chapter Fourteen

His wife was avoiding him again, Ryan thought grimly as he stood in her doorway. Ever since he got rid of the cars she had been distant. He had done it to take away her burden of working two jobs. He had done it so that they could spend more time together, but it seemed that his plan had backfired. She was skittish around him again. All the progress they had made over the past few weeks drifted away. He wondered what was going on in that head of hers.

She hadn't mentioned leaving him in quite some time now. Did she want to stay? The money was all hers as far as he was concerned. She had earned it by living with an asshole for ten years. If she decided that she didn't want this, he could go away knowing that she had enough money to survive on. He made it so she had a choice now. She wasn't bonded to him. She didn't have to stay with him as a sacrifice. She had freedom now.

He needed to know her choice. But more than that he just wanted to talk to her again.

The Major had sent him pictures of some of the men in his unit yesterday, including his commanding officer, Christian Howard. He couldn't remember their names, but their faces were hauntingly familiar. One was of a boy of about twenty-two, brown skin, big doe eyes, his name Terrell. Ryan couldn't remember a conversation or a time they shared, but he knew he liked the kid. The boy was dead now and Ryan felt an emptiness in his chest.

He dreamed of them last night, but not the violent dream he had before. This one was simpler. He was sitting at a card table with three other men. They were playing poker in their sand-colored fatigues. One of the men was called Tex—but he wasn't sure who—and then the dream ended.

That man was not him.

He walked into her room after watching her doze for a few minutes. She looked so cute curled up in a little ball on her bed, her mouth slightly open. She looked vulnerable. She must have passed out after her shower again for she was wrapped in a bathrobe, her hair still wet and clinging to her head. Lexy worked all day at the library from opening to close, doing anything and everything that was asked of her all in an effort to avoid him.

He climbed into bed with her. He always liked her pretty little bedroom with its old-fashioned vanity and handmade quilt, and the dozens of dainty little pillows that were piled high on her bed.

Still slumbering, she snuggled close to his warm body for a moment before she realized she wasn't alone. Her eyes popped open and he saw fear immediately fill them.

"Damn it, Lexy."

It hurt him physically to see that she was still afraid of him. It had been nearly two months since they had moved in together and they were still at the same place. Her trust was not coming easily. He was at a loss. He moved away from her. If she didn't want him there he wouldn't be there.

"Ry—" She grabbed his hand. "I'm just not used to waking up to somebody beside me. I told you that." She pulled him back down on the bed. "All I can say is that I'm sorry." She pushed her body close to his as an apology. "You are supposed to warn me anyway."

He was still stung by her mistrust, even though he knew it would take time. Living like this—seeing without touching—was nearly unbearable. She leaned over and pressed a kiss to his scarred cheek.

"Don't be mad at me."

"I'm not," he said stiffly.

"You are. I can feel it."

He growled in frustration. "I'm going crazy, damn it."

"So am I," she snapped and rolled away from him. "Do you think I expected this? Do you think I'm torturing you on purpose? I'm not. I wasn't expecting *you* to come back. I was going to leave. The last thing I ever thought I would get was a husband." She left the bed and sat at her vanity, putting distance between them.

"Do you know what Glory said to me at the game? That you always loved me. But if you loved me, you wouldn't have thrown your affair in my face." She slammed her hand on the fragile vanity. "Damn you, Ryan. After you found out I couldn't get pregnant, you didn't come home. You turned cold on me. You said I was useless." Her voice caught and tears gathered in her eyes.

So this is why she put the distance between them. She couldn't let go of what was done to her. How could she?

He felt like shit. He should have kept his mouth shut... He should have understood. Every step they took forward they took two back. "I hate you for that. I wanted a baby, but you pushed me and I lost him. Him, it was a boy. I was three months pregnant. It was your fault and you blamed me. You beat me for years and you wonder why I can't trust you after a couple of months. My skin still crawls when I think about it. I can't forgive you."

He felt a deep dull pain in his chest, but he knew what he had to do.

"I'm not him!" He stood up and moved closer to her. "We look similar but not the same. Can't you tell the difference? Can't you see I'm nothing like him?"

"You were in an explosion. Of course you look a little different to me. But it's not just me. It's your mother. It's the whole damn town. They all think you are Ryan."

"If you can't see me for who I really am, if you can't trust me, then you need to leave me. I'll sign the papers. You can have the money. I won't come after you."

The tears flowed freely from her slanted eyes. "It's not that easy!"

"Why not! I can take care of myself. I don't need you anymore. You can go without guilt."

"That's not why I'm staying." She wiped her eyes. "I like the man you are, and when I'm with you I feel like a different person. Like I'm married to a different person."

He left the bed and knelt before her. "I'm not him, Lexy." He picked up her hand and placed it on his cheek. "Look at me. Can't you see that I'm not him? Can't you tell when I kiss you? When I touch you? Hell, I don't even have an accent."

"Then who are you?" she whispered. "I want to believe you, but if you aren't my husband, then you are a stranger."

She was right. The same terrifying thoughts ran through his head and kept him awake at night.

"You know me, Lexy. I gave you that ring. Eight weeks ago

you became my wife. The real Ryan might be dead or living my life somewhere, but right now it's me and you."

She surprised him by leaning over and kissing his nose.

"Comb my hair?"

"Excuse me?"

"Comb my hair before it gets tangled."

"That's it? That's all you have to say to me?" He was absolutely dumbfounded.

"Yep." She handed him a beautiful antique sliver comb and looked at him. "Don't you want to?"

It wasn't often he was invited to touch her. She was trying. He had to oblige. He took the comb from her and sat on the bed.

"Come sit here."

She did what he asked and sat between his legs on the floor. She had thick, dark hair that Ryan slid his fingers through. He felt the shape of her delicate skull, massaging her scalp slightly until she let out a thick moan, and just like that he was turned on. Taking the silver comb he ran it through her still-wet hair making sure he made contact with her skin at every opportunity. Her forehead. Her cheek. Her neck.

"You've done this before," she muttered.

Her comment sparked his mind. He saw the glamorous redhead with the sparkling blue eyes. He could see her clearly wearing a fluffy white towel. Her long wet hair clinging to her back. Who was she? Why did she keep popping into his head?

"What do you want for dinner?" she asked him.

"Let's go out. It's too hot to cook," he responded, trying to shake the image from his mind.

"I like the way you think, Mr. Beecher."

He swiped the comb through her hair again and watched as the waves began to ripple.

"Will you wear it down for me sometime?"

"Only if you're here to comb it."

"Deal. Where did you get this comb from?"

"Maybell gave it to me. It was her grandmother's."

He always heard her voice catch a little when she spoke of her grandmother. She was the only family member she ever spoke of.

"Tell me about her."

"She was mean." She smiled. "But I loved her. I'm not sure how I came to live with her but she raised me since I was an infant. She was the only person I had. The whole town loved her. People used to line up for a piece of her red-velvet cake. She tried to teach me how to cook but I could never be as good as she."

"I like the way you cook."

"Thank you." She grabbed his hand and pressed her cheek to it. "But Maybell's food was so much better. I have her to thank for my hips."

"I like your hips."

She turned her head to kiss his palm, and in that moment seemed far away from the world.

"She was big as a house. When I was little I used to plop myself on her and fall asleep. She had a smell I won't ever forget, baby powder and sugar. It was like sleeping on a giant marshmallow."

"You miss her." It wasn't a question. He could hear the sorrow in her voice.

"Yes, but I'm so damn mad at her for dying. She was it. She was my world. And one day I came home from school and found her dead on the floor in the kitchen. Flour everywhere, her hand on her heart. I was devastated. I lost my light."

"What happened to you afterward?"

"You happened. I met you and you promised to love me. We were married two months after she died."

So that was how it happened. Ryan, the man she had married, the man he was supposed to be, saw a sad teenage girl and promised to love her. Lexy wanted to believe that he would love and take care of her. He had done everything but.

"I'm sorry, Lex."

"Don't apologize. Things happen for a reason. I have to believe that." She tipped her head back and looked into his eyes. "Thank you for combing my hair."

"Anytime." He bent forward to kiss her forehead, the lump in his chest growing larger.

"Where should we go for dinner? I feel like Mexican." She stood, and as she did the tie from her bathrobe came undone, revealing just a glimpse of her lush body before she hurriedly retied it. In the back of his mind he knew that she was naked beneath it but now her pretty nude body was in the front of his mind. She may have been embarrassed, but he was intrigued. He grabbed her hand and pulled her into his arms, unable to stop himself.

"Please, Lexy, can I see you again?" He spoke in a whisper but it sounded like a plea. "Please, honey. I need to see you." He thought she was going to refuse him but she didn't. Instead she tugged on the little strip of fabric and let the robe slide along her body and onto the floor.

"Damn it," he breathed. "You're beautiful."

Her lips curved slightly at the corners. Apparently his compliment pleased her, pleased her enough that she wrapped her arms around his neck and pressed her soft body into his. "I don't know if I'm ready to go all the way with you, but I want to try."

He smoothed his hands over the bare skin of her back as an erotic flash of heat ran through his body. "I just need to touch you, that's all." He kissed her under her ear. "Do you know how often I think about you? All day, every day."

Lexy tilted her head back giving him free access to her neck. He gave her hot wet kisses, eliciting moans from her. Her pleasure filled him with life. She had been through hell and all he wanted to do was make life good for her, for them. He took a step back so that he could see her in all her imperfect perfection. Never had he seen a body like hers.

Beautiful curves, large breasts, small waist, round hips, long legs all covered in light brown skin. It called to him, her body; it teased him, begged him to touch it. He couldn't resist her any longer.

Pulling her down on the bed he kissed her mouth. She lay still, almost frozen, except for her lips that moved carefully beneath his. She didn't respond with the comfort of a woman married for ten years, or like the woman who was pulling him into bed last week. But then again he knew that things were changing between them. He knew that she thought if they made love there would be no going back.

Breaking their kiss he gazed down at her body, seeing the scars left behind by the husband of her past. He found the first one on her soft lower belly. This was the scar that had caused her the most pain and he kissed it lovingly, wishing he could erase the past that came with it, wishing she understood that he wasn't the person who had hurt her.

"Ryan," she whispered.

"Not yet. Please, not yet." He didn't want to stop. There was a square-shaped scar of raised flesh that decorated her side. He found it with his mouth and, instead of kissing, he traced it with the tip of his tongue. She gasped, but then relaxed underneath him.

Feeling triumphant he kissed his way up her body. Her eyes drifted shut and she ran her fingers through his dark hair. She was responding to him. He loved her for giving him that.

Her breast captured his attention next, a thumb-shaped scar marked her there. That scar hurt him the most. She said he had forced her. He hadn't. If he had married her he wouldn't have had to force her. He placed his own thumb there and just as he suspected his thumb was bigger than the scar. He didn't do this to her. His lips kissed that scar, two, three times, while he cupped her in his hand, his thumb stroking her nipple to a tight point. Not being able to resist anymore he took her into his mouth and suckled slowly, gently.

She moaned.

"Does that feel good, honey? We can love every day. I can make you feel like this every day." He found her mouth again before she could respond and kissed her with all the pent-up passion that he had stored since he had awoken. She matched his passion, kissed him back, clung to him. He moved his hand between their touching bodies, stroking the soft curls between her legs. She gasped and, taking advantage of that shock, he began to stroke that little pearl that was the center of her pleasure.

It was then she froze.

"Ryan, please stop."

He stopped immediately, even though he didn't want to. He was dying for her. Physically she was ready. He felt the telltale sign when he slipped his fingers between her lips, but mentally she wasn't ready to let go. It hurt him but he respected her wishes.

"With your mouth," she said softly.

All the hairs on the back of his neck rose. "What did you say?"

Her cheeks turned red. She looked away from him. "Nothing. Never mind."

"No. Please, tell me what you said."

"Will you put your mouth on my…"

"Say it." His cock grew. It strained against his zipper in anticipation of her words.

"I—I can't."

He pushed his hands between her legs and flicked his finger across her engorged clit, then he slid it down into her too wet folds where he lightly explored. She pushed herself into his finger, trying to increase her pleasure, but he pulled his hand away.

"Does that feel good?" He dropped a kiss on her lips.

"Don't stop," she moaned.

"Then say it. Say what I want to hear."

"Put your mouth on me," she whimpered.

"Where?" He trailed his lips over her collarbone, then in between her breasts, careful not to touch her anywhere else. "Here?"

"Lower."

He kissed his way down her torso, stopping at her belly button to run his tongue around the perfect circle. "Here?" He dipped his tongue inside and she shivered.

"Ryan…"

"Tell me where, Lexy. You're in charge. Tell me what you want."

"Kiss me between my legs. Kiss my clit. Please."

"Okay." He grinned up at her. "That's all you had to say."

He still continued his kisses downward, giving her hot openmouthed ones on her pelvis, on her inner thighs, anyplace above or below the one she asked him to. He was teasing her. He would give her what she wanted, but he needed a little revenge first. He remembered the day she tied him to the bed, torturing him with her kisses and touches. He would torture her, too.

"Ryan... Now!"

He chuckled then blew on her clit causing her to grip the back of his head. "Okay."

He took one long lick up her center. She tasted sweet. He licked again, her wetness filling his tongue. She was so responsive. Every lick, every kiss, every stroke elicited a moan. She couldn't keep still, bucking her hips against his mouth. He had to clamp his hands on her hips to keep her from rising off the bed.

"Stop it. It's too much. I feel too much," she begged.

That was the one request he couldn't grant. He stayed where he was, pushing his tongue inside her tight hot opening. Mimicking the movements of sex, of fucking, each thrust a little harder than before.

"It's happening again," she warned him. Then she was bucking against him, coming so hard he had a tough time keeping her on the bed. He licked her through each aftershock until she was panting and exhausted and perspiring.

"I knew you would like that." He gathered her into his arms and kissed her under her ear.

"Take your clothes off." She opened her eyes and rolled into him. "All of them."

"You sure?"

"Naked."

He stood, wasting no time stripping off his shirt. She sat on the edge of the bed and grabbed his waist, so that she could pepper kisses all over his torso.

He tugged his pants down, they got caught over his massive erection for a moment before he was free. His cock stood straight out, brushing her cheek, causing her to blush prettily.

"It's bigger than I remember," she muttered as she ran her hand down his length. "Sit against the headboard, please."

"You aren't planning to tie me up again?"

"No, but I would like to try something, if that's okay with you."

"Whatever you want, baby." He cupped her face in his hands to kiss her and before he realized it, he was on top of her, her legs wrapped around him, her beautiful wet sex rubbing against him.

"Wait," she panted, rolling away from him. "You didn't listen."

"Sorry." He grinned. "I got a little carried away. Lexy, you don't know how bad I want you."

"I do know, and you've been very patient. I want to make you feel good. Please sit up."

He obeyed, forcing himself to the back of the bed when he really just wanted to slip inside her warmth and lose himself. His cock sat straight up, waiting for her attention. He couldn't believe she was ready to take that final step with him, but he was too afraid to ask. The last thing he wanted to do was change her mind.

She knelt in front of him. "I'm new at this, but I have been thinking about trying this with you for a little while now."

He nodded, so aroused he could no longer form words.

She straddled him, but did not slide down on his erection like he desperately wanted. But she was open to him. He could see how aroused she was. He could smell it. It made him even harder. "I wanted you to hold me." She took his hands and placed them on her perfect ass. "Here."

He squeezed it. "No problem."

"And I want you to kiss me." She tapped on her lips. "Here."

He caught her lower lip between his teeth and licked inside her soft mouth. "Done."

"Good." She inched herself closer until her open sex was touching his cock and then she moved. With her hand she stroked the tip of him and with her hips she moved against him. Up and down she stroked him with her hand, with her body. She tilted her head back, her mouth opened slightly, her lips damp and swollen from his kisses. It was the most erotic thing he had ever seen. It was like his sweet little Lexy was made for sex.

"Kiss me," she ordered.

He did, long hard hungry kisses that caused her to lose control, and move her body against him at a frantic pace. He couldn't help himself, either. He moved her sweet little bottom up and down, pushing his cock against her, trying to get as close as possible.

She came hard. Trembles flowed through her sex. He couldn't hold back once he felt that. He came, too, spilling himself all over her belly.

He collapsed on the bed taking her with him, not wanting to be away from her for even a second. It took a few minutes for them to regain their senses and when she did her face turned a brilliant shade of red.

"Why do you get so embarrassed?" He kissed her hot cheeks. "That's what men and women do behind closed doors."

"I don't know. I think I got carried away."

"That's how you know it was good." He took his discarded shirt and cleaned them both up as much as he could. "I always want you to get carried away."

"I'm so confused, Ryan. I don't want to want to be with you. I don't want to like it so much."

"There is a reason you want to be with me and you know it." He pulled her blankets up around them. "But let's not argue about it. Go to sleep."

Chapter Fifteen

"Don't you look especially hot today," Lexy heard a slow voice say.

She shuddered, knowing the owner of that voice even before she looked up. Georgie was in front of her in a cream-colored cowboy hat and a black, fitted T-shirt that made him look like a sausage.

"Why are you here?" Of all the people who might visit her at work, he was definitely not one she expected. "Did hell freeze over? I thought that was the only way you'd end up in a library." She folded her arms. "We don't sell beer here, honey, but I can find you a book to teach you how to make it."

Georgie smiled and ran his eyes over her body. He made her skin crawl. She didn't think he was bold enough to try anything with her, but she still didn't trust him.

"Your mouth." He stared at her lips while licking his own. "Too smart for your own good. I thought you would have learned your lesson by now."

"What lesson would that be?"

Ryan may have slapped her around but he never beat the spirit out of her. She would never be silent. He would have won if she stopped speaking.

"Never mind. If you don't know by now you never will."

She sighed and tried to swallow the twinge of unease that

was growing in her chest. A visit from Georgie was not a good sign. "What do you want?"

He leaned over the circulation desk, his beady eyes traveling up her body. Suddenly she felt naked. "Georgie!"

His face grew serious in that moment, more serious than she was prepared for and for the first time she didn't see any sign of that dumb good-old boy she knew.

"It's about Ryan."

"What about Ryan?" She grew nervous. "Is he all right? Was he hurt?"

When had he taken over all of her thoughts?

"No." He frowned. "When the hell did you get so concerned about him?"

"He's my husband," she said, as if that explained everything. It didn't, not even to her. She wasn't sure how she felt but she knew her hard feelings were softening.

"Before you didn't care if he lived or died."

Georgie was right about that, but now she cared about him. Very much so. So much it scared her. He had seen her naked body, kissed her scars and told her she was beautiful. She found herself wanting to be with him, all of him. She wanted to feel that big heavy body on top of her, inside her, but fear stopped her. Which is why she prevented him from taking that final step he so desperately wanted. She tried to keep him satisfied with touch alone. Day after day he came after her and while they kissed and played and found sexual satisfaction with each other she could not let him inside her body. She was afraid if they slept together that he would turn into the monster she had been married to before. Or worse she would find herself in love with a stranger.

"What do you need to tell me about him?"

Georgie blinked. "He's different."

"Yes, very much so."

"He don't wanna hang out. He don't fix cars no more. Damn it, Lexy, he drives around in a Mercedes. That ain't even an American car. You're not worried about him?"

"No." A hysterical bubble of laughter burst out of her. He came home sober every night, smelling like things other than stale alcohol. He didn't hit her or debase her. For the first time she wasn't worried about him when Georgie was.

"How's he treating you?"

"Very good."

Georgie had witnessed one of Ryan's drunken slaps. He didn't move to stop him. He didn't say a word. He let it happen.

"He's not seeing Glory," he said, as if fidelity was tragic.

"I know." The affair was the sharpest blow to their marriage. It left her feeling completely inadequate as a woman.

"He got you a ring. He wears one, too."

She looked at her hand. It was still there. She almost believed it belonged there. "We are married. That's what married people do."

Georgie shook his big head. "He ain't the same. You're not even the same. You look different. You're pretty. Real pretty, Lexy."

"Thank you," she said, not knowing what else to say.

People had been telling her that lately. Her whole life she felt like an oddity, an ethnic enigma with slanted eyes and kinky hair. Today she wore it down, long and thick and curly; and instead of her worn muted clothes she wore a sundress with blush-colored flowers running over her body. Ryan had picked it out. When she first looked at it she thought it would be ridiculous on her, but it suited her, her body type, her skin tone. It was a halter-style that left her shoulders bare. It wasn't risqué but it was more than she was used to.

"He isn't hitting you?" Georgie said, almost sounding disappointed.

"No, he hasn't touched me."

Only lovingly.

"I should have never let him hit you."

His statement took her by surprise. He knew about it from the beginning but did nothing to stop it. She didn't want to talk to him about her abuse. She felt embarrassed by it.

"If he hits you again you can come to me, Lexy. I'll be there for you this time. I'll protect you. I can even make you happy if you let me."

She was stunned by his offer, but couldn't say anything to let him know it was unwanted. He must have taken that as a positive sign because he smiled, tipped his hat to her and left the library, whistling. What the hell was going on with the men in her life? Ryan was wonderful and Georgie didn't seem like such an idiot. They were both offering something she knew she couldn't accept. It troubled her.

She found herself needing to leave the library. She hadn't been to the place Ryan worked in years, but somehow when she turned on her car it took her there.

"Hey, there, Sexy Lexy." Lance whistled as she walked in.

"Ryan told you not to call me that, but it's not him you'll have to worry about if you utter that name again."

"That's my girl," she heard from behind her. She turned around to see her husband, all six feet of him, with a sexy grin on his face. But then he really looked at her for a moment. "What's wrong?"

Everything was wrong. She had begun to feel off balance since he walked back into her life.

"I wanted to talk to you. Can you spare a few minutes?"

"Yes. The books aren't going anywhere." He turned toward the back. "Pep," he yelled. "I'm going out with my wife. I'll be back in a little while."

Pep came out of the shop, a red rag in his hand, grease smeared on his cheek. In fact all the men in the shop were covered in grease except Ryan, who looked clean and sexy in a dark-colored shirt.

"My God, Alexa, I haven't seen you in here for six years. You're looking well, honey."

"Thank you. My husband is trying to keep me happy."

"Is is working?" Ryan asked.

She smiled at him. "I'll bring him back, Pep."

"Don't bother. Take the rest of the day, Ryan. Lexy is too pretty to leave."

Ryan agreed with him and they walked out.

"Good God, it's hot out today," Lexy commented as they walked up the street.

"I don't know how you Texans stand it."

"You're a Texan, too," she pointed out. "Plus you were in Iraq. It has to be hotter there."

"You're probably right but I don't remember."

"Oh, I keep forgetting that."

He smiled at her and grabbed her hand, interlocking his big fingers with hers while they walked.

"What did you want to talk to me about?"

"Nothing." She was enjoying the feel of his fingers locked with hers. They had never held hands like this, not even when they were dating. This seemed more intimate than sex.

"Then why did you want to see me?"

"Promise me you won't laugh."

"No, I won't promise. It might be funny, but please tell me anyway."

She frowned deeply at him, hating herself for what she was about to say. "I just wanted to see you."

They made it to a little park not far from Pep's shop. There was a bench there nestled in between two shady trees.

"You missed me?"

She nodded.

"You're starting to fall in love with me?"

Her heartbeat quickened. She couldn't answer him.

"Wouldn't you like to know?" She rested her head on his chest, seeking comfort even in the heat. He cradled the back of her head in his hand, encouraging their closeness.

"You look really pretty today."

Georgie had told her the same thing but coming from Ryan it made her feel renewed.

"You never used to say that. You used to call me a—"

"Mutt."

"You remember," she gasped.

"No." He shook his head as a flash overtook him. "Not all of it. I dreamed I was sitting around a card table with three guys from my unit. Their faces are fuzzy but I can see them clearer than before. 'My wife Lexy is a mutt but she was so damn hot when I met her I didn't care who her people were.' I know I didn't say those words, Lexy. Your husband did." He turned his gaze on her. "I won't ever call you that." He got quiet for a long moment.

She saw him drift away, saw a blanket of sadness fall over

him. Every time their turbulent past was brought up he seemed to drift a little further away.

"Come back to me, honey," she whispered into his ear.

"I'm so damned confused."

He seemed to hate the real Ryan Beecher as much as she did. He hated that when people looked at him they saw a man who was a monster.

"I know."

"This is not my—"

"Hush, I don't want to talk about it. Tell me how pretty I am."

He kissed her forehead absently. "You're gorgeous."

She tipped her face up to him, looking into his blue-gray eyes. "Will you—" She paused, biting her lip.

"What?"

She wanted him to be happy, as odd as it sounded. She had come to value his friendship.

"Will you kiss my neck?" She hesitated. "And maybe my shoulders." She hesitantly raised her hand and traced the fading scar on his face. "Maybe I could kiss you a little."

He grabbed her arm and began to pull her toward his car.

"Wait! What are you doing?"

"I'm taking you home." He didn't even bother to look back at her.

"Why?"

He stopped dead in his tracks and turned around to gawk at her.

"Why?" He shook his head. "I thought you wanted to—"

"Kiss you!" Her pretty eyes widened. "You thought I wanted to— What kind of girl do you think I am?"

"The kind of girl who has sex on her second date!"

"Well, neither of us are the people we were when I was seventeen, and if I remember correctly that sex wasn't so great. I'm tired of fighting it." She gently pressed her lips to his. "I want to start over. I want to take things slow."

"It's too late for slow. We've been intimate every day for the past week."

"I know."

"I want you, Lexy."

"Soon." She knew by admitting that, she was promising him some kind of future. She was telling him that she wasn't ready to leave. She should have been gone already. He should just be a part of her memory. Her eyes filled with tears as she wrapped her arms around him.

"Lex," he whispered into her hair as he pulled her close. "What happened? Why did you really come?"

"I wanted to see you."

"Tell me, honey," he urged.

"Georgie came to see me at work."

"What? Did he touch you?"

"No," she breathed.

"Lexy, tell me the truth. If he hurt you I'll fix him. Just tell me what happened."

"Nothing, Ryan. He didn't touch me. He told me I was pretty. He said that if you were mistreating me I could come to him. He said he would take care of me."

"Please tell me you didn't consider that for even a nanosecond."

"Of course not. How dumb do you think I am?"

"You're smart, baby. The smartest woman I know." He gave her a light kiss on the nose as a way of apologizing. "What else did he say?"

"That he was worried about you."

"Worried! He can't be too worried. He is trying to steal you away from me."

"He can't steal something that doesn't belong to you in the first place."

"Touché," he said, even though he was thinking that she was his from the moment he laid eyes on her.

"He kept saying how different you are. I think he really just misses his best friend."

"I'm not his best friend, Lex. I'm not the same man." He wasn't meant for this life.

"I know you're not the same man because if you were, I would have been gone already."

"I'm not Ryan Beecher. I'm not your husband."

He was starting to recall his memories. They were few and fragmented like broken pieces of glass. And in that glass he saw tiny glimpses of his life and none of those glimpses included Lexy. He wouldn't forget her. It wasn't possible.

"Then who are you?" Her voice was sharp. Immediately her shoulders went stiff and her eyes burned with anger and regret and some other emotion he couldn't identify. They could never discuss this without getting into an argument.

"I don't know who I am."

"Well, I know who you are, and you can't claim to be an entirely different person just because you don't like being a wife beater. Your memory lapse doesn't erase the past. Why can't you accept it and change?"

"I can't accept it. I won't." He gripped her arms. "You have to see it. You have to feel it. You have to consider that I might be a different man. Shit, even if I was him, I couldn't have changed so much that you don't see any traces of the man I used to be. Think about it."

Lexy looked down at her feet instead of in his eyes. She was considering the facts. She was on the verge of admitting the truth.

"Look at me, Lexy. Feel me. You can see the differences. You can tell just by the way I love you."

"Stop!" She backed away from him. "Don't you dare say you love me in the same breath you say you're not my husband. I see the differences. You feel different to me, but if you aren't Ryan Beecher then who are you and why are you still here?" She shook her head and he could feel her growing distress. "If you aren't my husband then you have no rights to me. I shouldn't be wearing your ring and holding your hand and thinking about being with you. I hated my husband and I never want him in my life again. If you aren't him—"

She shook her head and slipped the ring off her finger. "I shouldn't have started this. I shouldn't have let my guard down. If you aren't my husband then you shouldn't be here. You probably belong to somebody else and I have no right to be with you." She placed the ring into his closed hand and walked away.

Ryan could only stare at it. He was stunned. He didn't mean for their afternoon to turn out like this, with her shoving a knife in his chest. She was right. He might have a life and a family elsewhere. He just couldn't remember. And if didn't remember, he couldn't leave her. No matter what waited for him in the real world, nothing would change the fact that he had fallen deeply in love with Lexy and he couldn't let her go.

Chapter Sixteen

Lexy sat on the floor of her living room, colorful little squares of cloth decorated her lap as she tried to piece them together. She had four months to finish the baby quilt for Jemma's daughter. Baby quilts always made her sad. She would never feel the excitement of an expectant mother. That never stopped her from making a quilt, though. She loved walking into the hospital to see a new life. She prayed that the child would have a life that the one she lost couldn't.

Keys rattled in the door, followed by the sound of heavy footsteps. Ryan was home. The man who claimed that he wasn't her husband. They had barely spoken in days, functioning as roommates only. This is how it should have been from the beginning. She wouldn't have started to have feelings for him. It would have been easy to leave him.

He sat down on the couch behind her, his knees on either side of her body. He put the ring down on the coffee table in front of her.

"I want you to wear your wedding ring."

She shook her head. "Why do you care? You say you're not my husband."

"I'm not the man you married," he said softly. "But I am your husband. The moment I opened my eyes and saw you standing over me, I became your husband. I don't want to live like this anymore, Lex. Please wear it."

"Are you making demands?" Her temper sparked as she jabbed her needle through the yellow fabric.

"Yes, I am. You are my wife. You need to start acting like it."

"Fine, whatever." She slipped her wedding ring back on, hating that she missed seeing it there. She wouldn't tell him that she had missed him these past few days.

"Now quit being mad at me. It's getting on my nerves."

"Quit being an ass and I will." As soon as the words left her mouth she flinched, almost waiting for a slap that she knew would never come. She knew he wouldn't hit her but somewhere in the back of her mind the old Ryan lurked, waiting for her to let her guard down.

Ryan leaned close to her, placing his lips on her skin. She hurt him.

"I'm sorry," she whispered.

He didn't respond. She only felt his rigid body behind her. Finally after tense moments he picked up the braid that hung down her back and gently fingered the gnarled scar at the base of her neck.

"I won't hit you. Ever. I won't force you. Ever. I'm the man you are supposed to be with. I wish you would stop treating me like a monster."

"Ryan." Tears began to trickle down her cheeks. She had never cried so much as she had these past few months.

"Am I that bad?" He brushed the tears away with his thumbs. "Do you hate me that much?"

"I don't hate you at all. I'm just afraid that…"

"Tell me."

"I'm afraid that I'll fall in love with you and you'll turn back into him."

He swept her into his lap, cupping her face in his hands.

She wanted to look away from him. The expression in his eyes was so intense.

"Are you falling in love with me, Lexy?"

"Shut up." That was a question she didn't want to answer.

A slow smile spread across his face. "I'm going to kiss you now."

"You don't have to warn me anymore." She wanted his kiss; she longed for it.

"I don't?"

"No." She relaxed completely in his arms for the first time since he left the hospital. He pecked her mouth and tingles of warmth spread through her.

"I won't hurt you," he whispered against her mouth. "Do you believe me?"

"I want to, but—"

"No buts." He brushed another brutally soft kiss across her lips. "Let me make love to you."

She wanted him to. Only God knew how much, but there was something she couldn't let go of.

"I don't know…"

"I'll be gentle—I promise. And if you ask me to stop, I will."

She believed his promise and so when he lowered his mouth to hers, taking her lips between his own, she let him. He probed gently at first, taking his time, loving her mouth, loving her taste. She knew she could no longer let him go.

Her hand came to rest upon his cheek. He heard her sigh and knew that he had won her.

Be gentle.

He needed to be gentle because he couldn't afford to lose

her. If she knew how much he wanted her it would scare her. Hell, it scared him.

Lexy's mouth drifted open, her sweet tongue came out and brushed his, causing pure fire to shoot to his groin. She noticed. She felt his erection on her bottom and pressed herself into it.

"You never used to respond to me like this before," she whispered into his mouth. "It would take hours of dirty movies for you to come after me."

Come after her? He broke the kiss and stared down at her. The man Lexy had married had forced her into bed. No wonder she was afraid.

"I'm sorry." She looked apologetic for bringing it up. "Don't stop kissing me. I shouldn't keep bringing up the past."

She took his face in her hands and searched. For what? Signs of anger? Forgiveness? He did not know. She pressed a kiss to his mouth.

"I threw all the dirty movies in the trash the day you left."

"I don't need them. You're in every dirty movie that plays in my mind."

"I'm not sure if that's a compliment," she laughed.

It was a rare sound.

"It is. Let me tell you all my fantasies. There are about a thousand of them. We could be here awhile." His kissed her throat, still feeling the vibrations of her laughter.

"You're full of shit, Ryan."

"Fantasy number three," he murmured into her skin.

"What?" Her eyes danced with aroused amusement. He had never seen her that way before.

"You talking dirty. I love a girl with a filthy mouth."

"My mouth isn't filthy," she protested. "Just a little messy. Will you still love me?"

He kissed her forehead. "I will always love you."

In that moment a flash came to him. He was sitting in an office in one of those cushy leather desk chairs that cost a fortune. He wasn't alone. In his lap sat that redhead he saw from time to time. She asked him the same question—*Will you still love me?* He couldn't recall the answer to her question because the woman whose name he couldn't remember floated away and he was left looking at his current love, who was looking at him with concern in those slanted eyes.

"What is it, Ry?"

It was a memory, a glimpse into his past, and instead of rejoicing in recovering yet another piece to his puzzle, it troubled him. He was afraid, afraid that if he delved into his past he wouldn't get the future he wanted with the girl he was in love with.

"Ryan—" she placed her fingertips on his temple "—what is it, honey?"

"My head."

"Your head?" She jumped out of his lap and ran to the kitchen to retrieve the medicine the doctor had prescribed for him. "Take these and go lay down."

"I'm fine, Lex." He pulled her into his lap, sorry he said anything.

"Don't be macho, just take them."

"Lexy my head doesn't hurt. I had a flashback."

"Please—" She touched his cheek with her hand. "In all the years we've been married I've never asked you for a thing, but now I'm asking you to do something just for me. Take the pills and go lay down. You have no idea how much I worry about you."

She just revealed herself. Silly woman. She had no idea how good it made him feel.

"Why are you smiling at me like that?"

"You love me, don't you?"

He watched her mouth drop open. His chest swelled.

"You do!" He grabbed her hand and pulled her into his arms, causing the pills to drop to the floor.

"Shut up, Ryan," she said as he kissed her under her ear. "I love toe jam more than I love you."

"You can say no all you want, but everything you do tells me that you love me."

"No," she gasped as she tried to get off his lap. He tightened his grip on her. "Oh, go lay down," she growled in frustration. She wiggled a lot, managing to arouse him in the process. He let her go.

"I'm not going anywhere." He folded his arms over his broad chest and stared at her. She amused him with her denial. There was no way he could believe that she was apathetic to him.

"Please." She changed her tactic, speaking softly now. "Go take a nap."

"Only if you do something for me."

She eyed him suspiciously. "What?"

"Come to bed with me." He pulled her into his lap.

"Ry." She looked unsure again, even afraid.

"Let me love you."

"I'm afraid." She touched the backs of her fingers to his cheek. "What if you really aren't my husband, like you say?

What if you belong to somebody else? I can't be the person to ruin a marriage. I know how it feels."

"I'm your husband," he whispered. He almost wished that he hadn't said anything.

"What if you are my husband and I can't get over the past?"

"What if you stopped thinking and just felt?"

"Oh," she breathed. "I want to, but—"

"Shh." He stood and carried her to his bedroom. "Trust me, baby." He knew he asked her for a lot, but he couldn't wait any longer.

He laid her on the bed and slowly began to peel off her clothing. She was beautiful nude—thick and luscious. Not normally his type of woman. His girlfriend was neat and trim. But Lexy, she had a body he obsessed about. She was different and intoxicating and not his wife. But he was going to love her anyway because he just couldn't stop himself.

"Ryan?" She called him another man's name, a monster's name. She looked up at him with those big brown slanted eyes and he didn't know how anyone could hurt her.

"Yes, honey?" He smoothed his hands across her bare hips.

"I—" She broke off as he lowered his lips to that ugly scar on her breast. "What if I..." Words fails her as he took her nipple in his mouth, teasing it, sucking on it until it was a hard, little aroused pebble.

She gasped, not believing that this was going to happen. His mouth felt good on her. So hot and wet that she shivered, she trembled hard. She wanted him, the man she thought to be her husband.

"What if I can't do this?" she managed, trying to blink away the tears. He didn't answer, instead he dropped his head

Ginger Jamison

between her thighs and started to kiss her. Down there. Between her legs. In a place she never thought she'd be kissed until he showed her it was possible. That fact put another bit of doubt in the back of her mind. Her husband would have never taken the time to seduce her, to please her.

He parted her with his fingers and ran his warm flat tongue inside her. A moan escaped her lips and she grabbed on to the bed to make sure she wasn't falling off the earth.

"You're so beautiful, Lexy," he murmured as he began to bring her pleasure.

She never knew she could be treated this way by a man who spoke with no accent and was taller that she remembered.

He's not your husband.

I know.

A stranger was about to make love to her and she was going to let it happen. He ran his tongue in long deep strokes until something inside her broke. Waves of now familiar feeling shook her violently and a lovely warmth encased her. She orgasmed quickly. He was the only man to ever bring her to do so.

But before she had time to recover, the man had come inside her, filling her up in a way that was foreign. He moved in and out of her with deep, thick, long strokes. He called her beautiful and kissed her lips and her neck. He suckled her breasts and ran his hands over every inch of skin he could reach.

He wasn't hers. He couldn't be. One day he would remember and she would feel guilty—or worse, she would wait for her own husband to emerge. It was an ugly thought during such a beautiful moment.

She tried to think of other things but the tears started to form in her eyes. He was trying so hard to make her feel good, to make her feel loved. He was succeeding. She had been prepared to feel a lot of things when he came home but loved was not one of them.

"You're so sweet, Lexy," he whispered, kissing her shoulder and neck.

He was a good lover. That building feeling of passion was growing again. He was so much better than her husband, so much sweeter and kinder. He went to kiss her mouth when he stopped cold.

"What's wrong?" He looked down at her. "Am I hurting you? Why are you crying?"

"No." She grabbed him, feeling panicky. "Please don't stop." She had to get through this. He deserved the gift of her body. He had been so patient and sweet. He made her feel whole again. She wrapped her legs around his hips, bringing him closer to her. He was still hard inside her.

"Please, Ryan." She rolled her hips underneath him, causing both of them to feel that sexual force that was uncontrollable between them. He began to move inside her once more.

Touching his back, she felt his scars, the places where the hot debris burned him. She kept touching those places to remind herself that the Ryan she knew was gone. But she kept seeing visions of him, forcing himself on her after she lost the baby. She couldn't hold it in anymore. A sob tore from her throat. Pleasure and anguish fought for control of her body.

"I can't do this." He stopped. "I can't." He rolled off her and sat on the side of the bed, his head in his hands. "You hate me."

"No!" She scrambled to sit beside him but her tears wouldn't stop coming. "You've been so good to me."

"Then why do I feel like I'm forcing you? Tell me what to do, Lexy, because I don't know anymore."

"There's nothing you can do." She wrapped her arms around him. "You've been so good to me. I appreciate it." She could feel his hurt. She hated that she hurt him.

"You're supposed to be treated that way, Lexy. You don't have to thank me."

"I do, because you used to— *He* used to force me," she choked. "Hurt me, debase me. He used to…" She couldn't take the look in his eyes. She couldn't face him, this good man who didn't belong to her. She ran out of the room, no longer able to face him.

Chapter Seventeen

"Mad dog!" Georgie ambled into Ryan's office, lowering his big body into the chair in front of his desk.

Ryan was surprised he had the nerve to show his face here after the confrontation they'd had at the Calloway. Especially since Georgie had the nerve to visit Ryan's wife at work.

"What do you want?" he snapped.

"What the hell is wrong with you? Everybody's been saying you've been in a funk for days."

"So?"

He *was* in a funk. That evening with Lexy was a disaster. He'd made love to her and she started to sob. He saw her face every night when he closed his eyes. She was in pain, and instead of holding her and helping her through it, he turned away. He didn't know how to handle her tears at the time. It made him wonder what her husband had done to her to make her so terrified of him. Did she cry every time? Did the real Ryan force her through the tears?

"What's wrong with you, man?"

Lexy wasn't speaking to him, which was fine because he couldn't even look at her. She looked so...sad. She warned him. She told him she might not be able to go through with it and yet he ignored her. What kind of man was he?

"Stay away from my wife."

"What?" His eyes widened. "I haven't touched her in years."

"Years?" He gripped the edge of his desk to avoid lashing out at him. "You better not touch her ever again. Why did you go visit her at the library?"

"Uh, I was just making sure you all were okay." He swallowed.

Ryan watched Georgie's big Adam's apple move as he grasped for an explanation.

"That's not your job."

"It is," he spat. "You took her from me. I saw her first. You knew I loved her and then you had to marry her. You didn't even treat her right. You beat her—you called her names. If you would've let me have her she would have been happy."

"She didn't want you," he bellowed. "And you sure as hell didn't love her. If you did, you would have never let any of that happen to her. If you loved her, you would have kicked my ass. If you loved her, you would have treated her with respect instead groping her. She's too good for you, George. She never wanted you. She never will."

Georgie's lips spread into a thin line as cold fury spread over his face. "She's too stupid to realize it. I've been waiting for her to come to her senses. It's only a matter of time before she leaves you. I used to worry she was going to stay with you but I've seen her these past few days. She's just as miserable as she was before you left. You'll see. I'll finally get what's mine."

"I'll kill you Georgie. Dead. Don't fuck with me."

"Whatever, Ryan. I ain't scared of you. You only hit women." Georgie gave him one last hard look before he walked out.

He had to leave here. Texas wasn't his home but he wasn't sure where his home was. The only thing he could do was go back to the place he and Ryan Beecher had in common. He would reenlist as soon as he was able.

"Lexy." Di walked into the library and sank down in one of the cushy armchairs that were located in the fiction section.

"Hello, Di."

"Sit down, honey." Di motioned to the chair opposite her.

"What's wrong?" Lexy sat as a beat of concern passed through her. Di looked exhausted when she was normally so full of energy.

"I'm knocked up again."

"Di! You are? I'm so happy for you," Lexy said sincerely. She ignored the little knife of jealousy that stabbed her in the gut. They were the same age. Di was going to have four kids. Lexy still didn't have any.

"Yeah, yeah. I've got morning sickness. I'm exhausted and we're broke, but my husband is happier than a pig in shit." She sighed. "That's not what I came here for. You're miserable and you're making the whole damn town sad just looking at you. What's wrong?"

"It's nothing."

"Don't lie to me, Lexy. You wouldn't let me be here for you the last time. Let me be here for you this time."

"It's Ryan."

Di went on guard, her slender body rigid. "Is he hitting you again?"

"No." She shook her head. "He wouldn't hit me because he's not my Ryan. I don't know how he got here but he doesn't belong here." She smacked herself in the head. "I'm so stupid. I let this happen. I spend my days laughing and wanting to trust him so bad I ache. I ache for him but at the same time

I'm scared of him. I'm scared that he could be my husband and he's just putting on an act. I should have walked out months ago, but I didn't, and now I hurt him and he hates me so much he won't even look at me."

"Whoa, honey." Di shook her head repeatedly as if she was trying to make sense of it all. "Take a breath. What are you saying? You don't think the man you've been living with is Ryan?"

"He can't be."

"His eyes."

Lexy nodded. "And his accent."

"Plus, he's gorgeous," Di said, her eyes flying to Lexy's. "He's not an asshole. My God, Lexy, you might be right."

"I think so."

"Well, holy shit."

Lexy nodded. That was her thought exactly.

"He really can't be somebody else. It would be too crazy."

"I know that and I might be able to let it go if he wasn't so sure about it. He doesn't think he's Ryan, and more importantly he hates that everybody thinks he is."

"Who wants to wake up from a coma and be told they spent their entire life being an asshole? I know I wouldn't." Di leaned forward and took Lexy's hands in hers. "You can't let things go on like this. It's not good for either of you."

"I know."

"What are you going to do?"

"That's a good question."

"Well," Mary said, opening the door of her cozy little home that she spent the past thirty-five years of her life in, "this is a pleasant surprise."

"Hi, Mom." Ryan kissed her cheek and entered the house. "I wanted to talk to you."

She said nothing, only pressed a hand to her cheek in the spot he had kissed.

He turned to look at her. "What's wrong?"

"Nothing." She shook her head, coming out of her fog. "What did you need, sweetheart? Can I get you something to eat?"

"No, thank you." He sat on her floral-print couch. "Mom—" he rubbed his forehead "—I—"

"You never called me *mom,* and you've never been so polite in your life." She leaned close to him to study his face. "I think this war has been good for you. You're a better man now. I keep meaning to tell you that."

"You warned me," he started, "to be good to my wife."

"Are you? She doesn't look very happy lately."

"No, she doesn't. She's afraid of me."

A thread of worry crossed Mary's face. "Please tell me you haven't hit her."

"No, I haven't hit her. I would never hit her."

"No, I guess you haven't." Mary rose, pulled a picture off the mantel. "This man is my son." She showed him a picture of a man who looked ridiculously like him, same coloring, same build. They were alike but so different. "He had beautiful blue eyes just like his daddy." She looked from the picture back to Ryan. "You have beautiful eyes, too, but you aren't my boy. Hi, I am Mary Beecher. Who are you?"

It felt like a weight had lifted off his shoulders. He felt unburdened. "You know," he breathed.

"Of course I know. I know my child. I love my son, but you are too good to be my child. Who are you?"

"I don't know. I'm close to remembering, but I just can't."

She nodded. "I guess if you did you wouldn't be here, would you?"

"I've fallen in love with Lexy," he said helplessly. "But she's afraid of me and I can't be with someone who thinks I will turn into a monster."

"She's lost a child. He beat her unconscious. She'd be crazy if she wasn't afraid."

He knew that but it didn't change anything.

"I'm not him. She should be able to see me by now."

"Maybe." Mary shrugged. "You look like him. Your voice is deep like his… And who could really believe that the government could make a mistake like that?"

"You're right," he sighed. "I don't believe it myself half the time." He looked away for a moment, wishing he could accept this life without question. "I think Lexy's falling in love with me but she's fighting it."

"Wouldn't you? She was going to divorce him. All she had to do was get him to sign—and then you came along, and you treated her right. She's finding it really hard to go, and the thought you'll turn back into him always stays in the back of her mind. If she lets herself fall and you abuse her she won't be able to live with herself and she'll never forgive me because I asked her to stay."

Mary felt guilt. It was evident in her face. Apparently he wasn't the only one with regrets a mile long.

"Am I supposed to live in this limbo? We aren't really married. We don't even talk anymore, and I walk around so pissed half the time I can't stand myself. I can't stay in that dead-end job or be with a woman who cries when I try to make love to her. I can't do this anymore."

Mary shook her head sadly. "You'd both be better off if you moved on."

"Yeah." He nodded. "But I have no idea who I am or where I came from. All I see are little flashes. Everything is unrecognizable."

"So what are you going to do?"

"I've thought about it. I'm going to the place your son and I have in common. I'm going to reenlist."

Di had asked Lexy to babysit her little girl while she and her husband went to a doctor's appointment. She loved Alana. She loved the way the four-year-old babbled on about nothing, the way she smelled like baby powder and the way her mother dressed her hair in pigtails. She wanted a child so badly that it hurt to be around one. She should probably be thanking God. It would have been harder to leave Ryan with a child in tow. It would have been worse if her child had grown up with a drunk for a father. It would have been terrible for her baby to witness her being abused.

"Where's Uncle Ryan?" Alana asked as Lexy pushed her through the aisles of the supermarket.

"I think he's at work." They hadn't spoken for days. She was lonely without the man she thought she wanted to leave.

"Oh. I want him to read me a story."

"He might if you ask him nicely."

"Mama says he'll do anything for you."

"Did she now? Your mama has a big mouth."

"Yeah." Alana grinned. "Daddy says that, too."

Di was right about that. Her new Ryan would have done nearly anything for her. He said he would give her babies and she believed him. He said he would take care of her and he had. He said he loved her and he did.

But he wasn't her husband, was he? He said he wasn't, and she started to believe him. Sometimes when he wasn't looking she stared at him hard, trying to find that one thing off about him that would give her an *aha* moment.

"Can we buy Teddy Grams, Aunt Lexy?"

"Of course, baby." Lexy had spent years buying store-brand food. For the first time in her life she could buy name-brand products, and all because Ryan had sold his cars. Sometimes she felt guilty for splurging, but she knew the life she had now wasn't going to last forever.

"How about we make spaghetti and meatballs for dinner tonight? Uncle Ryan will be home soon."

Lexy heard Ryan's heavy footsteps a little past five-thirty that evening. Dinner was almost ready, the garlic bread baking in the oven.

"He's home!" Alana squealed and Lexy knew how she felt. She got that little flippy thing in her chest when he came home. It was quite annoying.

Lexy scooped the little girl up. "Let's go greet him." They met him in the living room and stood silently just looking at each other for a long moment. He was miserable. She could read it in his face, see it in every movement he made, hear it in his voice. It was her fault. She wanted to make it up to him but she didn't know how. She couldn't tell him why she sobbed when he made love to her.

"Alana's here!" He put on that charming smile that disarmed her and walked across the room to greet them. "How is my gorgeous little cousin?" He bent down to kiss her forehead. It was then that Lexy took the opportunity, and planted a soft kiss on his mouth. He looked at her critically and then kissed her mouth again.

"How's my gorgeous little wife?"

"We made you dinner!" Alana yelled proudly.

"I thought I smelled something delicious."

"Guess what it is."

"Um." Ryan tapped his chin, pretending to think. "Liver and onions?"

"Eww, no!"

"Hot dogs?"

"You're silly," she giggled.

Ryan took Alana from Lexy's arms and strolled into the kitchen, coming up with more ridiculous suggestions. Lexy watched them laughing together and felt her heart twisting painfully.

The next morning her heart twisted again. It was Friday, her day to visit her brother. She almost didn't want to go. She didn't want to get out of bed. She didn't want to make the drive. She didn't want to feel the heavy sadness of seeing her brother wasting away. She didn't want to be alone. But it was selfish to only think of herself. Kyle was all she had left of her family. She only had him for a little while longer. She needed to be with him every chance she got.

She put on one of the dresses Ryan had picked out for her and wore her hair down, needing a boost that day. Maybe if she pretended that things were okay, Kyle wouldn't pick up on her sadness. She needed to be happy for him. When she was ready she left her bedroom to find Ryan standing at the front door.

He stared at her for a long moment, seeming to take in every inch of her. Goose bumps raced along her arms. She missed him. Part of her wanted to launch herself at him and ask him to forgive her. But she knew she couldn't do that. There was too much keeping them apart.

"Did you forget something?"

"No. I thought I would drive you to see your brother."

"Oh." She put her hand over her beating heart. She was touched. She was more than touched—she felt her heart crack open. "You don't have to do that for me."

"It's not for you," he said softly. "I want to see Kyle, too."

She nodded. "He would like that."

He opened the door for her, but instead of passing through it she stopped, placed a hand on his chest and kissed his cheek. "Thank you for everything."

Lexy was crying. No, more than crying. She was sobbing again. Sobs of pain. Something was happening to her. Someone was hurting her. He started to run through the house. He would kill for her. He would kill whoever was hurting her.

A cold fury came over him as he spotted a man shaking his wife.

"You're a mutt, Lexy. A whore."

"Get off of me," she screamed.

"You don't get to tell me what to do." The man raised his large hand and slapped her hard in the face. He watched as her head snapped back.

"Lexy!" he screamed, but when he tried to move his feet were stuck to the ground. "I'm here," he called to her. "I didn't leave you."

"Help me," she cried. He wanted to help her. He was trying to. He couldn't move.

"Leave her alone," he roared. "I'll kill you, you bastard." The man who was beating his wife turned around to face him and he froze.

"You can't kill yourself." The man looked just like him. The same scars decorated his face. The man was him.

"No," he screamed. He wouldn't hurt her... He couldn't. It happened then.

It.

The explosion. The fire. The pain ripping through his head. He saw the men in his unit bleeding around him and a dying soldier. The same man who was beating his wife.

"Lexy!"

"I'm here, honey." He heard her voice nearby and when he opened his eyes she was there by his bed. He sat up and grabbed her hand. It was just a dream. Thank God. It was just a dream.

"Lexy." He still felt panicky. "I dreamt that..." He drifted off, unable to tell her what he saw.

"It was the explosion, wasn't it?"

"Yes." Tears ran down his face. He hated the weakness. He hated himself. He hated that he needed her. He had taken the day off work and driven Lexy to see her brother just to be with her. They didn't speak on the long car ride there or back, or at all that day, but he tortured himself with her presence because being away from her was more painful. And he knew that his time with her was coming to an end.

"Sweetheart." She cupped his face in her hands and kissed his wet cheeks. He could feel the franticness of her kisses.

She must feel it, too—she must know that their life together was ending.

She pulled her nightgown off, revealing her nude body to him. That shocked him out of his miserable thoughts for a moment. He stared at her in the darkness, just making out the shape of her curves in the moonlight.

"I'm here for you." She climbed into bed beside him, hugging him close to her body. "You aren't there anymore. You're with me now. You won't ever feel that pain again."

"They didn't survive, Lex."

"No," she admitted. "They found you next to another soldier. He didn't make it, but you did." She kissed his neck, his chin, the scar on his cheek. "You came back for me." Her hand wandered to his boxers, where she began to stroke him until he was hard.

"What are you doing?" he asked, shocked by her boldness.

"You need this." She came over him, taking him inside her warm wet space. "Go ahead. Make love to me."

He hesitated for a moment, not believing this was happening.

"Ry." She shifted her body so that her breasts were pressed against him. She moved her hips, unsure of herself. He knew she had never made love this way. She was clumsy with her rhythm and for a moment he saw her embarrassment. She shouldn't be embarrassed. She was beautiful and selfless and no woman had ever turned him on like this before.

He grasped her hips and rolled her onto her back, pushing himself deep inside her. Heaven.

"Don't hold back, Ryan. Please."

He wouldn't. He was too far gone, too emotionally raw to hold back now. She wrapped her legs around him and relaxed beneath him, allowing him to use her body. His strokes were strong and rhythmic, not meant to tantalize, but to make him feel—feel her, feel comfort and calm, and anything other than terror.

"My husband," she murmured, which caused him to lose all control. He came hard inside her.

"I love you," he said into her neck. He wasn't even sure if she heard him, but it didn't matter because he did. He would always love her even if he regained his memory. Even if he learned that this life was not his own. She brought him back from death.

The next morning Ryan reached over wanting to feel his wife's warm body, but she wasn't there. The only thing he felt was the empty space where she should be. Last night she had come to him, comforted him, gave him her sweet body with no apprehension, no hesitation, and afterward she slept in his arms. But now she was gone and he was confused. Had it been a dream like the one he thought she rescued him from?

No, the sheets smelled like sex, their sex, and her sweet scent. Why had she gone? He thought maybe this would be a turning point in their broken marriage.

He got out of bed looking for her in her bedroom, but she wasn't there. She wasn't in the house at all. He swore violently. Nothing had changed. He was going to leave here. Next week he would be gone.

Chapter Eighteen

Mary had called Lexy the night before, just as she and Ryan had gone to their separate beds, to tell her Ryan was going to go back into the marines. Lexy's blood froze. She knew things weren't good between them and she knew the fault lay with her. Going back was extreme. To risk life and limb just to get away from her was extreme. And it hurt her.

He taught her how to laugh, showed her how a man was supposed to treat a woman. She knew they weren't going to last forever, but she was grateful for the time they did share together. When she left him she would leave her bitterness behind and her anger, as well. But Ryan was ruining her plan by leaving before she could. He was going to get himself killed just because he hated her.

"What's wrong, honey?" Deidre, the other waitress working that night at the Calloway, asked.

"Nothing. I was just thinking."

They were short-staffed since two of the regular waitresses called out with the flu. Lexy agreed to work a twelve-hour shift right after she left the library. She was used to working a lot. And after she left Ryan she would have to start working long hours again to make ends meet. But that was fine with her. There wouldn't be much else in her life.

"We're really slow tonight," she commented. "It seems like every time they call you they don't need you."

"It'll pick up. The bowling league is heading this way when they finish."

Deidre looked over at Lexy, who wore a pink tank top and a denim skirt that Ryan had bought for her. "I should probably change, then. I won't get many tips with you looking like that."

Lexy looked down at herself. The tank top was simple. Light pink, slightly faded from the wash. "I don't look so great. Your boobs are bigger than mine."

"Mine aren't real, honey." Deidre rolled her eyes. "And you got your hair down. I'd kill my mama for hair like that."

She wore it down as an impulse. This morning she wore it braided, but when she got here six hours ago she'd unraveled her braid and finger-combed her wild hair into place, thinking about Ryan as she did.

"My husband likes it down," she told Deidre, not meaning to.

Last night she had offered her body to him after he had a nightmare. She knew he often dreamed about the war, but he had never called out for her before, and he never knew that she had often snuck into his room at night and stroked his hair until he fell into a more restful sleep. She wouldn't tell him that, either. She didn't want him to know that his nightmares haunted her, too.

"You mean the husband who's been sitting in the corner for the past half hour?"

"Ryan's here?" She whipped around and spotted him in the darkest corner of the bar at a small table. He looked brutally angry. He had always come here when she worked to make sure she was safe. Somehow it surprised her tonight. Before she went to him she had the cook prepare him a cheeseburger and a glass of cream soda.

"I didn't know you were here," she said, approaching him.

"You were in the back when I came," he said stiffly.

"Are you hungry?" She set the food on the table, not waiting for an answer. He had been angry with her since their first failed attempt at lovemaking. Now it seemed worse.

"I didn't get your message until a little a while ago. They didn't tell me at work."

"I called when you were out," she explained. "Damn it, Ryan." She sat on his lap and folded her arms around him. She was hurting. They both were. "I'm sorry," she mumbled into his neck. "I never thought I would apologize to you...but here I am." She looked up at him, his face still hard. He said nothing, only buried his fingers into her loose hair.

"You did this for me." It wasn't a question.

"Yes," she whispered, trying to reconcile the fact that he wasn't her husband. She had no right to feel the way she was feeling. She had no right to keep him.

"You care about me."

She said nothing to that, just kissed his mouth tentatively at first because she wasn't used to initiating kisses. He held his mouth still to begin with, but she kept kissing, kept moving her lips over his, running her tongue over the soft place that she used to rub cherry lip balm on.

Eventually he gave in and kissed her back, a deep soul-sucking kiss that left her breathless.

"Are you afraid of me?" he asked when she broke away for air.

Of course I am, she wanted to say, *but not for the reasons you think.* She studied his face, taking time to kiss the scars there.

"You've come so far," she said more to herself than to him.

She remembered when he couldn't speak or walk. She remembered when he needed her. Her lips trailed his chin and down his neck and then back up to his mouth again. He was a beautiful kisser, and he made her feel precious and beautiful whenever their lips touched.

"Lexy," he murmured. His expression hadn't softened but she felt his body turn on like a switch. He wanted her and for the first time in her life she knew she wanted him just as badly.

She could never really have him.

She had to stop growing attached. This would end. She rested her head on his strong shoulder, stroking his cheek with her thumb.

"I think—" she started before she choked "—I should be the one to leave."

"What?" She felt him go on alert. Before, she'd felt cold anger, and now she felt his heat.

"I don't want you going back to the marines. I'll leave so you don't have to."

"Why would you leave, Lexy?" he asked sharply.

"You're reenlisting to get away from me. So I'll go. You just finished healing. I watched you hover between life and death. I won't let you get yourself killed."

"Well, how about not asking me to go, damn it? Sometimes I hate you, Lexy. Where is your self-respect? You don't have to give up everything. You would leave your job and family and friends because you don't want me to go? Why do you get to be the victim all the time? You let him walk all over you. You let him destroy your dreams. You're not a doormat. You need to stand up for yourself."

"I did," she cried, "and I got beat unconscious for it. Don't you dare act like I asked for it. Don't you dare say that I played the victim. I did the best I could. I did it because I didn't have a choice."

His silver eyes blazed with fire. "You let it happen. You let bad things happen to you and good things walk away. You're determined to be miserable for the rest of your life."

Miserable was something she never wanted to be again. She was trying to take charge of her life.

"I had to stay for Kyle!"

"Don't bring him into this. You had a choice. I paid his bill to take that excuse away from you. You could have left me weeks ago. This is all on you now. This is about what you want. But you're too scared to decide."

"I don't want you to go, Ryan. Are you happy now? I invested my life in you."

"You shouldn't have." He shook his head sadly. "You should invest in yourself. You should have left years ago. You should have left as soon as I could walk. You should have started over already. But you waited and everything turned to shit again."

"How," she breathed, "could you blame this on me?" She stood, now enraged.

"You cry when I make love to you. You tense when I touch you and other nights you crawl into my bed. Sometimes I feel so close to you I could crawl inside of you, and other times you throw up a wall so high that I can't climb it. That's why I need to get away from you—because I can't live like this anymore. Either we live together as man and wife or we go our separate ways forever. I can't take the in-between. I can't live with a woman who is half terrified of me."

It was just after midnight when Lexy walked out of the Calloway. The air had grown chilly and she shivered in her tank top and short skirt. Somehow she managed to blow it with Ryan. He was going to walk out of her life. She should be relieved, but she wasn't.

She had fallen in love with him, but she knew he wasn't hers and she felt too guilty to ask him to stay.

"Lexy." She heard her name called by a male voice.

"Georgie?" She strained to see him. There weren't many lights behind the Calloway.

"Yeah, I came to see you." He moved closer to her and she could smell the beer and sweat on him.

"Why?"

"Why?" He moved closer, invading her space. "I wanted to see you. Can't one friend visit another?"

"We're not friends, Georgie." She tried to push past him. He grabbed her and pushed her against the wall. She gasped in shock.

"What's your damn problem, Lexy? You spend all the fucking time acting like you're too good for me. You're just a mutt. You ain't no better than anybody else. You shouldn't be so picky."

"Let go of me, Georgie." His grip tightened and she felt fear slice through her.

"You were mine, damn you." His eyes glazed over with anger. "You were mine and Ryan took you away from me."

"I was never yours." She struggled. "I never even liked you. Why would you think I ever wanted you?"

"You were sweet to me." He pushed her harder into the wall, the bricks scraped her back.

"I'm nice to everybody. Let me go!" She began to fight him but he had her pinned.

"No! You picked him over me and he beat you. You're a stupid bitch. I would have loved you."

Fear began to build in her chest, but she warned herself not to let it get the best of her. He would win if she did. "You let him beat me. If you loved me you would have stopped him, but you let him nearly kill me."

"You deserved it!" Spittle flew out of his mouth and into her face. "You betrayed me. You both did and because of you I lost my best friend."

He was insane. He'd snapped. She wasn't going to get away from him unharmed but she wouldn't go down without voicing the truth.

"He chose you over me," she yelled in his face. "Every day. He lost all of our money for your stupid schemes. He chose to go out drinking with you every night. He loved you more than he ever loved me."

"He's changed. He joined the marines for you. He comes back and doesn't want nothing to do with me. He tells me to stay away from you. Who does he think he is?"

"My husband!" she spat. "Get off of me."

"No." He forced his big smelly body against hers. "Your husband walked out on you. I saw him go. I knew it wouldn't last. I knew you would end up with me."

"End up with you!" She struggled harder, bucking her body, fighting him until she was breathless. "Let go of me, you son of a bitch!"

He was big, nearly as big as her husband. Too big to fight off. He grabbed her neck. If she moved he would choke her.

"I loved you, Lexy." He forced his mouth on hers, kissing her hard. "I hope you can make it up to me."

"Stop it," she sobbed and before she knew it his hand shot

up her skirt. "No!" She tried to scratch at him, her nails clawing at his skin, but he didn't seem to notice. He just tightened his grip on her neck. He grabbed her through her panties, kissing the side of her face.

Something, a glimmer of light, made her look to her left. She saw Ryan looking at her and a piece of her died. He locked eyes with her. He was going to let it happen. The tears came now. She had no idea he hated her enough to watch her get raped.

"Get off of her," he growled deep in his throat. Georgie looked up completely shocked. Suddenly Ryan was at Lexy's side, delivering massive blows to Georgie's face. "I told you to leave her alone." He smashed Georgie's head against the brick wall. "She's my wife. You're a dead man."

Ryan delivered blow after blow in cold fury. Georgie's eyes were blackened and swollen. His lips were bleeding, a tooth on the ground. Ryan was going to kill him.

"Ryan, stop," she cried.

"He tried to rape you." He kicked Georgie in the stomach. "I told him not to touch you. I warned him."

It was clear Ryan wasn't going to stop.

"Please, Ryan. I want to make love to you."

He stilled.

She was shaking violently. "Ryan, my heart, come home with me right now and make love to me. I need you."

He stepped away from Georgie, who was moaning in pain. It was then the door burst open—one of the line cooks and the bartender rushed out. "We saw you through the window." He looked down at Georgie. "At first we didn't know it was you, Lex."

"We thought it was just another couple making out. And

then we saw Ryan" the bartender said. "We would have never let him near you if we had known."

Georgie groaned again and tried to sit up but his body was too weak to manage it. Lexy was afraid he was badly hurt, that his injuries could be serious. She didn't feel sorry for him. She just didn't want Ryan to be charged with his death. "Can you get him to the hospital?"

"You sure you want us to do that?" the cook said. "We can take him out in the woods."

"No. Please. Just get him fixed up."

"All right. But he won't be bothering you anymore. We'll make sure of it."

Chapter Nineteen

Ryan sat on the edge of the bed waiting for Lexy to return with ice for his swollen hands. Something had told him to go back for her. Maybe it was God or conscience or common sense, but he was glad he did. He wouldn't have been able to live with himself if Georgie had hurt her. It was odd, at first he thought they were kissing, that Lexy was so upset with him that she would let Georgie kiss her. But then he came to his senses. She would never do that. She wouldn't betray him. He could have killed Georgie.

He would have, if Lexy hadn't stopped him.

She returned. "Honey." She knelt down before him placing an ice-filled towel on his open knuckles. "Are they broken?" She gingerly picked up his hand. It burned with pain and was swelling at a rapid rate.

"I'm fine."

"Yes, you are." She lovingly kissed his palm. "You are a good, fine man but you are hurt."

She kissed his hand again, his palm, his middle finger, his pinky. Soft sweet kisses that were arousing him immensely. He touched her face with his free hand, stroking her cheek, even though his knuckles were aching. It was the way she was looking up at him with eyes that were almost worshipping. He didn't want her to worship him. He wanted her to love him.

"I'm so sorry, Ryan." They were always apologizing to each other. That would have to change.

"Kiss me," he told her. He expected her beautifully formed lips to touch his, but they didn't. Her hand sneaked into his jeans and pulled out his cock. He was hard before the air touched his skin, and when her lips touched his throbbing manhood he nearly died. "Lexy..." he choked when she took him into her sweet wet mouth.

"You don't want me to kiss you here?"

"If you stop I'll—I'll divorce you."

"Oh?" She looked up at him, mischief in her eyes.

"Please don't stop."

She pressed a kiss to his head, causing his whole member to twitch.

"Okay, but only if you tell me you love me."

"I love you," he said honestly. "I love you. I love you. I love you."

She smiled up at him, an easy smile, one that told him that she was no longer afraid of him.

Finally.

She took him in her mouth, her movements unsure, unrhythmic. He knew she had never done this before, only for him. She was giving him a gift and it was beautiful. Her mouth was soft and wet; her lips were warm and full.

"I'm going to—" he warned her.

"Mmm-hmm," she moaned. That was it—he was going to have to marry her. His last girlfriend, Caroline, would never have been so—

He finished with a shudder before that thought was fully formed. Greedily he grabbed her off the floor and began to undress her. She had such beautiful hips, curvy and round and life-giving. When he took off her skirt and panties he kissed her thighs. Just the outsides at first, but the more attention he paid the wider her legs spread, and soon he was taking her hard little nub into his mouth. She stood there letting out contented sighs, running her fingers through his hair.

"Take off your bra," he murmured, kissing her belly. It brought back memories of the first time he had kissed her there in the hospital. Soon she was naked, her lush honey-colored body was warm and waiting for him. "Get under the covers."

She obeyed him and he disrobed, climbing in beside her. They huddled close together. Skin to skin, their warm bodies touching, their hands gently caressing. This moment was so close to perfect, but something was bothering him.

"You didn't think I was going to stop him, did you?"

The tears came immediately and he knew he was going to have to kill Georgie. "He was drunk. You— They both were. When he grabbed me between my legs. You— He saw him do it and watched him for a moment before he walked away. I yelled and Lance pulled him off of me and took him home."

Ryan shook his head. He couldn't blame her for not trusting him.

"You aren't him," she continued. "I have to stop treating you like you are." She closed the gap between their mouths and kissed him. "I want to try, Ryan. I want to be your wife. I want you to stay."

"Stay?" He kissed her nose. "I don't think I could have actually walked out. I couldn't even leave you tonight."

"I'm glad you came back," she whispered. "He's lost it."

"I know." He touched his lips to the spot on her neck where Georgie's fingers were still visible. "I'm going to kill him. He's a dead man." He tried to kiss away all traces of the brute. He would try to kiss away her bad memories.

"Don't. He's not worth it."

"Did he hurt you?" He brushed the curls between her legs.

She sighed in pleasure. "I seduced you so that you would stop thinking about it."

"You did a good job." He stroked her cheek, thinking about her sweet unsteady movements. "You've never done that before, have you?"

She scrunched her face adorably. "Was it awful?"

"No, baby," he laughed and kissed her face. "I don't think that can ever be bad, especially when you do it. Thank you."

"Ryan never let me do that to him. He said only whores do that, and he married a virgin not a whore."

"What an idiot." He slipped his finger inside her lips and rubbed her clitoris lightly. "You should have left him then."

"If I did I would never have met you." She moaned as he played in her wetness. "Plus, I love naked war heroes."

"They like you, too." He captured her mouth and sucked deeply. She melted into him, moving her hips beneath his stroking hand.

"Ryan," she moaned when he came up for air. "I don't want to— I'm going to— I need you inside of me."

"No," he refused, slipping his finger deep inside her.

"You son of a bitch," she moaned and promptly climaxed. He continued to stroke her through the aftershocks, feeling stupidly happy. "That was just evil," she said when she finally got her breath back.

"I don't think it was." He grinned, dropping a kiss on her forehead.

"I want to tell you something." She looked up at him. "I want you to know why I cried."

"I was wondering," he said flatly.

"It was just that it felt so good, and you were so sweet and I've never had— I've never—"

"Felt loved before?"

"I felt like a virgin all over again. And raw. It wasn't you. I was waiting for him to come back. I was waiting for a reason to leave but you never gave me one, and I wondered what I got myself into." She looked away for a moment. "You were very good."

"And you were a basket case."

She kissed his hurt knuckles. "Yes, I was."

"Were you really going to leave?"

"Yes," she answered without hesitating. "If it would have kept you from going back into the marines." She touched her fingertips to the burn on his stomach, the place where his skin was puckered and ugly.

"I'm not going anywhere. I love you." He was serious. To him, love was not something to take lightly.

"Nobody has ever said that to me and meant it."

"Your grandmother loved you. I know that for sure."

"Yes. She wasn't good with her words, but I knew she loved me. She showed me."

He took for granted that his childhood was happy and filled with two parents who loved him and each other. He was told daily that he was loved.

"Tell me what you dream about." She meant his nightmares—the ones that caused him to awaken in a cold sweat.

He swallowed hard. "I'm on fire in some of them. The heat rushes up my skin and I'm being burned alive in the desert.

Other times I see a young kid with no arm and half a face calling my name, telling me he was going to marry some girl. That he was going home in three months…"

"That's enough."

She placed her fingers over his lips knowing that he was starting to get panicky. The doctors had warned them that this would happen, that he would have flashbacks, dreams, frightening thoughts. But those doctors also said that he would need to talk about his time at war. Just a little bit. Just enough to relieve some of the burden on his mind. "We can talk about it later." She snuggled closer to him, throwing her leg over his hip. "Make love to me," she whispered. "I like the way you feel."

He rubbed his cock against her wet opening but did not enter. She trembled hard, never before had she looked forward to making love to a man she was in love with. Yes, she loved him. It was new and scary and so powerful that sometimes she couldn't breathe properly just thinking about him. He was her husband for now, but one day he would remember, and when that day came he would leave her. Until that day came, she would love him as her own.

He kept rubbing his engorged penis against her wet opening over and over, causing her insides to quake.

"Please—" she begged. "You're torturing me."

"I know," he grunted. "Now you know how I felt for weeks, spending my nights in pain because every time I thought about you I got hard." He entered her shallowly, with little quick strokes so she never felt full of him. She had never made love in this position. It was a different sensation. It was driving her insane. "You made my life miserable."

"You should have left," she moaned as his strokes took on a delicious rhythm.

"I couldn't. I was too in love with you to go." His hand came up to cup her breast. He kissed her lips but kept his thrusts controlled and shallow. "I spend every night thinking of ways to make love to you. There are thousands of ways. I will show you all of them."

"Thousands?" She thrust her hips forward, trying to take him in deeper. She wanted him closer. She wanted to feel all of him.

"No." He grabbed her hips, keeping her at a distance. "I'm showing you what we can do."

"Please," she moaned. "I dreamed about you at night, too. I think about you—this—all the time. I wanted to climb into your bed every night."

"Why didn't you?" He thrust deeply just long enough to fill her once before going back to his shallow, torturous strokes.

"Because—" She lost her train of thought as her pleasure spiked. He tweaked her nipple with his fingers, bringing her to the present. "I didn't know how to approach you. I didn't know how to make love to you."

"All you had to do…" He slipped and began to give her slower deeper thrusts, filling her up with his hardness. He felt delicious. "Was come to me. We would have figured it out. It would have been beautiful."

"Like now?"

"Like now," he agreed. He was panting, a thin sheen of moisture was beginning to coat his body. She could tell how hard it was for him to control himself. She forced her hips forward meeting his strokes with fervor.

"Relax," he said through gritted teeth. "Let me."

"Damn it, Ryan." She was so close, but he was still playing games.

"I'm paying you back." He kissed her face.

"I came to you last night," she cried as she gave herself over to him.

"But you left me. I was going to make love to you again. Last night I only took from you. I wanted to give."

"You did. I felt needed."

"Did I hurt you? Is that why you left?"

It was getting harder for them to talk, their breaths shortened by their intense lovemaking.

"No. Mary called and told me." She cried out in pleasure as he quickened the pace. "Told me you were going back. I was so angry that after all your nightmares you'd rather go back to war than stay with me."

He rolled her over to her back, burying himself deep inside her. His gray eyes locked on her and she shivered. "I would rather die alone than not be able to touch you."

"Ryan."

Tears threatened, but she held them back. There had been too many tears shed between them. This was a time for love. He lost control at that moment, driving into her, taking her in insane heated movements. It only took a few moments before she climaxed. He kept going, taking his fill of her until she came again even harder than the last time. He finished, filling her with his hot seed. They lay there still connected in a mass of sweaty tangled limbs.

He looked down at her, brushing a light kiss across her mouth. "That was the best sex I've ever had."

"Love," she murmured. "I'm flattered, but how would you know? You don't remember past two months ago."

He blinked and rolled off her.

"Believe me, I know."

She grinned up at him, and within moments fell asleep in his arms. Sleep didn't come so easily to Ryan. He lay awake for a long time thinking about what his life had become and what it could be.

Ryan woke up the next morning reaching for his wife. She wasn't there. The bed was empty except for him. He had a flashback of yesterday morning. This is like a real-life version of *Groundhog Day*. He swore violently.

"What's wrong, Ry?" She appeared at the door wearing a silk robe that was open, revealing her very nude body.

"I thought you went to sleep in your bedroom."

"Nope." Placing the mug she was holding on the nightstand she crawled into bed with him. "I went to make you some coffee and brush my teeth. I was here the whole night."

"From now on we sleep in the same bed."

She looked up at him with her slanted eyes.

Feeling uneasy about her silence, he asked, "You want to, don't you?"

"Yes, but I hate this room."

"Would you rather sleep in the other one?"

"No." She bit her lip. She only did that when she was anxious, which made him worry. "Would you mind if I redecorated?"

"You can do whatever you want. This is your house."

"But the money…"

"Don't worry about the money."

"The money from the cars won't last forever."

"It won't, but I can get money if we need it." He kissed her mouth. Money was not something they had to worry about anymore.

"You gonna rob a bank, champ?"

"No." He kissed her mouth, lingering a little longer. "I have an ace in the hole."

"Do you?" She gave him a seductive smile and wrapped her arms around him.

"Yes. I kept one of the cars, and I got offered a job at a dealership in the finance department."

"Would you really leave Pep's?"

"If we needed the money, I would."

"Oh." She cuddled close to him, resting her head on his chest and allowing him the freedom to run his fingers through her thick hair.

"Would you be open to moving to a bigger place?"

"And leave this palace? No freaking way." She laughed. "I would love to start over with you, but for a little while I want to keep things the way they are. I just want you to be my husband."

Her husband. They came so far since he woke up in the hospital. He had come so far. His life had changed forever.

"Can I take you on a little vacation?"

"A little vacation? How about a big one? How about many big ones? I've never been on a vacation before."

"Where do you want to go?"

She had lived an eventful life but it was sheltered. He could show her the world.

"Austin."

"Austin? You don't want to go to Acapulco or the Caribbean? You want to drive two hours to Austin?"

She looked up at him and frowned. "I've never been."

"Okay." He rolled her over, peppering kisses on her neck. "I'll take you to Austin but not for vacation. We are going away. How about South Pedro Island?"

"Wherever you want. Mmm, that feels good," she moaned.

"You feel good." He placed himself between her bare thighs. "Why don't you marry me?"

"I'm already married to you." She stiffened and looked up at him. "Aren't I?"

He didn't mean for it to come out the way it did. He didn't want to deny that he was her husband, but he wasn't a wife beater or a drunk. He knew he wasn't her husband. His memories were coming back in little jagged pieces, but they were there. And all the things he remembered didn't line up with the life he was in now. But he loved Lexy. He knew there was a reason he was put here. And it was to be with her. He almost wished he never remembered his whole life, because he knew once he did, once he remembered, things would change for them. Their life would cease to be simple. She would no longer be his wife.

"I just said that to get in your pants," he lied.

"Oh." She grinned up at him and relaxed, wrapping her legs around his waist. "Well, since I'm already naked that was unnecessary."

Chapter Twenty

"I'm getting fat as a cow," Di complained to Lexy on a trip into town with Di's daughter, Alana, in tow.

"Well, that's why we are here, Di. To get your big ass into some maternity clothes."

"I hate maternity clothes. Why can't I be pregnant and not look pregnant?"

"Well, you should have pondered that question before you got yourself knocked up."

"I blame my husband," she sighed. "Alana, I love you, child, but if you don't stop picking in your underwear I'm gonna swat you."

"Sorry, Mama," the obedient girl said.

"You love being a mama, don't you?" Lexy asked.

"Some days," she sighed again. "I just hate being pregnant. I vomit in the mornings. I'm exhausted in the afternoons. I don't fit any of my clothes."

"I'm sorry."

"Fat lot of good your sorry does me. I wish this on you, Alexa Beecher."

"When pigs fly." She hadn't been able to get pregnant since her miscarriage. Ten years she had been married and that was her only pregnancy. It would never happen for her.

They stopped in front of Laurel's Consignments, which had a pretty porcelain doll in a pink lace dress in the window.

"Oh, Mama," Alana cried. "She's so pretty."

"Darling, it's beautiful, but you aren't getting it."

"I don't want it, Mama. I rather have a cell phone."

"Ha!" Di laughed loudly at her daughter's extravagant taste. "You aren't getting that either, but mama loves you anyhow."

Lexy's heart pulled again and she looked away from Di gazing at her little girl with her heart in her eyes. A man in a dark green shirt caught her eye. She only saw him from behind but his powerful build and muscular back attracted her to him.

"That looks like Ryan," she muttered to herself.

"It does," Di replied. She must have heard her. "He looks like he just walked out of the lawyer's office."

"I wonder why."

He couldn't be planning to divorce her. She wasn't even sure if they were married. But she was sure of her happiness the past two weeks. What she had now was what she thought a marriage should be. Partnership, companionship and love—and it had taken her ten long hard years to get it.

Her cell phone rang.

"You have a cell phone!" Alana clapped. "See, Mama, Aunt Lexy has a cell phone."

"Your uncle gave it to me." She looked at the caller ID. "Hello, Ryan."

"Hey, honey. I'm in town. I just came out of Jay Tanner's office. I was setting up a will."

"You were?" That surprised her.

"I just wanted to make sure that you would be taken care of if anything happens to me."

"I do not want to think about that now, thank you."

"I was just letting you know," he laughed. "By the way I'm standing in front of the bakery and was wondering if you wanted me to pick up one of those cinnamon rolls you like so much."

"I would love one. You won't have to bring it very far because I'm standing fifty feet behind you."

"Excuse me?"

"Turn around."

He did…and smiled when he saw her. Her damn heart raced. He walked toward her, all sexy confidence, and she couldn't help but return his smile.

"My three favorite ladies," Ryan greeted them. He grabbed Alana and threw her in the air and kissed Di's cheek. And when it came to Lexy, he cupped her face in his hand and kissed the tip of her nose, then her forehead and then her mouth.

I love you, she thought. He finally broke her. She loved him and he was worthy of her love.

"What are you up to?"

"Shopping. Di's fat. She can't fit her clothes anymore."

"I'm pregnant, not fat!"

Lexy grinned up at Ryan while Di fumed.

"My wife thinks she's funny. Congratulations, by the way. I haven't gotten the chance to tell you that. You're a great mother."

"Thank you." She blushed. Di wasn't used to Ryan being this way. The Ryan she knew was an asshole.

"I'll bring the rolls home. Do you want me to pick up dinner?"

"You don't want me to cook?"

"You cooked three nights in a row and you made me pancakes this morning. You do enough."

Di made a barely audible noise in her throat. The sound conveyed what Lexy was feeling.

"Shrimp?"

"Crab legs, scallops and hush puppies, too?"

"Perfect."

He leaned forward and pecked her mouth. "I'll be home around six."

"I'll see you later."

He said his goodbyes to Di and Alana, and walked off.

"So," Di said conversationally, "how are things at home?"

"He loves me, Di. He tells me ten times a day and shows me a hundred times more."

"I can see that," she said softly.

"I love him, too."

"Ah," she said, knowing all of Lexy's doubts. "What are you going to do now?"

That was the million-dollar question. She was living on borrowed time. She knew he would remember soon and when that day came he would walk right out of her life. She prayed that day would never come. She didn't want to lose out on the only piece of happiness she ever had.

Ryan sat in the living room reading *East of Eden* when Lexy walked through the front door. He smiled upon seeing the pretty woman he lived with. The past month had been one of the best in his life.

"Hey, babe."

She hung her keys on the hook near the door and sat beside him on the couch. She smelled familiar, good, like soap and skin and air. She looked good, too, wearing a simple sundress that he'd insisted on buying her. Her hair was swept into a cute ponytail and for the first time she looked truly relaxed and happy. She let him take care of her. She made him feel like her husband.

"Hey." He dropped a kiss on her forehead as she rested her head against his shoulder. "Are you all right?"

"Yes." She kissed his neck. "I missed you today."

"Did you?" He tossed the book he was reading onto the coffee table and wrapped his arms around her.

"I know it's only three o'clock but do you think you could make love to me now?"

He just looked down at her. She was sexually adventurous, always ready for him, always willing to give her whole self to him.

Silly woman.

"Of course." He smiled at her. "You never have to ask me." He pressed a kiss to her face, wondering why she looked distressed. "What's wrong?"

"You don't have to."

"Have to what?" He frowned.

"Make love to me."

"Excuse me?"

"You can say no." She shook her head. "I think there is something wrong with me. I think about being with you all day. Even when I'm reading to the kids, dirty thoughts pop into my head…and you are always doing very dirty things in those dirty thoughts. I want to have sex all the time. Twice a day should be enough, but it isn't."

She looked so distressed, so cute that he just burst out laughing. Laughing so hard that his body shook and his chest ached.

"Don't laugh at me, you ass."

"You're crazy." He squeezed her against him. "We love

each other and people in love want to make love all the time. There is nothing wrong with you."

"I've never felt like this before." Her husband wasn't worthy of love, so for her these feelings were brand-new.

"You've never been in love before," he said quietly. He kissed her throat. "And I think about you, too."

She melted into him. Her body was familiar and welcoming.

"All day. I'll always want to make love to you." He pulled her dress over her head, revealing her very pretty, very pink bra and panties.

"Take me to bed." She was kissing him, touching him, rubbing her body against him in a hurried hungry way.

"No. Here."

"On the couch?"

"Yes." He unfastened her bra, taking one of her breasts in his mouth. She moaned.

"I want you on top of me. I love the way your heavy body feels. I love the way you look at me."

"You'll like this, too." He stood, quickly stripping them of their clothing. He sat again, his erection standing straight up. "Sit on top of me, Lexy." He grabbed her hips. "Trust me." She looked unsure for a moment, but then her eyes locked with his and she slowly lowered herself. Every time they made love it was an experience. It was fine with Caroline but it had never been all-encompassing like it was with Lexy. He needed Lexy liked he needed air.

"Promise me..." She lowered herself slowly, ridiculously slowly. "Promise me you'll love me forever."

"You know I will." He grasped her hips and pulled her down.

"No matter what happens." She moaned slightly, trying to

fit him in her tight wet space. Something was causing her to doubt him. She was holding on to something. She was worried about something. He wondered if it was the same thing that terrified him.

"No matter what."

She leaned in and kissed his face—not a sexual kiss, despite their position, but a love kiss.

"You're very good to me." She sank all the way down, filling herself with him.

"Move on me, honey. Anyway you like."

Her hips rocked back and forth giving him pleasure so acute it was painful. She draped her arms around his shoulders, letting her head fall back, while her hips rocked in a deliciously seductive motion. He let her take control, take her pleasure from him, and all he did, all he could do, was sit back and enjoy the exquisite torture. Soon she shuddered, whimpered and climaxed in such a sexy way that it made him more aroused.

"That was good." She looked into his face and smiled.

"It was." He was still rock hard inside her and was nowhere near done. He lifted her slightly, and lowered her slowly. "But we're not done yet." He fluttered kisses along her throat. "I'm going to make you scream." He set a slow rhythm, allowing her to feel every hard inch of him as he slid in and out of her.

"I don't scream," she panted.

"Not yet, you don't." He captured hers lips and sucked deeply. Her tongue was sweet, her mouth was warm and wet and he couldn't seem to get enough of her.

"Ryan, I'm going to…" She gasped. "Again."

"Say it," he said through gritted teeth. "You're going to

come again." He pumped harder, sliding her furiously over his cock.

"I'm going to come," she cried. And then she did. Violently.

"Good." He finished, too, spilling his seed inside her.

"My God." She kissed his damp hairline. "My God." Sweet exhaustion overtook her and she rested her head on his shoulder. "My God. My God. My God," she breathed, causing him to laugh.

"It must have been good if you're taking the lord's name in vain."

"My God," she laughed.

"Don't you wish you would have given in two months ago?"

"I do. I wish I would have met you ten years ago."

Chapter Twenty-One

"What's wrong, Ryan?" Lexy Beecher asked the man she called her husband. She found him lying in bed, eyes closed, hands folded neatly over his hard belly. "Ryan?" She touched his face, finding him slightly clammy. Her alarm went off. Ever since he came out of the hospital she had worried that he healed too fast. And now that they were close that little niggle of worry ballooned into full-blown anxiety.

"Ryan, please answer me!"

"My stomach is upset. It must have been the Mexican food."

They had gone for an early dinner at Pena's, a little hole-in-the-wall restaurant that made authentic Mexican food.

"I told you." She smacked his chest. "Why on earth did you order a three-pound burrito?" Just then his stomach let out a monstrous gurgle. This was going to be a rough night.

"It was damn good," he said, his face twisted in discomfort. "You ate some, too. Why doesn't your stomach hurt?"

"My poor baby." She kissed his handsome but moist face. "What can I do for you?"

"Can you bring me some Pepto and maybe sleep in the other room tonight?"

"You mean you're not going to make love to me?" she teased.

"Lexy…" he whined.

"Okay, champ. I'll bring you the medicine, and a glass of

water." She opened all the windows. "Call me if you need me." She took off his shoes, loosened his pants and covered his face with kisses before she left him.

"Stupid, damn burrito," Lexy thought miserably as she rested her head on the cool rim of the toilet. For two days now she had been pitching her guts into it. It was worse in the morning. As soon as the sun rose a wave of nausea smacked into her and she rushed to the bathroom; but the sickness lasted all day. She finally gave up sleeping in her bed and moved into the bathroom just off the garage. She hadn't eaten anything in days. Even the thought of toast made her throat fill with bile.

"Lexy." Ryan peered around the door.

"Get out!" She had banned him from seeing her. She was unshowered, pale and all-around gross. Plus she was furious with him. He inhaled a three-pound burrito and only suffered with a night of indigestion. She had four bites and the porcelain pot was her best friend.

"Honey." He stepped closer and she hurled the toilet brush at him.

"Go away."

"You haven't eaten in days. You haven't gotten off the floor in hours."

"Leave me alone." Suddenly her stomach rolled and she held her breath hoping to quell it.

"You've seen me at my worst. I was near death and you took care of me. Let me do the same for you."

"Go," she ordered, and promptly heaved into her new friend. He finally obeyed and she was glad he was gone. She wished he hadn't seen her at all, but she was sure he would let her be now. It was exhausting to be sick.

"If you are going to stay in here all day then you might as well be comfortable." Ryan appeared again, surprising her. He spread a large down comforter on the cold floor, picked her up and deposited her on it. He had brought pillows from his own bed and a blanket to cover her. Perched on the sink was a tray with ice water, beef broth and a bell.

"I'm not going to work today," he told her. "You had better get some of that down by the time I come back. Ring if you need me. And if you aren't better tomorrow we are going to the hospital."

"But—" She didn't get to finish because he walked out.

"Lexy?" A sweet voice drifted above her as she lay on the bathroom floor.

"Mary?" Was she dreaming?

"Yes, honey."

"Did you come here because I'm dying?"

"You aren't dying. I'm here because you are being mean to your husband. Why won't you let him take care of you?"

"Because—" Lexy's head swam from weakness "—I get food poisoning while he gets gas. Where is the justice in that?"

"Honey, if a bomb didn't get him, a little Tex Mex won't. Why are you keeping him away?"

She looked up at her mother-in-law as her stomach rolled. "I look like hell. I smell like hell and I don't want him or anybody seeing me tossing my cookies every five minutes."

"But he loves you," Mary said simply.

"I want to keep it that way."

"Lexy, pay attention to me. Nobody has ever loved you as much as this man. He's worried and hurt that you are pushing him away. A little vomit isn't going to turn him off, and if it does you are better off without him."

"He's not really my husband," she said softly, almost fearing what would happen if she said it aloud.

"God sent him to you for a reason, and as far as I'm concerned that man who kisses my cheek and treats me nice is my son." Mary reached down and tugged her hand. "Now you're going to get off the floor, get in the shower and eat something before you waste away."

Ryan came home from the supermarket and the first place he checked was the bathroom floor. It was blessedly empty. Mary came through for him. He went to their bedroom and found Lexy in bed asleep on top of the covers. She wore a bathrobe instead of that blue nightgown she had been wearing for the past few days. Her hair was wet and curling around her face. He picked up the quilt that hung over the chair and gently placed it on her. He was glad she had gotten up. If she hadn't, he would have dragged her to the hospital and she would have fought him. She was feisty, but that's what he liked about her. He kissed her nose.

"I love you," she murmured in her sleep. He froze. She had never said it before. He had known she did. She showed him in every way, in everything she did. He felt her love and even though she was clearly asleep he knew she meant it. He climbed into bed beside her, kissing her face softly.

"Ryan." She burrowed her body into his.

"Yes?"

"I thought I was dreaming." Her breath smelled minty, her body like soap. Was it wrong to be turned on? She was naked beneath her robe and her skin was so soft and her body his.

"How are you feeling?"

"Guilty." She looked at his chin. "I'm sorry I threw the toilet brush at you."

"Don't apologize. I just missed you. I thought I was going to have to drag you to the hospital by your hair. Are you feeling better?"

"Yes." She smiled softly. "I'm just exhausted. Thank you for sending your mama and making me comfortable. You're a good man."

"You literally kept me alive. Don't canonize me for bringing you a glass of water."

"You've been taking care of me since you walked out of the hospital. It's in your nature to take care of things. You are a fixer."

A fixer.

Somebody had said that to him, but in anger. *"You're a fixer, Cooper, but it's not your job to fix everything. You can't bring your brother back. Your duty is not to your country, but to me. You need to fix our relationship."*

"I love you, Ryan."

He jolted and looked down at the woman he was in bed with.

He remembered everything. Everything. His name was Cooper. Not Ryan. He was thirty years old. His birthday was the same day as Abraham Lincoln's. His father had died two weeks after his brother was killed in Afghanistan. He was from New York. He had a mother, who was waiting for him to come home, and a former fiancée, who had given him an ultimatum when he decided to go off to war.

He remembered. Every broken memory was now whole. It all came rushing back to him, so many thoughts and faces and words flooded his mind that it made his head spin. It made him feel like he was falling off the earth.

Without his memories he felt like half a person. But now…

"Are you okay, honey?" Lexy stared up at him, her face twisted in concern.

Lexy was not his wife—she was Ryan Beecher's wife, but he was dead. He remembered Ryan clearly now. He could see his face burned into his mind. They weren't friends. Yes, they were bonded in brotherhood by service but they weren't friends. There was always something about Ryan he didn't like.

My wife's a mutt.

She thinks she's smarter than everybody else.

I had to remind her who the man of the house is.

If Cooper had known… If he had known that Beecher had nearly killed his wife in a drunken rage he wouldn't have died in an explosion. Cooper would have killed him first.

But maybe things happened for a reason. He was here now. He met her and loved her. And they made each other happy. Cooper had thought he had been in love before. He had even thought he was ready to spend his life with that woman, but what he felt for Caroline was nowhere near what he felt for Lexy.

He shut his eyes. He didn't want to go back to his old life. *Not yet.*

He didn't want this to end when it felt so good.

"Ryan." Lexy gripped his shoulders. "You're scaring me."

She called him another man's name, causing his stomach to churn. He always knew he couldn't be the man who did those things to her, but he didn't want to seriously think about what not being him would entail. It meant that Lexy wasn't his wife. They had lived as man and wife but they really weren't. He needed all of her, not just in name, but physically, legally, entirely.

He had to tell her. He opened his mouth to, but the words wouldn't come out.

Not yet.

His brain kept warning him to keep it to himself. To think about everything. To process. To plan. He knew if he told her now it would all be over. It wasn't going to be simple. He needed a little more time with her before the outside world infiltrated, before things got too hard.

"Ryan!"

"Say it again. Tell me you love me." This was what he wanted. His entire life he wanted to be with somebody who loved him without conditions. Lexy was the only one. His parents, his fiancé, the world expected so much from him. Maybe that's why he joined the marines. Not just to honor his fallen little brother, but to get away from the world. To find out what kind of man he really was.

He knew deep in his gut, he was a better man with Lexy.

"I love you." She pressed her lips to his. "I'm in love with you. I feel safe with you. I want to make you happy."

"Lex." His eyes burned, tears threatening.

"I love you."

"I need to stay with you." He pressed soft kisses to her jawline, trying to block out the nonstop flood of memories. "I need to."

He wanted her forever. She untied her robe, inviting him to touch her soft body. He did, feeling her soft tummy and hips.

"You're skinny."

"Am I?"

"I don't like it."

She grinned at his comment.

"Tomorrow I'm going to feed you mashed potatoes and gravy."

"That sounds good." She reached out to touch his stomach, feeling the brutal scars. "Make love to me." She kissed his chin, his neck, the top of his chest. He was hard and throbbing, wanting her despite the turmoil that was going on inside him.

"Are you feeling up to it? We can wait until you're one hundred percent."

"It's been three days. No waiting. I need to make love to you." With that final comment she wrapped her leg around him and freed him from his pants.

"Damn it, I love you." His mind was made up. He couldn't go back to his old life yet. He wasn't sure he would ever be able to.

Chapter Twenty-Two

She had never been on vacation before but Ryan had insisted that they take a long weekend to go to South Padre Island, a little vacation spot on the coast of Texas. She sat next to him on the beach, soaking up the end-of-summer rays. Then, leaning over, she kissed his shoulder.

"You've been quiet lately. Are you feeling okay?" *Quiet* wasn't the right word for it. He still spoke to her. He still made her smile. If anything, he had been even more attentive to her this past week. But he seemed pensive, worried almost, and she couldn't figure out why.

At first she thought it was about money. She had asked, but he showed her their bank account. He even went through the trouble of setting one up just in her name, which she thought was strange but he assured her it was necessary.

Then she thought he was sick. She knew his head still hurt him. She knew that sometimes his scars still throbbed. But physically he seemed fine. He even went out jogging every morning this past week. That was odd for him, too. There was something off about him, but she couldn't put her finger on it. She tried not to worry about it. Part of her knew that she distrusted happiness, because she hadn't had much of it in her life. She was always waiting for something else to go wrong.

"I'm fine." He set his beautiful gray gaze on her. "I'm just wondering what life would have been like for you if you hadn't gotten married at seventeen."

"I never thought about it. I was so devastated by Maybell's death that I didn't think about what my life could have been like. I wanted somebody to love me and so when Ryan came around I jumped."

"Didn't you have a dream as a little girl? Didn't you want to go to college or be a hairdresser? I don't believe that you didn't want more from your life."

She had dreams but they were never clear or definite. They were just dreams of a better life, a different life.

"I love books. I love the way they smell, the way the paper feels on my fingers. I always wanted to write a book. I always wanted to tell a story with mythical creatures in a far-away land where kids could escape to. I think I would have liked to have been an English major in college."

He reached over and stroked the curve of her cheek. "Why didn't you?"

"I couldn't. I had to work to help us stay afloat. Plus, it wasn't like anybody was encouraging me to start writing." She was afraid to tell Ryan then. He would have laughed at her.

"Is there anything you dream of now?"

She shook her head. "When I was first married I dreamed of this. I dreamed that you would be you." She was embarrassed about her admission. "I don't dream anymore. Right now I'm just focusing on remembering how happy I am in this moment."

Ryan reached over and pulled her into his muscled arms, so her back rested against his bare chest.

"What about you? What do you want out of life? What do

you dream of? What did you dream of?" He was silent for a long moment.

"I think my whole life I did what was expected of me. And then I joined the marines and that was something nobody expected me to do. Some people even fought me on it, but I had something to prove."

"I'm glad you went in." She snuggled into him, trying to get closer.

"Me, too," he said softly. "You are what I dream of now."

"You don't have to say that, you big liar. I already admitted how much I love you."

He chuckled softly in her ear. "I was dreaming about you in this bikini." He snuck his fingertips into her top, brushing her nipples and making her squirm.

"I'm getting fat and you know it." She could barely button her pants and her breasts seemed to be swelling daily.

"I love your body. I can't keep my hands to myself. It's verging on obsession."

"I noticed, you perv. You were ogling me the other night in front of Mary. She turned three shades of red."

"I know." He cupped her tender breast in his hand. They felt heavy and slightly sore but he was always gentle. "I can't help myself. You are just about the sexiest woman on the planet." He slid the fingers of his other hand between her legs, stroking the soft skin of her thighs.

"Just about?" she teased.

"Excuse me. You are the sexiest woman on the planet and I'm very much in love with you."

"I love you, too..." she moaned as he started to rub her through the fabric of her swimsuit. "But if you don't stop that I'm going to—"

"Come? Well, darling, that's the whole point of this."

She laughed, feeling light for the first time in a very long time, and kissed him deeply until he was jelly in her hands.

"We need to get off this beach," he panted. "Before we get kicked off."

"Are you going to make love to me?"

"What the hell do you think?"

They had a beautiful weekend together. The best week-end she'd ever had, Lexy thought to herself as they drove up to their home. Ryan was insatiable, and tender and sweet and he kept looking at her like she was going to slip through his fingers. Even at night, when they slept, he wrapped himself around her, not letting her go, keeping her with him, as if to keep her safe. She appreciated the attention, the affection. It was something she had never experienced before. She never felt safe before. Even when she was a small child. She was always looking after Maybell, worried one day that the old woman wouldn't be there. And then when she met Ryan and he hit her, he took away her security and replaced it with fear and self-loathing. But now it seemed she was healing. Her heart was healing. And her mind.

And her body.

Her period was late. For years it had come like clockwork, but now she had missed it for over a month. Her breasts were sore and she was gaining weight, but she couldn't be pregnant. Ryan had tried over and over to get her pregnant after the miscarriage but she didn't think it was possible.

But maybe it was possible. Maybe God had finally given her her blessing. Maybe he was telling her it was time. Maybe he was giving her what she had always wished for.

Ginger Jamison

"Did you have fun this weekend?" Ryan asked her, pulling into their driveway. He looked at her for a long moment, seeming anxious about her answer.

"It was the best weekend of my life." She smiled up at him, meaning every word. "Thank you. Thank you for making me happy."

He smiled softly back at her. "Do you think you can take a few days off next week? I still want to take you to Austin. There are so many places I want to take you." The way he said it, almost wistfully made her feel...sad. Like he was trying to squeeze so much life in to such a short amount of time.

She was going to ask him what was the matter, but she stopped herself. She had asked him before. He had assured her it was nothing. "Can we afford another trip?"

"Yes." He stroked her cheeks with his thumbs. "Don't worry about the money. You'll never have to worry about money again. You don't have to work anymore, Lexy. Not if you don't want to. I can take care of you now."

She believed him, he was that sure of himself. So she pushed all those tiny little uneasy thoughts from her mind. She stepped out of the car, leaning against it and let the early September sun warm her skin. Placing her hands on her slightly rounded belly she thought about the possibilities. Praying for them.

I want to be a mommy. She had always wanted a baby, her own big family. She wanted what most took for granted.

"What are you thinking about, Alexa?" He tilted her backward, wrapping his body around hers.

"Would you like to be a father?"

He grinned. "You know I would."

"I want you to be the father of my children. Would you be okay with that?"

She saw the happiness bloom in his face. "I'm more than okay with that. So are we going to try for a baby?"

"I don't think we'll have to try hard. We've been practicing a lot." She didn't want to tell him just yet, because she wasn't sure herself. But soon. She would find out for sure soon.

"You're right." He fluttered kisses across her chin. "I'm excited to give you a baby. I want to kiss your belly and hold a little piece of you in my arms. I want to make a family with you."

He continued to kiss her. Her neck, her cheeks, the bridge of her nose. He had to tell her. He had to come clean about his memory. He had a whole life left in limbo—a good job, a fast-paced lifestyle, money. He had respect in his old life. It was a good life but not a better life than the one he shared with Lexy. Texas was a place he had grown to love almost as much as the pretty woman he called his wife. The thought of leaving her was unbearable, but exposing her to the life he had before the marines was something he couldn't do.

They had to make a new life of their own. They would make a new life. Lexy wanted to give him babies. *Him,* not the brute she married, the man who died at his side. She loved *him,* wanted to spend her life with *him.* He wanted to hear her call him Cooper not Ryan. He longed to give her everything he was capable of giving.

He was going to tell her, next week, just as soon as he heard back from the military. He wanted to be sure he did things the right way.

"I love you," she whispered, tearing him from his hazy thoughts.

"I love you, too, honey."

"Cooper?"

He heard his name, his real name, and at first it didn't faze him.

"Cooper!"

He froze.

Not now.

He wanted to tell Lexy on his own terms. He wanted to break it to her gently and map out their new life together. He had a plan. He had already taken the steps. He just needed a few more days.

He looked to his left and there was his former life staring him in the face and he knew his plans had just gone up in smoke.

"Caroline. Mother." He couldn't describe the feelings that raced through him at seeing them. Love and guilt and anger and sorrow and regret, and even more, all mixed together.

It had been so long. So long since he had heard his mother's, Helena Thomaston, voice or spent a holiday with her or said *I love you* to her.

Caroline looked the same and he barely spared a thought as to why she was there because he couldn't pull his eyes off his mother. She had aged so much in the nearly two years he had been gone. Her hair was all white now, her skin ghostly pale, almost gray. She was so thin he could see her bones. She looked frail and old and not at all how he pictured her when he saw her in his mind. She was not the mother he had three years ago.

He knew it was hard for her to keep her vitality. Jacob was her baby and her favorite. She loved him, everybody loved him. She had a special soft spot for her baby that she didn't have for Cooper, and then he was killed—accidently,

in friendly fire—and she lost him. And in those days right
after Jake had died, Cooper saw a wall go up in his mother.
It was high but not insurmountable. He understood why she
put it there.

Then her husband two weeks later, a massive heart attack
at the dinner table. Cooper was there. Together they watched
Edward Thomaston die, and instead of coming together in
such a tragic time they grew apart. He had tried to bridge
the gap. He had made an attempt at closeness, but his mother
wanted none of it. She went on with her life. She went shopping with her friends. She had dinner parties at her house, but
she never talked about Jacob or her husband. She never talked
to him. She never wanted to.

Cooper thought she had gone cold. For a while he hated her
for it. He went away to war thinking his mother was so cold
that she didn't care if he went, if he died, too. She didn't try
to stop him. She didn't say a thing. But he had thought a lot
about her in the two weeks since his memories had returned.
He thought about seeing her again. If it was better for him
to break it to her that he was alive, or if it was better to have
the military call first.

He wondered if she would be happy to see him, or if she
would even care.

But then he thought about his mother, about his childhood
with her. They may not have been as close as she was with
Jacob, but he knew she loved him. He never doubted that.

The coldness. The silence. The pushing him away. It must
have been how she grieved. It took seeing her again, seeing her
drained and frail and so happy to see him to figure that out.

He realized he had been stupidly selfish.

The guilt hit him hard in that moment.

He turned to Lexy who looked so stoic for a moment. Then her face drained of color and she doubled over, clutching her stomach, causing his guilt to multiply tenfold. He grabbed for her, but she stood up straight, placing her hand out to keep him away. She looked betrayed.

He knew then he had done the wrong thing in making them all wait.

"Cooper—" His mother rushed toward him. "Is that you, sweetheart? Please tell me it's you."

He nodded, letting her clutch his face, closing his eyes while she kissed his cheeks.

"You look so different, sweetheart." She held on to him, hugged him as hard as her frail body could manage. "You don't know how I've missed you. I'm sorry. I'm so sorry." She started to sob and he held her, trying to remember the last time he had hugged her. She didn't do it when he had come to say goodbye right before basic training. Or at Jacob's and his father's funerals, or the days each of the men had died. It made so much sense now. She didn't because she couldn't.

He felt eyes on him and looked up to find Lexy staring at him, bewildered.

"You remember." It wasn't a question, and in those two little words there was a world of hurt.

He nodded, knowing their quiet little world was crashing down around them.

"You're alive," his mother chanted while he held her. "Thank goodness. You're alive."

In that moment he felt like he was torn in two. Torn between the old life he had foolishly run away from and the new life he had come to love.

"The military contacted us," Caroline started. She looked

just the way he remembered with long red hair and a slender body. She was classically beautiful and graceful and wealthy. She was everything the girl he fell so hard in love with was not. "They told us that there had been a mistake, that a soldier in Texas contacted them saying he was you. That you had Ryan Beecher's dog tags in your hand and that's how the mistake had been made. They—they checked the dental records. They said it was Ryan Beecher who died. Not you." Her eyes searched his face as if trying to see if he were real. "I knew you weren't dead. Thank heaven I was right."

Caroline fixed her eyes on Lexy and the compassion he saw just a moment ago melted away and was replaced by ice. "I assume the woman you were kissing is Ryan Beecher's wife. Hello, Mrs. Beecher. I'm sorry to inform you that your husband is dead. The man you've been passing off as your husband is my fiancé."

"Wait a minute," Cooper spoke up, not at all liking her implication. "You gave me an ultimatum before I left. You broke it off. Lexy didn't pass me off as anything. I'm here because I want to be."

"I still wear your ring." She showed him the flashy diamond he'd given her six months before he left. "I was just angry that you chose the marines over a five-year relationship."

"You belong to somebody else?" Lexy said. "For five years?"

Yes, it had been five years. And he had loved Caroline, but the love they had was different than the one he had with Lexy. It was based on mutual respect and similar lifestyle. He never longed for Caroline. He never felt like he needed to be with her. He had only asked her to marry him, because it was expected. After five years he owed it to her, not because she was the only one he could picture spending his life with.

And she didn't like kids. She didn't want the life he wanted. The life he was planning to have with Lexy.

"No." He grasped Lexy's shoulders, looking into her watering eyes. "That part of my life is over. We can start over."

"Cooper." When Caroline called to him he could hear the hurt in her voice and that made him take his eyes off Lexy.

She was crying. "I was planning my life around you."

"I'm sorry, Caroline, but you shouldn't have. You haven't spoken to me since I enlisted. You made it clear that when I left I couldn't come back to you."

"I was angry! What did you expect? One minute I'm planning a wedding. The next, the man I'm supposed to be marrying tells me he's going off to war. You weren't meant for that life, Cooper. That was your brother's path. You were supposed to take over your father's company. We were supposed to go places together."

"That wasn't the life I wanted."

"It was. It was until your brother died. I didn't realize that the day we buried him we would lose you, too."

"I didn't lose myself," he countered. "I found myself. I know what kind of man I am now. I want to create my own legacy."

"How are you doing that?" She gestured toward their house. "You want to spend your days living like trash, instead of coming home to New York and taking your place in the world?" She focused her clear blue eyes on Lexy. "With her? Somebody else's wife? You should be ashamed of yourself, Mrs. Beecher, for seducing a man you knew wasn't your husband."

"Caroline," his mother gasped. "Now is certainly not the time for this." She swayed on her feet, but as he took a step toward her Lexy moved and wrapped her arm around her first.

"This must be a lot for you, Mrs. Thomaston," Lexy said,

supporting the older woman. "I'm very sorry. I really didn't know."

"Please call me Helena. Of course you didn't know." His mother gripped Lexy's hand, studying her face and then Cooper's as if she couldn't believe that either of them were real. "He does look different. The blast must have changed him."

"I'm so sorry that you've had so much loss," Lexy said softly as they walked toward the house.

"And I'm sorry for you, dear," she said softly. And then, as if she realized it for the first time, she said, "That means your husband is gone. I'm so sorry, dear."

Lexy turned her eyes on him. "Yes. He is."

Cooper could see it in Lexy's eyes. She was shutting down and in the process shutting him out.

His heart slammed against his chest. His hands shook. The old him was calm, always controlled. The old him didn't let life spin out of control. The old him always had a plan, but this time he didn't know how to stop things. To stop Lexy. He didn't have to speak to her to know that she was going to try to give him up, to throw away what they had, just because his old life had come to find him.

"Lex…I would have died it if weren't for you. You know that. I need you."

"Yes," his mother said very calmly as she patted Lexy's hand. "You've saved my son's life. The hospital told us, that they thought they were going to lose him before you walked through the door. Look how we pay you back. Barging into your home, and informing you of your husband's death this way. I'm ashamed." She looked at Cooper. "But when I heard there might have been a mistake, I had to come here and see for myself. I couldn't wait for the military to tell me. Thank you for being good to him. Thank you for keeping him alive."

Lexy looked stricken but she managed to pull herself together. "Please come inside. It's very warm out here. Can I offer you something to drink?"

Cooper reached out to touch her but she avoided him. He felt like dying right then. He had hurt her. She would never trust him again.

She wanted to vomit. Bile kept rising in her throat. Ryan was Cooper. The man she was desperately in love with wasn't her husband and he was engaged to someone else.

But you already knew that.

He had known who he was but he'd kept it from her and that was by far the worst feeling. She had known something was off with him the past few days. That he had been quiet, and wistful and almost sad.

Why couldn't he have just told her instead of letting this happen? Instead of making her look like a fool? Like she was too stupid to know that the man she was sleeping with was not her husband.

She wanted to have a baby with him. They couldn't be a family. He didn't belong in her world, but in another that was so far away she couldn't even touch it. She studied his mother, who was lovely, with the same bluish gray eyes as her son and classically cut white hair. His supposed bride was lovely, too—educated, elevated. Caroline looked like she belonged on Cooper's arm. Everything about them screamed money, education and sophistication. The way they sat with their heads held high, and spoke with their crisp syllables.

The way they looked around her house in wonder, like it was unfit for humans.

It was so obvious that Ryan—no, Cooper—didn't belong here.

"This was my husband," she said finally, pulling herself together enough to speak. She was holding a photograph.

They were sitting in her shabby living room. Helena, Cooper's mother, sat at his side. Her arm linked through his. His hand in hers. His mother. It must have been so hard for her all this time. To think her son was dead.

She thought about Mary. How was she going to tell her Ryan was gone? Deep in her heart Lexy had known her husband was gone, and even though she spent so much time hating him, she still felt sad for the loss. How was Mary going to feel? It had to be the same way Cooper's mother felt when she thought she had lost her son. When Lexy lost her unborn baby. The grief she felt had threatened to swallow her whole. She could only imagine what it felt like to lose a child you had known and loved and held.

She handed Helena the photo of Ryan that was about eight years old, before Ryan let the alcohol really grip him, when he was thinner and handsome and looked so much like Cooper. "As you can see, they look very much alike. I just couldn't believe he wasn't my husband."

"My word," she breathed. "Of course you couldn't have known. Caroline, you have to see this."

Caroline looked at the photograph, but said nothing. Lexy couldn't miss the coolness in her demeanor. Caroline blamed her. How could she not? Lexy should have been able to tell that Cooper wasn't hers, and she *could* tell. She just didn't want it to be true.

"You raised a wonderful son. I need to tell you that. He is kind and gentle and it has been a pleasure to know him."

Tears slid down her face in hot splashes. She swiped at her eyes, trying to stop them. He was going to go home. He was going to disappear from her life.

"Don't say that, Lex." He stood up, gripped her hands and squeezed. "It's not over yet. We can make this work."

He sounded so sure of himself. Like everything would be normal again after today. The only comfort she took from this was that he must have loved her. That was the only reason he would stay here, in this shabby little house, in this town that had nothing for him. He loved her when she had never really been loved before.

"Cooper," Caroline said, her voice softened when she talked to him. There was love there, too. Of course Caroline wouldn't want to let him go. Being loved by Cooper was too good. "Everyone except you realizes that you cannot live this life. We've come to take you home. It's time to tell Mrs. Beecher goodbye."

"You don't get to tell me what to do. I'm not a child and I'm not leaving here. How can you expect me to just pick up and leave the woman I've spent the last three months with? She saved my life."

"You spent the last thirty years of your life with your mother and the past five with me. Are you just going to throw us away for her? For some stranger?"

"I may not agree with everything that Caroline said," Helena started, "but she's right on that point. We haven't seen you in over a year. We thought you were dead, sweetheart. Your time is ending here. I know you must be fond of Lexy but this is not your life. This is Ryan Beecher's life."

He shook his head. Lexy could see his resolve. She knew that he wasn't just going to leave no matter what they said.

"Can I have a moment with you, Ryan?"

He nodded and she led him away from the house, all the way to the garage where Ryan Beecher had kept his shop. The real Ryan. The Ryan who was dead.

Her real husband was dead.

Being in the now-empty garage made it really hit home.

She hadn't mourned him or accepted the fact that he was gone before she had fallen in love with another man, with a stranger.

"Lexy."

"What is your name?"

"Cooper," he said almost regretfully.

"Your whole name, please." She put her hand over her eyes not wanting to look at him.

"Cooper Thomaston." She looked into his face. His name was familiar.

"You're the—" Her stomach rolled as she remembered the details about him. "They wrote stories about you. I read about you. Your brother was Jacob Thomaston. He died in friendly fire, so you enlisted to honor him."

Normally that tale wouldn't have picked up so much press but it had because the man she was looking at was the golden boy of his family's dynasty, the CFO of a huge telecommunications company. "Your grandfather was a senator. You don't belong here."

"I love you," he said, as if that explained everything, as if love was all they needed. "I never belonged with them. I only felt right here."

She ignored his beautiful but meaningless words. It would

never work between them. It would kill her but it would never work.

"How long have you known?"

"Two weeks."

"Two weeks!" He flinched as the sharpness in her voice. "You knew and you made love to me? You let me tell you I loved you? You let me think that we could have a family when you knew that you weren't my husband? How could you? How could you lie to me like that?"

"I didn't lie to you. Not about anything. I just couldn't tell you until I figured some things out. I was going to tell you, Lexy. You have to believe me. I knew this was going to be hard. I just wanted a little more time with you before it got hard, before I had to merge my lives. I love you. I want a life with you. I want to be married to you. I want kids with you. Nothing has changed but my name."

"Everything has changed. You have a family and a fiancée."

"Caroline and I are done. We have been for a long time. Even if we weren't, we would be now. I don't love her."

"You have a life that is so much better than this. You don't belong in this hellhole."

This place had been hell once upon a time. At least for her. There was no way they could live here. In this house. In this town with little traces of Ryan everywhere. Her tears came again and she hated herself for crying. She wished she could have turned them off. She wished she didn't feel.

"Honey, you're killing me. Please stop."

"I knew, Cooper. I knew the whole time you weren't my husband. You could never have hit me and I knew that. But I wanted you for myself, so I took what didn't belong to me.

You have to go home. You have to live your life the way you were meant to."

"No!" He gripped her shoulders, shaking her. "I was put on this earth to be with you. God brought us together. This is all too crazy to be a coincidence. I was supposed to be the one who loved you. I knew Ryan. He didn't deserve you."

"And I don't deserve you. Go home, Cooper."

"Why are you saying that? I can make you happy. Are you afraid of that?"

"Go home!" she screamed. She was afraid. She was afraid he was stupid enough to give up his life and choose her and this place, when he had so much more waiting for him. When he had a mother who suffered needlessly because she was too blind to see that he wasn't the man the world thought he was.

"No!" He grabbed her and held her tightly against him. "I love you," he breathed. "I love you. I'm not going without you."

"Without me?" She blinked up at him.

"You can come to New York—"

"No." She cut him off, shaking her head, knowing that what they had was over. She wasn't meant for his life, just as he wasn't meant for hers. "It's time for you to go."

He had to. They were over.

"I love you, Cooper Thomaston. I love you." She had to tell him before he went. She couldn't live with herself if she didn't say it.

He shook his head stubbornly. "We can make this work."

She shook her head, feeling acute pain. "We can't. We're strangers."

"We aren't. You know my heart, the real me. Without the money and my family name and all the expectations. You're the only person in this world who knows me. Everything else is meaningless."

"You have to get back to your life. Thank you for coming into mine." She kissed his face. "Now I know what it feels like to be loved."

"Lexy, don't do this to me."

His eyes filled with tears and it was nearly unbearable. He was in as much pain as she was, but it had to be this way. It had to end.

"Goodbye, Cooper." She ran out of the garage and away from the house, not stopping till she reached the car. Cooper had left the keys inside. Her bag from their weekend trip was still there. She knew he wouldn't go, so she had to. She could no longer be in a place filled with so many memories.

Chapter Twenty-Three

Cooper stayed in the garage for a long time after Lexy ran out. He felt heavy. So heavy that it was hard for him to leave his spot and walk back to the house to face his mother and Caroline.

He couldn't blame Lexy for walking out, for leaving him. This was his fault. He should have told her sooner. He should have forgotten his plans and just come clean. But even if he had, he wasn't so sure the outcome wouldn't have been the same.

Lexy didn't think he belonged in Liberty and maybe he didn't, but he belonged to her. And as long as they were together they could make it work wherever they were. He wasn't going to stop going after her until he made her see that.

"Cooper." His mother rose from the sofa when he finally walked back in. "You've been crying. Oh, honey. What happened?"

"I'm not going back with you."

Seven days had gone by since she sent Cooper away. It had been seven days since she had been home. Seven days since the bottom of her world dropped from beneath her. She couldn't go back to Liberty while he was there. And she knew he was there, living with the ghost of her dead husband. Maybe she wouldn't be able to go back ever. There were too many memories there, good mixed with bad, memories of a life she shared with two men.

Cooper called her cell phone a thousand times since she walked away from him. At first she listened to the messages.

I love you.

Come back.

We can make this work.

But listening to his voice, knowing that he had another complete life somewhere else with a family that loved him was torture for her. So she stopped listening and the messages piled up until her phone became too full to take anymore.

She looked back to her brother, Kyle, after the phone stopped ringing this time. He was lying in his bed, blankly staring up at the ceiling and she wondered where his mind was. What his thoughts were. She had come to him when she left Cooper. He needed to be with his family and so did she. Kyle was her family. Her only family.

She rented a little room near the hospital and came to see him every day, talking to him, brushing his hair, feeding him at mealtimes so the nurses wouldn't have to.

She thought she would feel happier doing this, a sense of completion being here with him all the time. This was her original plan. To leave Ryan. To move closer. To spend time with her only family. She thought being with her brother would make her happy, and make her forget about Cooper. But it didn't take her mind off him, it just heaped more sadness onto her chest.

She knew he was sick. She knew he was dying, but spending so many hours with him she was forced to see how ill he really was. He was going to need a feeding tube inserted, the nursing staff told her. It was becoming harder for him to swallow. His dystrophy was progressing. Every time she touched him, he felt softer. It was more difficult for him to move even his head. He was having more seizures. He was dying slowly in front of her and she felt lonelier than ever watching it happen. Before she had work and Di and Mary to take her mind off things. She had a goal she was working toward. She had leaving Ryan to look forward to. And then when Cooper came into her life she had him and Kyle. She had somebody to lean on.

Now she was truly on her own.

"Lexy."

Kyle's doctor walked in with a pitying look on his face. Only the pity wasn't for Kyle, it was for her.

"You're still here?"

She nodded, offering no excuse for her constant presence for the past few days.

"I don't think you should be."

"What?" She looked up at Dr. Herbert, shocked by his words.

"He's not going to change, Lexy. He's not going to get any better. And you keeping this vigil over him is not helping. You're sad. You think he can't feel your sadness? Of course he can feel it. This whole hospital can."

"I'm sorry," she said, knowing he was right.

"You've got to live your life, Lexy. I don't know what happened to you, but you have to find a way to find happiness. If not for yourself then for Kyle. He deserves more than to spend his last few years of life with somebody who can't even smile."

"You want me to stop visiting him?"

"Of course not. I would never say that. I'm telling you to fill up your life. Make yourself happy. You deserve it and so does he. He's the happiest when you are." He went to Kyle's bedside and touched his shoulder. "It's beautiful outside today. Don't you think your sister should go out and enjoy herself while she can?"

Kyle's eyes focused for a moment and he looked at Dr. Herbert as if to say yes.

Lexy almost laughed. Her misery was affecting everybody. Even Kyle wanted his space from her.

Dr. Herbert was right. She couldn't hide here forever. She couldn't really ever leave Liberty. It was her home. She had been happy there for bits and pieces. She was just going to have to learn how to make a new start there.

"Okay, I'm going home." She stood up and kissed Kyle's cheek. "I'll see you soon, though. You can't get rid of me."

"I'm glad. It's for the best." Dr. Herbert walked her to the front door. "A man called for you here a few minutes ago," Dr. Herbert started in a low voice. "I informed the staff to say they hadn't seen you."

She didn't have to ask who it was. She already knew. "Thank you. I appreciate that."

"Is that the man I met a few weeks ago?"

"Yes."

"That man is not your husband, is it?"

She looked up at Dr. Herbert, shocked by his insight.

"I remember your husband from the first time you came to see Kyle five years ago. He said if it was up to him he would pull the plug. That man was not him. The man I met recently cares too much for you to say that."

She nodded, knowing it was true, feeling an acute pain sneak up in her chest. "He has another life that I don't fit into."

"I'm not one to give love advice, but if somebody loves you that much, is it really the right thing to let them go?"

She said nothing to that question, but she knew in her case it was.

Cooper dropped his keys on the kitchen table of his hotel suite when he walked in the door. He had been to Di's house again, and then Mary Beecher's. He had been all over this town, looking for Lexy. He had even gone to see her brother yesterday only to find she wasn't there. She had been. Even though the staff told him she wasn't, he knew. There were signs of her everywhere, the clothes Kyle wore. The way his hair was combed. She had been there hiding from him. And he couldn't stand it.

He stood there staring at the keys while he thought of her, the Mercedes emblem reflective in the light. He shook his head as his thoughts broke. He shouldn't think of them as his keys anymore. They weren't. They were Ryan Beecher's keys and Liberty was Ryan Beecher's town. And this was Ryan Beecher's borrowed life.

He wasn't sure how word had gotten out so quickly that he wasn't the man he thought he was, but everybody knew. And the whole town looked at him like he was some kind of imposter, an alien that had come down and taken one of their own. He had always known that Liberty wasn't his hometown, but the place had become like a home to him. But every time he walked down the street, every time he heard a whisper about him behind his back it felt less like one.

Liberty was Ryan's home. He was their son, who had died in combat. The town was mourning him. His friends were mourning him and every time they looked at him they felt confused or scared, like they were seeing a ghost. He knew his presence was hurting the town, but he couldn't go yet. Not without Lexy.

"Cooper—" his mother patted the sofa "—come sit next to me."

She hadn't gone home. He hadn't expected her to—in fact he had asked her to stay with him until he saw Lexy again, but Caroline left. She left because she was fed up with him and he didn't blame her. But even if Lexy never came back into his life, he knew he and Caroline were over for good. He was a different man now than he was then.

"You haven't been sleeping," Helena said as she ran her fingers through his dark hair.

"No. I don't sleep much."

She, on the other hand, was looking slightly better than when he first saw her. Her skin no longer contained that deathly pallor and he was glad for that.

"Is it because of Lexy that you don't sleep? Or is it because of the blast? I talked to your uncle before I came. He hasn't been in Vietnam for forty years but he says sometimes when he dreams it's like he's never left it. Is it like that for you?"

"Sometimes." He nodded. "Lexy helped me through it. It's better now."

"She must be special, son."

"She is." He fell quiet, not sure what else he should say to her. He was glad to see her, but there was some awkwardness there. He felt more comfortable around Ryan Beecher's mother, even today when he went to go visit her just to pay his respects. She hugged him and kissed his cheek and treated him how she always had. Why couldn't things be so easy with his own mother?

"We're like strangers, aren't we, son?"

He blinked at her. She had read his mind.

"It's my fault. I didn't know how to handle your brother and your father going. So I shut down. I closed myself off to stop the hurt. You don't know how it feels to lose your child. It's like the pain is a gushing wound and it keeps bleeding and bleeding until you're all dried out. And then your father… I married him at twenty. I grew up with him. I spent my life with him…and he was just gone. No warning—" She snapped her fingers. "Just like that. I thought I was going to die. I tried to bury myself in things and shut out feelings and love and anything that could possibly hurt me and in the process I forgot about you. I hate myself for forgetting about you."

"You don't have to." He shook his head. "I was just as guilty. I could have tried harder."

"No. You couldn't have. It wasn't until you were actually overseas that it hit me that I could lose you, too, and then it was too late. I should have said something. I should have tried to stop you."

"I wanted to be a marine. I liked being one. I liked the men in my unit, the feeling that I was serving my country. I wish they hadn't died, but I wouldn't take my service back."

"No. I know that. You're a good man, Cooper. I don't tell you that enough but it's true. You make me so proud."

A knock at the door stopped him from responding. They looked at each other for a moment.

"Did you order room service?" he asked her.

"No. I was waiting for you to get back so we could go to dinner."

The knock sounded again and Cooper left his mother to open the door.

Lexy was there, looking weary and sad, but she was there. His first impulse was to pull her into his arms, but he didn't. He was so surprised to see her he couldn't move, because he knew she wasn't here to come back. She was here to say good-bye again.

"How are you?" he asked after a moment.

"I've been better," she said with a sad smile.

"I've been looking for you."

"I know. I want you to stop, Coop."

He shook his head unable to agree, unable to face the thought of life without her. "Not until you come home with me."

"Where's home?" She shook her head this time. "Is it here? Where my husband and his family are from? Where they're mourning him? Where he was loved? It would be a slap in the face to stay here. To love here."

He knew that. He had never been more aware of anything. "Then come with me to New York."

"I don't belong there. I couldn't be happy there. Texas is in my blood. And I need time, Cooper. I need time. He may have been a bastard, but Ryan was my husband and he's dead. And his mama is hurting really bad. I need to be here for her. I love her. She's my family. Just like your mama is your family. You owe her some time. She thought you were dead. She mourned you. You owe her some time. Away from me. You need to get your life back on track. You need to know yourself away from war, and this place and me. Cooper, you really need to figure out what you want out of life."

He wanted her in his life.

He shut his eyes, knowing she was right but not wanting to admit it. He was being selfish. Hoping for the impossible.

Right now. They were impossible.

He leaned toward her, setting his mouth against hers one last time. Sucking her in. Tasting her sweetness, needing to capture this moment for his memory. "Okay," he said after a long kiss. "Okay."

She nodded and turned away, but looked back at him for a moment. "I do love you. You should know that."

"I do. And I love you, too. Don't forget that. Or me. Please don't forget me."

"I won't."

She stepped forward and hugged him tightly one last time before she stepped away for good. There was no turning back. He just stood there watching her until she was out of his sight.

"Come here, son." His mother was there, behind him, and when he saw her and the sadness in her eyes for him he broke.

She took him into her arms and he cried. The best part of his life had just walked away from him.

"Honey," Mary said softly as she stroked Lexy's hair. "I'm worried about you." She looked up at her mother-in-law and blinked. "You haven't slept in your house in weeks."

"I can't go back there. My husband is dead and the man I love is gone. The house is filled with both of them. I feel like I'm suffocating when I'm there. I wanted to leave Ryan, but I never really wanted him to die. I never expected to fall in love with a stranger, but I'm miserable without Cooper."

"He's a good man, Lexy. You'd be crazy not to miss him."

"I'm pregnant," she admitted for the first time. "Three months now."

"Oh, Lexy!" Mary cried. Lexy pulled up her shirt to reveal her small round baby bump.

"There are two babies in there. I found out yesterday. Two heartbeats."

"What are you going to do?"

When she found out, a thousand feelings ran through her head, but overall she was happy.

"Raise my babies. Would you help me? I know they won't really be your grandchildren but I want you to be their grandmother. I need a mama now more than ever."

"Of course." Mary's voice was choked with tears. "I'll take care of you. You can move in here if you want."

"I would like that." Her eyes filled with tears. "I love you, Mary. Thank you."

"Don't thank me. I should have never let my son hurt you. I should have raised him better. You don't know the shame I feel."

"I don't blame you. Your husband hit you, too."

"I should have stopped the cycle. I should have called the sheriff the first time he hit you."

"Don't do this to yourself. If it wasn't for you, Ryan would have never went to the marines and I would never have met Cooper. And if I never met him I would not have my babies or known what it was like to be loved." She rubbed her belly, feeling her miracles grow inside her.

"Are you going to tell him?"

"No. I thought about it but I can't. He has another life, a job, a family. I don't fit in anywhere."

And it killed her.

"How are you going to manage?"

"I'll have you," she said uneasily. Mary wasn't young anymore but she had so much love to give. "Cooper put a lot of money in the bank for me after he left. At first I was going to give it back, but I'm going to raise his babies with it."

Cooper had settled into a routine. Finally. It took him a while, almost two months of being back in New York, for him to feel any sense of normalcy. But for some reason, even though he had grown up there, Manhattan didn't feel like home. His apartment didn't feel like home. There was no handmade quilt on his bed. No cheery, colored curtains on his windows. No worn-in couch that was perfect for naps. No sweet-smelling woman to fill the place. It was just an apartment, where he slept and bathed and ate alone.

But he was surviving.

Those first few days after he had gotten back he wasn't sure he would. He was miserable but as the days passed he slowly got better. He slowly returned to life. He wasn't happy, necessarily, or even content…but he was going on. He spent a lot of time with his mother. They had dinner together at least once a week. They went to museums and plays. They talked. She gained some of her weight back. She was becoming the woman he used to know and he was glad for that.

But something big was missing in his life. He walked around with an emptiness that was almost consuming, and the feeling never left him. He wasn't sure it would. It amazed him how he managed to be lonely in the biggest city in the world. He met up with his old friends to combat it. He kept himself busy working in his old job. He went out at night after work. On weekends he stayed out late so he didn't have to go back to his empty, quiet apartment.

That's when he had met Olivia. At a dinner party. They exchanged emails for a few weeks. And then she suggested they go out for dinner. At first he was surprised by the offer. He had been in such a fog, in such an odd state that he hadn't looked at her as any normal man looked at a woman. He didn't see her with interest.

There was something wrong with him. But he agreed, thinking that maybe it was what he needed. And as they sat across from each other in a cozy Italian restaurant he tried to find his attraction for her.

She was a beautiful woman. Dark hair, big brown eyes, a sweet Audrey Hepburn face. She was interesting. She worked as a college professor, teaching humanities to freshmen. He even found himself laughing that night. For many men she would be perfect. But he kept comparing her to another woman. Olivia had smooth porcelain skin, but he liked skin that was a mixture of coffee and milk. Olivia had straight hair, but he found himself wanting to run his fingers through hair that was curly. She wore tailored, designer dresses but Cooper preferred a girl in a tank top and a pair of jeans.

"I'm being unfair to you," he said. He had tuned out of the conversation as he studied her. It was rude, but Lexy was on his mind. She was always on his mind.

"Oh?" Olivia smiled prettily at him. "I hadn't noticed."

She would make some man happy. Just not him. "I wish I weren't in love with somebody else."

Her eyes went wide and he knew he could have stated that better. "Of course you're in love with somebody else." She gave him a self-deprecating grin. "Every man I like is. Story of my life."

"I'm sorry. I'm trying to live without her, but it seems I can't. I could try with you. I would like to try with you, but it wouldn't be fair to you. I haven't seen her in months, but nothing has changed. I still love her."

"Then why are you here? If somebody loved me like you love her I wouldn't want them sitting around. I would want them to tell me that."

He blinked at his date. There were a million reasons he couldn't go back, but there was one reason he was going to. He loved her. His life wasn't good without her.

The library had been extremely quiet. Libraries were normally quiet but there hadn't been a single person there all morning. She was the only one working besides Jemma, and she was downstairs doing inventory. Lexy had checked in all the books and now she was incredibly bored.

When her hands were idle her mind drifted to Cooper. He haunted her. She touched her ever-growing belly. One of Cooper's babies was moving. She hoped one of them would have blue-gray eyes, that way she could look at them and see the man she loved every day.

"So I was thinking…" She heard Cooper's voice and didn't believe her ears.

Her heart was playing tricks on her. She was missing him so badly that she conjured him up in her mind.

"I promised you a trip to Austin and I never took you."

"Cooper?"

"Yes." He smiled softly, leaning over the circulation desk where she was sitting. "I miss you, Alexa. My life sucks without you."

She was silent for a moment, not sure she could trust her eyes, but he was there. He looked the same as she remembered him. The scar she liked to kiss was still on his cheek. He still had that gleam in his eye. He still looked at her like she was meant for him. It was almost too much to take in. But then he reached across the desk and took her hand in his. Those feelings she got whenever he touched her raced along her skin. He eyes weren't playing tricks on her. Her heart hadn't made her imagine things. He was back. "My life sucks, too."

"Do you still love me?" he asked hesitantly, almost like he was afraid she was going to say no.

"I still love you. I couldn't stop."

"Good, because I can't function without you. I just go through the motions. I don't live. I'm not happy without you."

"Cooper—" she dashed the tears away from her eyes "—I missed you."

"I'm moving back here. Or if you don't want here, tell me where you want to go. I was thinking we could build a big house after we get married."

"Married?" Her heart pounded in her chest.

"Oh—" he grinned "—did I forget to ask you?" His eyes twinkled and her heart hurt.

"You don't have to ask. I will."

"You're damn right you will." He came around the desk and pulled her into his arms, hugging her tightly against his hard body, and she nearly died from pleasure.

"Uh…" He froze and then shifted his hand to her ever-growing belly.

"I'm pregnant," she confessed.

"I can see that."

He gawked at her big belly. He looked so surprised and adorable that she had to kiss his face a dozen times.

"You gave me two babies." She backed away and lifted up her gauzy shirt to reveal her pregnancy.

"Lex." His eyes filled with tears. "Twins? You're going to have my babies?"

"Yes." She took his hand and placed it over her belly. "You did this."

"Amazing. How far along are you?"

"Four months."

His mouth dropped. "Were you ever going to tell me?" Hurt flashed in his eyes. She never wanted to hurt him but she needed to tell him the truth.

"I didn't want you coming back just because I was pregnant. I wanted you to come back because you loved me. I would have always wondered if you would have rather been with someone else. Or if you would have resented me for keeping you here. But now I know."

"I never wanted to leave you, damn it!" he yelled at her. "I love you."

"Then why did it take you so long to come back? I was worried, you ass. I didn't want to raise these kids without you."

His face broke out in a smile. "You're a nut, Lexy. Do you know that?"

"Of course I know that, but you are the one marrying the crazy lady."

"I am." He brushed a soft kiss across her mouth. "This afternoon. I want to make love to my wife as soon as possible."

Epilogue

Lexy lay with her head on Cooper's chest, her hand rested on his stomach underneath his T-shirt. This is how he and his wife spent every evening. It was their way of unwinding, of simply being together.

"Are you hungry?" Lexy looked up at him. She was just as pretty as the day they met. "I made a peach pie, or if you don't want that I bought mint-chocolate-chip ice cream."

He ran his fingers through her loose hair that had grown so long it was now down her back. "You hate mint-chocolate-chip ice cream."

"You like it, and I like you so I bought it."

He kissed her forehead. "I love you, Lexy." He didn't tell her enough, or if he did it was automatic, like saying good morning or good night, but he did love her. She was the best thing that ever happened to him.

"I love you, too, Coop." She grinned up at him, raising her head slightly so she could kiss his mouth. A spark caught and the kiss grew into something more than either intended. He rolled her over on the couch, wrapping her leg around his hip.

"You always get me, you witch," he muttered before he took her mouth again.

"I didn't even do anything," she giggled. After twelve years he could still do that to her.

"You were born," he retorted. Her hand wandered up his shirt, stroking his still-scarred back.

"What are you guys doing?" they heard a voice say. Cooper lifted his head to look at his irritable twelve-year-old daughter holding their nine-month-old son.

"I'm making out with your mother. Go away."

They had five beautiful children: twelve-year-old twins, a boy and a girl; a nine-year-old daughter; a four-year-old daughter; and a baby boy. He never thought they would have so many. They never thought they would be so old and still be having kids. Lexy was forty. He was forty-three. She thought she would have trouble conceiving, but they were as fertile as a rainforest. Their last two children were unplanned, due to his inability to keep his hands off his wife.

But there were some bittersweet times in between their happy times. Kyle had passed away just after the twins were born. It was sad but it really was a blessing. Kyle had suffered more than one person should. But he had got to see his niece and nephew before he went, and that made Lexy happy.

"I would love to go away but Conner is making noise."

"Ma!" He squealed and held out his chubby baby arms to his mother.

"Hey, booger," she said, still trapped beneath her husband. Conner broke out in jubilant baby giggles as he always did whenever his mother spoke to him. He would be a mama's boy. Conner looked just like Lexy, with caramel skin and dark curls, but he had Cooper's blue-gray eyes.

"I'm trying to do my homework," Lacy whined.

"You waited till eight to do your homework?" Lexy asked.

"Um, no?"

"Tell me another lie." Lexy looked up at Cooper. "Get off of me."

He frowned at her. "I don't want to."

"You already have five kids," Lacy complained. "You don't have to do it anymore."

"Yes, we do," Cooper answered. "And if you don't like it you can move out."

She wouldn't be going anywhere. They had the biggest house in Liberty, Texas. He had fulfilled his promise and built Lexy the house of her dreams. She had been easy to please. They had money. He ran his own accounting firm and she wrote for a living. She could have whatever she wanted, but she still shopped at Wal-Mart and insisted that the kids earn their allowance by doing chores.

"Dad!"

"Cooper!" Lexy poked him.

He looked down at Lexy, still wanting her, and she nearly blushed. They still made love every night and some mornings if they managed to wake up before the kids. "Coop." She kissed his cheek, and when he still didn't move she tugged on his hair. He sighed and rolled off her. There was always tonight.

"Come to Mommy." She held out her arms to their baby, who was pumping his legs in excitement as Lacy brought him near. "How's my little love?" She smothered his face with wet kisses.

"Daddy?"

Their four-year-old came into the den wearing her blue footie pajamas, rubbing her eyes as if she had been crying. He loved all of his children tremendously, but May stole his heart. She was his look-alike and she had him wrapped around her finger.

"Charlie smashed the cricket that was in my room and now I've got guts on the wall. I told him not to kill it." Her lowered lip trembled pathetically, which caused Lexy to roll her eyes.

"Come here, princess." He collected the little girl in his arms, kissing her tears away.

"Charlie!"

A boy, big and healthy-looking, appeared. He was a mix of his parents. "Yeah, Dad?"

"Please clean the guts off your sister's wall."

"No problem." He shrugged. "I don't know why she's crying."

"Because dumb-dumb. Girls don't like guts on their walls," his twin informed him.

"Yes," Cooper added. "Now tell her you're sorry."

Charlie obeyed, giving May a loud kiss on her cheek. He was good to his sisters. Cooper was proud of his boy. He pulled him down next to him and ruffled his hair.

"Come here, Lacy," Lexy called. "Give Mama a kiss."

"Do I have to?" the increasingly fresh child said.

"If you want to live to see tomorrow, you will," her mother replied. Lacy came over and squeezed her mother tightly. She gave a lot of lip but she really adored her mother. They were best friends. "I love you, Lace."

"I love you, too, Mommy."

"Hey!" Their nine-year-old, Corey, entered. "Nobody told me you guys were having a meeting."

"Trust me," Cooper assured her, "it was not planned. Come sit with us."

She squeezed herself between her parents, resting her dark head on Cooper's arm.

This was heaven.

Twelve years ago he nearly died, when a dark angel came and gave him a reason to live. And he owed it all to Ryan Beecher, who not only gave his life for his country, but for Cooper, too.

★ ★ ★ ★ ★

Watch for the next title in Ginger Jamison's
REDEMPTION *trilogy, coming this*
Autumn 2014: JERICHO.
Don't miss this compelling, emotional story!